TOMMY BLACK

AND THE
COAT OF INVINCIBILITY

JAKE KERR

Currents & Tangents
Press

Cover design, illustration, and
interior illustrations by M. S. Corley

Edited by Eric Jackson & Lea Zukas

ISBN 978-0-9971950-0-2
[1. Fiction: Fantasy-General. 2. Juvenile Fiction:
Action & Adventure-General, 3. Juvenile Fiction:
Historical-United States-20th Century]

10 9 8 7 6 5 4 3 2 1

Published by Currents & Tangents Press

Dallas, Texas

For Mom & Dad

PART I

England

1

Visiting
an Old Friend

As the watery mud seeped into my shoes I couldn't help but laugh. I had expected an unpleasant visit. I just didn't expect it to start the moment I stepped out of the taxi. The driver stayed in the warm, dry car, holding his hand out the window, his palm collecting rain drops. "Are you certain you don't want me to drive you closer?" he asked. "A storm is brewing."

I motioned over my shoulder as I paid him. "It's a surprise visit." He nodded but then stopped as he caught sight of my cane. He continued to stare as I started up the road, but I couldn't tell if it was because he recognized me as the Archmage or whether he just thought it was strange for a sixteen year old to be using a cane.

Setting a brisk pace, I approached my destination, the mighty Citadel of London. With each step the tapping of my cane on the cobblestones made small splashes. My hope was to get the whole unpleasantness over with as quickly as possible.

It had been two years since I had walked through the gates of the Citadel. The previous time I had the help of friends. This time I would be on my own. I didn't want to be alone. My friend Naomi had helped me escape before, and I wished she were with me now, but I hadn't seen her in a long time.

I knew that she was studying magic in England, but I didn't know where, and she didn't seem interested in letting me know. I was in England, too, and Naomi knew that she could reach me through my great grandfather at Balmoral. Every visit to my great grandfather I would inquire about a letter or telegram from her, but he would shake his head, shrug, and change the subject. I eventually stopped asking if Naomi had contacted him, and the fact that she didn't made the distance seem an unbridgeable chasm between us.

She was an extraordinary magician, and I missed how she would casually prep dangerous spells to relax herself. I missed her wit and sarcasm. I missed her strength and spirit. I missed how beautiful she was, and I missed how she drove me crazy.

Naomi never said so, but I believe she left because I had saved her life. While she was thankful, it seemed like she saw it as a challenge or even an affront. When she went off by herself to study it was my belief that her goal was to never have to be saved by someone ever again. I admired that, but I still missed her.

The modest entrance to Fort Belvedere—the Citadel—soon revealed itself. It was an illusion, of course, hiding a mighty fortress behind the facade of a country estate, an illusion created at the hands of the man I was going to meet: Cain.

I still didn't know Cain's role in the English government. I assumed he was some nebulous member of the Army Council, in charge of magic. With magic all but gone from the world I figured everyone just left Cain alone.

And Cain left alone was dangerous, as I had experienced first hand.

During my previous visit, Cain had done his best to intimidate me into giving him the artifact I now carried. Rather than work with him I had spent the past two years freeing the enslaved Marids—magical creatures that powered the trains in England and the United States.

He had sent master level magicians to stop me, but I had learned much and escaped them easily. My power with the staff, which I initially considered to be the useless ability to create light like a mere lamp turned out to be much much more—by manipulating light I could defeat practically any creature, magical or otherwise. Each day brought me more confidence.

Having freed the Marids, I intended to move on to the next victims of magical oppression, whoever they were. Were the mighty furnaces in Forest of Dean powered by Ifrit? I didn't know, but I had an idea that Cain would. Hence my visit.

I decided it was safest if I stopped time from flowing around me. It was an extraordinary power I discovered by accident and was one of many things that turned the seemingly useless trick of manipulating light into something much more powerful. Inspired by the words of my great grandfather, who nonchalantly asked me if light could bend, I studied Einstein, whose theories of space and time were based on the constant of the speed of light. Einstein taught that my power with the staff was truly awe-inspiring.

As powerful as it was, I hesitated to use the Staff. My great grandfather had also told me that the staff was ultimately in control of its own magic, and as I used it over the previous two years I could sense it more and more—the staff was affecting me. How, I didn't know, but it was there. But there were times when I had no choice. Facing Cain was one of them.

I closed my eyes and stopped time, the motion of light held still by the power of the staff. I opened my eyes to a frozen tableau. It was always uncomfortable living in a world of stopped time. The sense that it was wrong seemed to permeate everything. Still, I never failed to marvel at the stillness of the world around me.

Splashing mud from marching boots looked like chocolate milk. Rain was suspended in the air like glass beads. Even the dark clouds above me appeared to be blobs of paint smeared across a drab canvas. The activity around the Citadel appeared frantic even as it was frozen in time around me. We were at war with Germany, and troops were everywhere. The expansive lawns of the estate, which had been mostly empty during my previous visit, were full of columns of soldiers. Everything smelled of gunpowder, and the grass lawns were ground into dirt under the constant pounding of boots.

There were no magicians in view, just soldiers and guns and cannons. Technology had eliminated the need for difficult-to-learn magic, and magicians were for the most part nothing more than street performers—certainly not powerful soldiers.

I approached the door that led to Cain's office and paused, holding the cane tight. Despite my developing power, he was still frightening. He truly was an awesome illusionist, as great as any among the ages.

The last time I had visited him he had set me on fire with nothing more than his mind. I was sure that he was still outraged that I had freed the Marids, and with his power I needed to keep him off balance. I didn't want to find myself on fire again.

I passed through the doorway and into Cain's section of the building. There were no magicians on duty, which surprised me. The entry was guarded by a bored looking soldier, his hand caught in the act of scratching his bushy mustache. I wondered if there were any powerful magicians remaining in England.

There was one other change I noticed: The electrical lights that were previously attached to the pillars of the long hall that led to Cain's office were gone. They were no longer necessary, as I had created a home for the ominous Shadow creatures, creatures that could absorb anything and move it to a place without any feeling at all. Their leader, Vingrosh, had requested a home without light, and I had given them one. The Shadows had not been seen since.

Opening the door to Cain's office, I walked over, and sat in the chair facing his desk. I leaned forward and looked at him. Even with Cain frozen in time, my hands clenched the staff. He looked older—more drawn and with thinning hair—but he still oozed power. He was writing a note, the pen stopped mid-stroke. The office itself was little changed. As I looked around, I tried to assess what Cain's role was with the English government, but it was impossible to tell.

I took a deep breath and let light flow again.

"Hello, Cain." His head jerked up, but only for the slightest of moments. As a magician, his self-control was extraordinary. He looked me over, smiled, and leaned back in his chair.

"Tommy Black. What a pleasant surprise." He put his pen down and folded his arms across his chest. His shoulder twitched in one of the tics that I was told were a sign of his years of doing illusions. "Why look how you've grown. How old are you now?"

"Sixteen."

"Sixteen years old, imagine that. Did you know that when I was your age I was helping our war effort in France by creating illusions to fool the German scouts?"

I shook my head and remained alert. Cain's power was not to be underestimated.

He frowned. "Contrast that with you, a traitor and coward by any definition. You've destroyed our rail infrastructure while we're in the midst of a war." Cain stared at me, his eyes narrowed in a challenge.

My confidence withered under his gaze, but in the end I knew that what I had done was right. "I freed slaves, Cain. That is all. There are other ways to power locomotives."

Cain leaned forward and slapped his palm on his desk. I flinched at the sound. "There is blood on your hands, Black. Mark my words."

I shrugged, doing my best to present nonchalance, although the idea of having caused deaths troubled me. There was a war, after all. Still, I held my ground. "I was helping others."

Shaking his head, Cain replied, "You foolish boy. Do you know how long it has taken to refit our trains? While we were rebuilding our supply lines, Germany took over half of Eastern Europe. If you had any honor at all you would use your powers to assist us." Cain picked up the pen and started writing again. "I don't have time to deal with children."

"I am not a child. I am the Archmage." Even as I said it, I felt rather embarrassed. I was relying on my title and not my actions or the moral power I felt lived behind them.

Cain calmly placed his pen down, and looked at me again, his intimidating stare only interrupted by a twitch of his eyebrow. "You are nothing but a coward."

I tapped the end of the cane on Cain's desk and he glanced down at it, startled for the barest of moments. His fear, fleeting as it was, helped restore my confidence. "I am not a coward, as you well know. I simply disagree with your methods." Cain said nothing, and I continued. "I would like to help, Cain, but there are other battles. My legacy demands that I free the enslaved magical creatures."

I had returned the conversation to the reason for my visit. I didn't expect Cain to understand, and if I were honest I didn't expect him to help. But I had hoped he would respect my mission.

Cain lowered his head and squeezed the bridge of his nose between his thumb and forefinger. "I'm tired, Black. I have a war to fight and don't have time to pander to some pointless crusade to restore your family's honor." He looked up, appearing more disappointed than angry. "The legacy of the Archmage demands no such thing of you."

I had expected this reply. Cain's comment was true at its heart. My family had wielded the cane for centuries, and our only true legacy was to use its power. But it was my great grandfather who told me the truth about our history, of a magical artifact—the staff in the form of a cane—that had been stolen from Persia. When I realized that the most powerful magic in the world originated not from magicians but from powerful magical creatures that had been enslaved to do the bidding of man, I realized that the stain of my family legacy could be only be erased by doing good and freeing them.

I was about to explain this when Cain held up a finger. "However, perhaps our goals are not in conflict."

"What do you mean?" I had expected further argument. I was hard-pressed to consider any common goal with someone like Cain.

"You do realize there are trains in Germany?" Of course. I had focused on my own home of America and ancestral home of England, but there were enslaved magical creatures across the globe. I was guilty of the blinders of nationalism that I was trying to remove from others.

I nodded. "And they are powered by Marids?"

"Marids, smaller ones by Ifrit. You don't think the vaunted German productivity is simply due to calloused hands? Their abuse of magical creatures is well-known." I expected that Cain would exaggerate to get me to be in line with his goals, but the concept that there were enslaved magical creatures in Europe made sense. My former teacher, Mister Ali, had told me the story of how the Shadows were hunted down by the Germans over the previous centuries.

"I will travel to Europe, but I don't trust you, Cain. I will do nothing without my own confirmation." Cain once again leaned back, smiling.

"That's the least of my concerns." He laughed. "My goodness, I'll even arrange transportation. I had hoped on using you to support our offensive, but this may be even better." He stared at me again, only this time the intensity was of excitement, not intimidation. "What if I told you that the ironworks in Volklingen uses scores of enslaved Ifrit to power their furnaces?"

"I would say that I would free them." If possible, Cain's smile spread wider.

"I can have you escorted to Reims. From there you can find your way to Volklingen. Free those Ifrit, and you will have England's undying gratitude. After that you can do whatever you like."

"Cain, I will do whatever I like regardless."

He shook his head. "The arrogance of the Archmage and the impetuosity of youth. But it matters not—of course! Do whatever you like! There are enough magical creatures there that will need your help to keep you busy for years. Frankly—and I'm sure you share the sentiment—I'll be glad to have you far away from me."

I couldn't help but smile. "I think we have an understanding." I stretched my legs. I hadn't realized just how tense I was. "When can I depart?"

"Give me a few days to make the arrangements. In the mean time I'll have Lord Ainsley find you lodgings." Lord Ainsley! I fondly remembered his kindness toward my grandfather and me. I looked forward to seeing him again.

"That works." I stood up, while Cain remained seated. I didn't expect him to see me out.

Before I turned to the door he spoke up. "Black, did you know that I talked with your great grandfather after you escaped the Citadel?" I turned and looked at him. He looked bemused as I shook my head. "He didn't say much, but he did say one thing that I considered interesting."

He paused again, so I played along. "And that was?"

"He said I should fear you." Cain scratched his chin. "Do you think I fear you?"

The idea that someone as powerful and arrogant as Cain would fear anyone was laughable. I shook my head. "I don't think you fear anything."

"Ah, Black. Such an attitude is foolish and a recipe for dying young. You would do well to remember that on the continent. Be that as it may, I do not fear you. Do you know why?"

I shook my head, not even bothering to answer. I had no desire to take part in any verbal games. "I don't fear you because you have a good heart, Black. You are predictable that way." He waved his hand as if dismissing me. "But I know more about magic than anyone else on the planet, and I assure you that while I don't fear you, I do respect your power." He nodded. "So I have confidence that you'll be able to handle what you are about to face, even if you cannot fathom just how dangerous it is."

I left and walked down the path to the wing with Lord Ainsley's office. I didn't spend much time thinking about Cain's warning. I had faced master magicians, Shadows, Djinn, Ifrit, and even mighty Marids. I couldn't wait to get going.

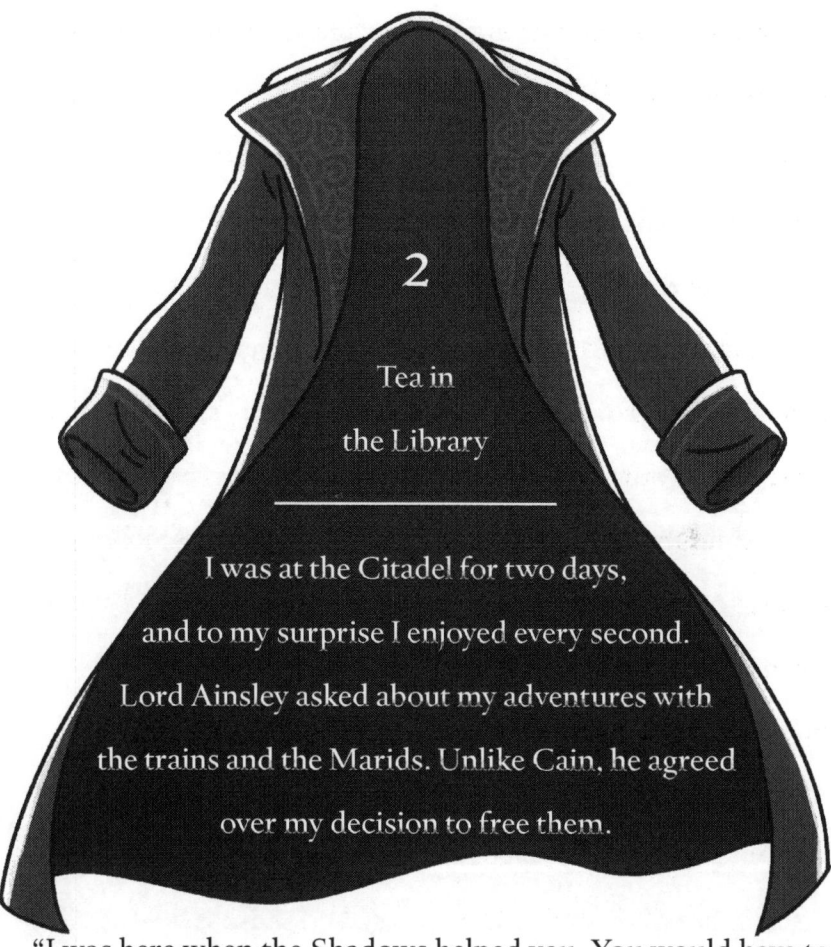

2

Tea in
the Library

I was at the Citadel for two days,
and to my surprise I enjoyed every second.
Lord Ainsley asked about my adventures with
the trains and the Marids. Unlike Cain, he agreed
over my decision to free them.

"I was here when the Shadows helped you. You would have to be foolish not to know that our knowledge of the magic creatures is incomplete. Were they soulless animals or slaves? Well, with new information comes new understanding. Would I have done things differently than you did? Maybe, but I think freeing them was the right thing to do."

We were in his library having tea. He leaned forward, and his hand shook slightly as he tried to keep his teacup steady. He was very old and reminded me of my Great Grandfather, one of the greatest Archmages in history.

"What were they like, Tommy? I've never seen a free Marid." His voice was full of youthful curiosity and tinged with awe. His eyes sparkled as he asked the question. He waved his hand around the room and its shelves of books. "I've read about their terrible might but also their majesty. It must have been extraordinary to see them so close." He took a sip of his tea. "We were always taught to fear them."

"They are fearsome," I replied. "When they emerge from the trains you can see them changing from a kind of compressed energy into their true being, and it is amazing and horrible. Their screams are of triumph but also rage and sadness. I've seen people faint as they hear it. They always fly straight into the sky and then off toward the South."

"Always to the South?" I nodded. "Interesting. So how did you free them?"

"I took control of the train and simply told them they were free. The master of the train is also the master of the magic binding the creatures." I raised a finger. "However, before I would free them I would ask their forgiveness and request that they not hurt anything."

Lord Ainsley shook his head. "I heard about Southhampton."

The Marid in Southhampton was the only one that took out his wrath on the surrounding area. I tensed as I remembered the scene. "The Marid was old and mighty. Maybe he had been enslaved for centuries. I don't know, but he was full of uncontrollable rage. Most of them would destroy the train, tearing their prisons apart and leaving behind a ruin of twisted pieces of metal, but the Marid in Southhampton didn't stop there. He destroyed the station and started to demolish nearby houses. He only stopped after I said I would free no more of his brothers or sisters if he continued. The Marid landed in front of me, and I was certain it was going to kill me, but it howled loud enough that my ears rung for hours afterward before flying off." I shuddered. It was the most scared I had ever been in my life.

Lord Ainsley stared at me for a few moments and then put his teacup down. Waving a finger at me, he said, "The Marids respect you, Tommy. I don't think there is anyone in history that can say that."

I nodded, wondering if that mattered much when it turned the entire country against me.

Captain Rechin came to see if I had any need of supplies. I was finally able to tell him the story of how his magic glasses had saved me, which made him so happy that I thought he was going to cry.

After spending two years wandering across England without friends being chased by government magicians, I felt like I was at a place that was at least something like home. I didn't spend much time with others at the Citadel, but those I did treated me well.

I took one last look around as I was about to climb into the car that was to take me to a naval base on the coast for my trip to France. The illusions were as strong as ever and completely baffled me. Was the wall near me or in the distance? Was the gate to my right or to my left? I couldn't tell. All I knew was that the Citadel was a towering achievement in magic, and it was due entirely to Cain.

Shaking my head, I turned away from the wall, which moved once again out of the corner of my eye. To my surprise, Cain approached. His arms were behind his back, and he looked his normal gloomy self. I turned to meet him.

"Cain," I said.

He stopped and looked me up and down, shaking his head. "You're on your own from this point forward, Black."

"I thought you were providing an escort?"

He shrugged. "Sure. An escort."

I had no patience for another Cain mind game, so I tapped the staff on the ground and asked the direct question. "Anything you're not telling me, Cain?"

"Yes."

When it became clear Cain wasn't going to add anything to his comment, I replied, "Anything that might be helpful?"

He stared at me for a moment, and then smiled. "Just be yourself, Black. I'm sure you'll cause maximum damage that way." And with that he turned and walked away, his steps made awkward by one of the spasms caused by his illusions.

3

"Chin Up, Black."

A day later I understood what Cain meant by my being alone. I was escorted by two soldiers on my way to meet with a Vice Admiral named Bruce Fraser, and the walk to his office was full of suppressed laughs and audible whispers from the soldiers about wasting time with another magician. They made little effort to hide their disdain. I clenched my fists around the cane, knowing that there was nothing to gain by teaching them a lesson in the power of magic.

We reached Fraser's office. He was a high-ranking officer and the person who was supposed to oversee my transit. The door closed behind me, and I was alone with the Vice Admiral. He stood behind his desk, staring at a document spread across his blotter. He looked intimidating and hard, as if he believed sitting at his own desk was a sign of weakness. He didn't look up as I walked toward him.

His office was huge and not unlike Cain's. There were maps of the English Channel, the North Sea, and the North Atlantic on the walls, while one side of the room featured a long table with papers spread all over it. The other side included a couch with some wingback chairs and a coffee table. The side with the couch was mostly tidy, although there were a few papers spread on the table. A teapot and some empty teacups stood beside the papers.

I stopped in front of the desk, which had a single uncomfortable looking chair in front of it. Those who met with the Vice Admiral were clearly split into two groups—those that were meant to sit in the uncomfortable chair with Fraser towering over them from behind his desk, and those he entertained with coffee or tea while sitting on the sofa.

I was clearly in the former group.

Fraser continued to ignore me. I had dealt with this kind of rudeness while meeting with Cain, so I cleared my voice and kept things simple. "Vice Admiral Fraser, I am Tommy Black. Cain sent me to see you."

The Vice Admiral looked up at me, a deliberate and slow motion that was rather intimidating. "Ah, the traitor. I notice that you are not taking a train for your important trip. I wonder why that is?" I said nothing. "Perhaps you should swim to Calais as a lesson for your traitorous destruction."

Did everyone in the government hate me? I closed my eyes and took a breath. There was no need to fight with this man. Cain said he would get me to Calais. That's all that mattered. I had to make every effort not to let him upset me. "I was told you would arrange my transportation to France." The Vice Admiral didn't reply. "Swimming is not transportation."

Fraser sighed and sat down, placing his hands on the desk. "This is absurd. I can't believe Cain expects me to devote two men from the Special Boat Section to escort a child across the Channel."

I stood tall, refusing to sit down as the admiral lounged behind his desk. "I am the Archmage."

His eyes narrowed. He looked like I had insulted him. "I don't know why London keeps sending me magicians. Your lot are useless. Do you know what happened to the last magician I sent out on a ship?" I shook my head. "He created an illusion that the small ship he was on was a mighty battleship."

"That's impressive!" I felt a need to defend magic from the ignorance of those like the Vice Admiral.

"Then the Germans focused all their attacks on that ship, and he died in the fusillade." Rather than seem sad, Fraser smiled. "At least one good thing came out of that."

"And that was?" I replied.

"I had one less magician to deal with."

The comment was appalling and beyond acceptable. I tapped the end of my cane on Fraser's desk, but unlike Cain he didn't react, not knowing the power he faced. "Your disrespect over the loss of life of someone whose only desire was to help the defense of England is treasonous and wrong."

Fraser's face turned red, and he stood up. "You dare talk to me about treason?" He walked around his desk while unsnapping a holster that held a gun at his waist. "I know of you, Black. We did a good job keeping it quiet so that the populace wouldn't riot, but I know what you did. Sabotaging our rail lines." He rested his hand on his pistol. "I don't know why you haven't been executed."

I glanced at the hand on Fraser's pistol. He looked under control, but I didn't know if he was unstable enough to shoot me. I was tempted to stop time and flee, traveling to Germany on my own, but I also knew that not only would I get there faster with the help of the military, but it would be good to at least have the appearance of them on my side.

"I freed magical slaves. No more." I could see Fraser's jaw muscles clench and unclench. "I am here to help, Vice Admiral. Ask Cain if you doubt me."

Fraser's hand moved, and I was nearly positive he was going to pull his gun on me, but he just tapped his fingers on the holster. The tension in the room was overwhelming. Just as I again considered freezing time, Fraser nodded his head. "At least all I have to do is transport you to Calais. Even a magician would have a hard time messing up a mission that simple."

"Perhaps you haven't seen the power of true masters of magic." I tapped my cane, but the admiral ignored it. "Then you would be more grateful."

That evoked a laugh from the Vice Admiral. "Grateful? Let me teach you of magic. Here's all you need to know." He quickly pulled the pistol from its holster, but rather than aim it at me, he held it up and stared at it. "Do you see this? This is magic. There is nothing you can do to stop the magic of a bullet. Any man with a gun can defeat you."

My patience was at an end. I had to teach this Vice Admiral a lesson. If magic was dying in the world it wasn't due to technology—it was due to the lack of understanding and respect of its power. I could change that with Fraser easily.

I smiled, and re-arranged my grip on the cane. With a thought I stopped time.

Fraser lowered the pistol and returned it to his holster. "I see I've made my point." I glanced down at the cane and once again made the utterly natural movement of stopping time. I had done it many times before. It was something I understood. It was something I had total confidence in.

And yet time didn't stop.

I started to sweat and my hands shook. Behind his desk, Fraser noticed. "Chin up, Black. You'll face more than a pistol on the Continent. If you lose your composure over this, how do you expect to face down the Germans?"

Desperate and fearful that I had lost all of my power I tried the most basic of the staff's abilities in my hands—creating light. I held up the cane, and a bright beacon of light shone from the top. I was so full of relief that I almost broke down in tears.

"Ha! Good one, Black. Light has its uses. Maybe you're not completely worthless."

I cleared my throat. "I need time to prepare." I needed time not to prepare for the trip but rather to figure out what had gone wrong. I couldn't stop time. What else couldn't I do? What scared me most was that I knew there were a number of things I could do with the staff, but I had relied on stopping time so much that I felt defenseless, even if the staff could do everything else.

Even if I could do the other things… what had changed? Why could I make light but not stop time?

"You leave tomorrow. If you need time, use your own, not mine or that of my men."

I barely acknowledged Fraser's comment. I stood up straight, clutching the cane. Thinking of what I could learn from it while alone, I wanted nothing more to get back to the room I had been given at the naval base. "Yes, sir."

Fraser smiled. "Very good, Black. Dismissed."

I didn't remember the walk out of Fraser's office. I think I was escorted back to my room. Maybe the soldiers talked about me.

Maybe they didn't. All I remembered was that my connection to the staff seemed normal. I could sense that it was. Yet it somehow wasn't.

I didn't know what was happening, and that scared me more than the Shadows, Djinn, Ifrit, Marids, and even Cain.

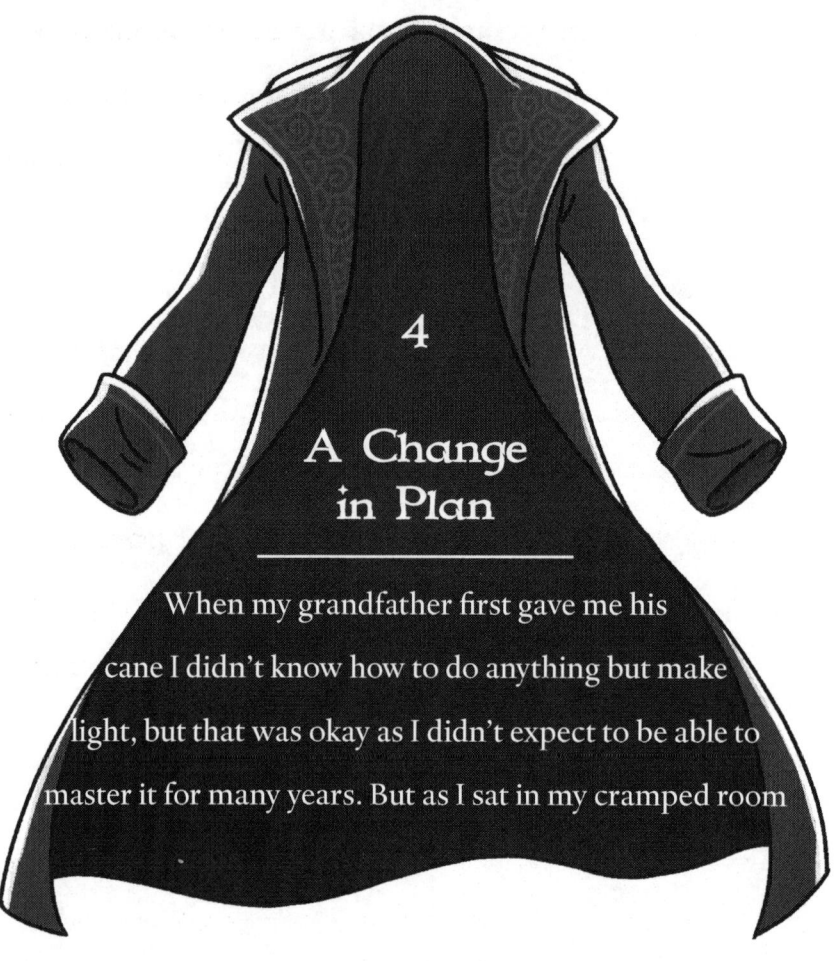

4

A Change in Plan

When my grandfather first gave me his cane I didn't know how to do anything but make light, but that was okay as I didn't expect to be able to master it for many years. But as I sat in my cramped room

in the naval base, I was near tears in frustration because I was in the exact same spot as that first moment with my grandfather. I could make light. I could remove light. What I couldn't do was stop light from flowing.

Which meant that my most powerful weapon, the one that had saved Naomi's life and had saved my own a number of times, the one that I counted on to help me defeat the Germans, was no longer under my control. I squeezed my hands on the cane so hard that my knuckles turned white and the outline of the runes pressed into my skin.

It didn't help.

I lay down and held the cane in my hands with my eyes closed. I relaxed and did my best to communicate with the staff, to understand it, to beg it to give me some kind of guidance as to what was wrong. I still had a deep connection to the staff, and that was perhaps what made the current situation so frightening—that connection didn't seem to change. It was still there. The staff remained a part of me. I could feel it.

It was the ability to stop time by stopping light that was no more.

I questioned whether I could defeat the Germans without that power. What use was blinding them with light or filling the area with darkness? Bullets are not stopped by darkness. Blind soldiers can still shoot.

The words of Vice Admiral Fraser became a nightmarish reality for me. I was no longer even as powerful as a single man with a rifle.

I was nothing more than a streetlight.

That thought made me think of Naomi. She was an extraordinary magician when I met her, nearly a master already at illusions, shields, and offensive magic. How much more powerful would she be two years later? Maybe she would join me and use her powerful magic to help. And, as humbling as it was to admit, it was clear I needed help.

As I considered asking Naomi for help, I realized that I was tired of being alone. I had spent two years by myself, running around, evading magicians and the military as I freed the Marids. My grandfather supported my mission, but had moved back to his home in New York. I missed having Naomi beside me, blowing things up and teasing me. I missed her calling me names. I even missed Mister Ali, the man who had betrayed my grandfather.

Still, more than friends I needed more information about what was happening with the staff, and I could think of only one person who could help me—my great grandfather. He was retired and living at his cottage in Balmoral. I had seen him every few months, and he was his same crotchety self, part inspirational and part insulting. I decided I should visit him and ask him about what may be happening with the staff. Of all the people in the world, he would know.

I had last seen him four months earlier. He was frail then and probably not long for the world. That depressing thought made me want to see him even more. Even if he knew nothing, I could at least say goodbye.

Vice Admiral Fraser was dismissive of my request, but within a few hours a soldier showed up at my quarters, telling me to pack. Cain had overruled Fraser and stated that a visit to my great grandfather should be accommodated. I wasn't sure if it was because he felt he owed my great grandfather for being willing to help him or because he felt it would help me in my cause in fighting the Germans. In the end it didn't matter—I was in a military automobile being driven to Balmoral, where I hoped to find answers.

5

The Retired Gardener

On every visit to my great grandfather I
challenged myself to find something that was
different. The path up to the cottage was always
perfectly manicured with the same razor sharp lines, while

the flowers and plants sat in the same beds and pots. Sometimes they were blooming, while other times they were awaiting
spring, but they were always there in some form or another. The
cottage itself didn't change at all.

In a world of violence, being hunted, and never knowing where
I would end up next, the stability and familiarity of visiting my
great grandfather was comforting to me.

This visit, however, was different in two key ways: A male nurse opened the front door instead of my great grandfather, and his cottage smelled strongly of antiseptic and medicine. Normally Great Grandfather would open the door, squint like he was pondering whether to let me in or not, and then I would walk in to a room fragrant with fresh flowers.

I followed the nurse through the living room, which was devoid of its usual vibrant plants, and into Great Grandfather's bedroom, where he lay in a bed under thick blankets. As I entered, his normal snarl was nowhere to be found. He smiled widely and lifted a skeletal hand. "Tommy! I'm so pleased you came to visit before I become fertilizer for my garden." He laughed, which turned into a cough. The nurse tried to hand him a glass of water, but he just waved it off.

"Nonsense, Archmage. You will outlive me!" I liked calling him Archmage, as it was a title he had been stripped of as a teenager and yet one he deserved even more than my mighty grandfather. My great grandfather could manipulate life itself with the staff.

"Bah. If I outlive you it will be because you did something stupid, which is quite possible, mind you." Even ill, Great Grandfather hadn't lost his bite.

I walked over and sat at his side. I rested the cane on the edge of the bed next to him. He didn't reach for it, which was his normal response. Ever since I had proven my ability with the staff, he wouldn't touch it without my permission. "How are you feeling?" I asked.

"Well, my entire body hurts. I'm hungry, but can't seem to eat anything. I'm thirsty, but they won't give me beer, and, as perhaps the final insult, the nurse they provided me is male."

I laughed. "I'm sure he's quite capable."

"Capable? He's not going to stop me from dying, so they may as well have given me someone pleasant to look at." I shook my head. Great Grandfather was blunt if nothing else. "Speaking of pleasant to look at, have you finally worked up the courage to go see your girlfriend?"

"I don't know where she is, and besides Naomi is not my girlfriend!"

With a wave of his hand, Great Grandfather dismissed my objection. "Sure she is. You two just haven't figured that out yet." He squinted his eyes and waved a finger at me. "I'm old, but not blind. I saw how you two looked at each other after I healed her." He closed his eyes and lay back on his pillow. "But I don't care.

I'm going to die soon. If you two want to be miserable, by all means stay miserable."

I didn't like talking about Naomi, so I changed the subject to the main reason for my visit. "I have a problem, Great Grandfather. You're the greatest Archmage I know, so I was hoping you could help me."

"Just go visit her. Problem solved!" Great Grandfather laughed again, which caused a coughing fit, a longer one this time. When he finished the nurse handed him a glass of water, which he took, drinking a few gulps before handing it back.

"I'm afraid it's quite a bit more serious than that." I reached over and picked up the cane. "I've lost the power to stop light and affect time with the staff."

"Eh? What do you mean?"

I outlined the circumstances of seeing the Vice Admiral, and how when I tried to stop time it didn't work. "I've been able to do it many times, and it has never failed me, whether I was facing an opponent or just practicing in my room. The staff always answered when I needed time stopped."

Great Grandfather's eyes peered at me with an intimidating intensity I hadn't seen in over a year. "And it is just this one ability?"

"Yes. I can create light, remove light… I've tried everything! It all works except for the one thing that provides me power over others."

"That's nonsense."

"Excuse me?" I had no idea what his objection could mean.

"You have power over others still. Your power is much greater than just stopping time. Please don't tell me you've been lazy in your study of the staff." If it were possible, Great Grandfather's stare was even more intimidating as he spoke.

"Uh—" I didn't know how to answer. Once I figured out how to stop time I hadn't worked on any other powers. "—I've studied Einstein. So I do understand how light can affect space and time."

"Lazy! Simple-minded! Uncreative!" His voice, which had been firm but weak, rose in anger. "Light is fundamental to many things, Tommy. I am disappointed in your lack of commitment to understanding your power."

"Okay, I get it. I can do more with the staff than I thought, but can we please focus on what is happening with stopping light? Why can I no longer do that?"

"I don't know. The staff is its own master. It is foolish to think you can control it. This is an excellent reminder of that." He looked down at the cane sitting on the bed next to him. "May I hold it?"

"Of course," I replied.

He reached for the staff, but the moment he touched it he pulled his hand back and cried out. His body started to spasm, and the nurse ran over. "What is happening?" I stood up and watched as the nurse pulled Great Grandfather up into a sitting position.

"I- I'm okay," Great Grandfather wheezed as he caught his breath. "It knocked the wind out of me is all." He slapped at the nurse's hand. "Leave me alone, you oaf. I said I was okay."

"It's time for you to rest, sir. I'm afraid your great grandson will need to leave." The nurse, who was about my size, gave me a pleading look.

"Nonsense. It's more important for us to talk. Go sit down and leave me alone." The nurse shook his head and walked over to his chair. Great Grandfather looked at me. He appeared frightened. "Tommy, the staff hurt me. It hurt me on purpose. It didn't want me touching it."

"What does that mean?"

"I don't know. Something big is happening. Something big. I know of our family's history with the staff. It has never hurt one of us. Ever. It refused to work for some of us, it worked in odd ways with others in our family, but it never hurt one of us."

"Is it dying?" I couldn't think of anything else. Maybe the Staff's power was in decline and it couldn't connect to anyone but me anymore.

"No. This is something bigger. More ominous." Great Grandfather struggled to sit up. The nurse hurried over but returned to his seat after my great grandfather shot him a glare. I helped him sit up and placed pillows behind him so he could rest against the headboard.

"What do you think it is?"

"I don't know, which is why you need to see Mister Ali. He will have some ideas as to what this may be."

The mention of Mister Ali filled me with conflicting emotions. I still hated him for betraying my grandfather, as well as his own son, but he was an important part of my introduction to the staff. He helped me in ways that I probably still didn't even realize or appreciate. "I refuse to see him. He betrayed our family. He betrayed your son!"

"Bah. My son. He deserved it. Declan was never smart enough to understand the politics of the world." Before I could object, he put his frail hand on mine, inches from the staff. "But there is a time when you seek out help, even if it requires you going to someone who did you wrong."

"When is that?" I asked, my voice clearly full of suspicion.

"When they are the only ones who can help you."

"Mister Ali knows less of the staff than I do," I replied. "His lessons were wrong and pointless. How can he help?"

"He doesn't know of the history of the staff with our family, and you are right—he doesn't know how it works. But he knows the older stories from Persia. He knows the myths and the legends. He can provide you with tales that may provide insight into what you are experiencing."

"Tales and legends?"

"We call them that, but doubtless many of them are based on truth."

"I don't even know where to find him," I answered, hoping my dismissive tone and simple response would end the conversation.

My geat grandfather would have none of it.

"Sure you do. He works for Cain."

I didn't know if I was more disappointed or surprised. My former mentor was now working for my enemy. "I will not beg a servant of Cain for help."

"Fine. Then you'll never find out what is going on with the staff." He shrugged, and with that the topic was closed. He had given me guidance, and that was that. If I didn't follow it, that was my problem.

His dismissiveness soon fell away as he took a raspy breath and closed his eyes. "I am old, Tommy. I have earned my selfishness. Find your own path. What I would like you to do now is tell me about your most recent adventures. Tell me how you did good with our family curse which has done so much evil." He crossed his hands and rested them on his chest.

My great grandfather was talking of the staff, of course, which he had taught me was stolen from others and used often by our family for glory and selfish reasons. I outlined the story of the Marid I had recently freed, the last enslaved Marid in England. Great Grandfather nodded and smiled at the point where I berated the Waymaster for trying to stop me by explaining that magical creatures deserved to be enslaved for the good of the country.

By the time I finished the story Great Grandfather was asleep, his breathing shallow. I looked over at the nurse. "Is he okay?"

"He's tired and in constant pain. I was surprised at how composed he was while talking to you."

I was stunned. I didn't realize he was so ill. "Is he dying?" The nurse nodded his head. "How much time does he have?" It felt wrong to be talking about Great Grandfather's future with him right next to me, but I needed to know.

"Not long."

I picked up the cane, wishing nothing more than that I could heal him with it or that I could just hand it to him and he could heal himself. But that was now impossible. I didn't want to leave. Maybe I could just stay by his side during his last final days. But I knew he wouldn't want that. He'd mock me for wasting time when I should be fighting to restore our family's honor.

Still, I couldn't leave. I sat on the bed as the sun went down. The nurse came and went, tidying, adding ice to the water, and basically keeping busy.

I had been absent-mindedly running my hands over the staff's runes, wondering what secrets I had overlooked when a gruff voice broke my reverie. "It's dark. You should be looking for your girlfriend."

I couldn't help but smile. "I just wanted to keep you company. I enjoy it."

Great Grandfather's voice was a whisper but still had a power. "Bah. Don't lie. Look, Tommy. I don't need you to babysit me. I'm too old for that. I'm tired. I'm not good company. You need to go. Find Naomi. Talk to Ali. He knows. You've created an honorable destiny. Don't sit here and waste it."

"All that can wait," I replied.

"Sentimental fool!" Great Grandfather's voice was loud and commanding, but the effort drained him, and he started to cough again. When he finished coughing, he added in a barely audible whisper, "I will miss you, Tommy, but you need to leave. This is not a room for a young man."

I stood up, and Great Grandfather closed his eyes and smiled.

I watched, and in moments I could tell he had fallen back to sleep. "Thank you," I whispered, but it didn't seem enough. So I shared all the bottled up thoughts I had been too intimidated to share with him. I told him I loved him, that he was my greatest inspiration, that I didn't want him to go. I told him that I wanted him to join me, even if it was just to insult me when I made mistakes. I wanted him to see Naomi again, to perhaps see that we weren't a couple or that we were. I thanked him for always giving me good advice. I told him that I'd visit Mister Ali and find out about the staff.

I told him I'd never forget him.

The nurse was standing next to me and handed me a handkerchief. I wiped my eyes and turned back to my great grandfather.

"Goodbye, Archmage," I said. I walked out and told the driver we were heading to the Citadel of London.

6

A Reunion
in the Library

The driver and I didn't arrive at the
Citadel until late the next day. By then I had
worked through every emotion, had planned every
plan, and had considered every challenge. In the end, I

decided to follow Great Grandfather's simple advice: Talk to
Mister Ali and then find Naomi.

We drove up the stone roadway to the Citadel. To my shock,
Cain was waiting just inside the front gate. I peered at my escort,
and he wore a grin which told me everything I needed to know
about how Cain knew I was coming.

As I looked back toward Cain I was surprised to see Mister Ali at his side. Mister Ali looked uncomfortable, and I felt embarrassed for him. He was such a proud man and yet he stood there fidgeting. At least he was dressed the way I had remembered him from the Persian Garden restaurant and our adventures—in his colorful robe, which I knew hid armor underneath.

The automobile stopped, and I climbed out. The moment Mister Ali's eyes caught mine, his jaw dropped, and he staggered back. Cain had a huge smile on his face. "Oh, there was no chance that I was going to miss this reunion." He turned to Ali. "Your student returns!"

I gritted my teeth and walked forward. I didn't look at Mister Ali. As hurt as I still felt over Mister Ali's betrayal, he did not deserve to be used as entertainment. "Enough games, Cain. I didn't come here for your amusement."

"Yet I am so amused." He couldn't take his eyes off me as he spoke. "It must be interesting to see the man who betrayed your grandfather, nearly killing him." I glanced at Mister Ali, who was staring at his feet. "Oh, wait, how could I forget? He also betrayed his own son." I tapped the staff angrily, but that didn't stop Cain. "Please, please, enjoy your reunion. I'll just sit back and watch as you two tearfully hug."

"Enough, Cain." I raised the staff, and Cain took a step backward. "Mister Ali does not deserve your mockery." Mister Ali looked up at me, surprise on his face.

"Fine. Fine. If you want to defend the man who betrayed you and your family, who am I to argue?" Cain laughed. "Besides, I'm sure you two have a lot of catching up to do." He turned to Mister Ali. "Ali, you can tell Black how you've helped me organize my magicians to catch him." Cain sneered, spun on his heel, and marched across the field toward his office.

There was an awkward silence as I looked at Mister Ali. I had grown much taller than him, and although his hair was still black as pitch, the wrinkles were deeper and seemed to frame his face in sorrow. That, more than anything, weighed heavy on my heart. I had been so used to Mister Ali's joy and laughter that seeing his deep sadness drained the anger I felt and replaced it with compassion.

He looked up at me, his eyes catching the reflection of the setting sun. "Tommy, I did not help anyone in trying to catch you. I cheered you on." His voice was missing the joyful cadence and tone I was used to. "I'm sorry, Tommy. I never meant to harm anyone. I've always loved Declan. I had no idea that Vingrosh would turn to violence."

I said nothing, and just looked at him. The truth was that I didn't know what to say. I was a mess of emotions. I couldn't deny that I still felt a deep fondness for him, and I knew his apology was sincere. He comforted me through frightening moments when I didn't know what I was doing, and his joyous laugh and positive attitude always made me feel better. At the same time I just couldn't understand his motivations. On one level I knew that he felt he was trying to help by ridding the world of the staff, but on the other hand he was willing to sacrifice friendship and possibly lives to do so.

Realizing that I wouldn't reply, Mister Ali added, "I don't deserve your forgiveness, Tommy, and I apologize that I let Cain fool me into using you and me as entertainment. If I knew you were visiting I wouldn't have left my quarters." Mister Ali turned to walk away.

"Wait!" Mister Ali stopped, waited a moment, as if deciding whether to listen to me or not, and then turned and faced me. "I need your help."

Mister Ali's eyes went wide and a look of concern filled his face. "Anything, Tommy, anything. Just tell me what you need." He walked toward me and stopped a couple of steps away.

I looked around, my military escort from Vice Admiral Fraser was behind me, and it looked like Cain had a soldier trailing Mister Ali. "Let's talk in Lord Ainsley's library." I figured Lord Ainsley had the authority to kick out any eavesdroppers.

"Of course."

We walked in silence, and I followed Mister Ali's lead. I was still befuddled by the illusions of the Citadel. I was completely incapable of seeing through even basic ones, and the illusions that were woven throughout the Citadel were sophisticated enough to make a two minute walk take me twenty minutes.

Mister Ali opened a door that I saw as a blank wall, and we were in Lord Ainsley's library at the edge of the Academy of Magic. Did the Academy of Magic even exist any more? I doubted there were any more students remaining. The few that were there during my stay two years ago had certainly long since been drafted as soldiers.

Our escorts followed us in, and Mister Ali held up a hand. The commanding presence I remembered returned. "Go! You two can wait outside."

"I'm sorry, I was told not to leave this young man's side."

Mister Ali's brow furrowed, and he frowned. When he wanted to look, he could look very intimidating. This was one of those moments. "Do you want me to call Lord Ainsley to have you forcibly removed? This is a library. What possible harm could come to your charge here?" The man stammered, and Mister Ali turned to his escort. "William, you are dismissed."

Mister Ali's escort thanked him and left, while mine looked back and forth between me and the open door. Finally he shook his head and walked outside.

"I'm surprised Cain's lackey just followed your orders like that." I sat down in one of the leather chairs.

As Mister Ali sat down in a chair near mine, he replied, "Oh, he is my servant, not Cain's. Cain likes to think he controls me, but I have too many friends here. I stay because this is the best place to stay informed of your—" Mister Ali shut up and then added, "—the best place to stay informed of the war."

Did that sound like I thought it did? Was Mister Ali keeping an eye on me? I had grown a lot in two years. I was able to treat Cain as an equal, and I was able to ask difficult questions. I took a breath. "You said your. Are you tracking me?"

Mister Ali shook his head as he replied. "Not tracking you, Tommy, applauding you. This was the best place to learn about your latest accomplishments. I am so incredibly proud of everything you've done. You are a beacon of goodness in this world of magical decay, a decay that is rotting even the best of our intentions, as my own behavior illustrates." He rubbed his forehead with a hand. "I told Cain I could help him track you down, but really all I did was listen to him rage about your successes and give him useless advice on where I thought you would be next. Of course, I didn't know. You are too clever for all of us, Tommy." He looked up at me and peered into my eyes. "Knowing the good you were doing with the staff made me even more aware of my foolishness in trying to rid the world of it." He folded his hands together and pressed them against his chin, as if praying in gratitude. "You gave the Shadows a home, Tommy. Remarkable. Nothing could have done that but the staff. In that simple act you proved how foolish and sad I truly am."

I didn't know how to reply. At every word spoken by Mister Ali any lingering anger drained from me. He followed me. He cheered me. He was proud of me. I was proving him wrong, and he was thankful for it. I had turned his greatest fear—the staff—into the one thing that could achieve what he could not, free and save the magical creatures.

And yet it still hurt. The attack in the alley, the one on the restaurant, perhaps even the attack that killed Naomi's mother—I would need to ask him about those, to demand an answer, to let him know that forgiveness did not mean he was absolved of blame or that trust was that easily regained. Still, the first step was to forgive.

"I accept your apology." I said the words, and they just seemed right. It was a first healing step toward him moving beyond his past, and my accepting his return to my life.

Mister Ali hadn't said anything, so I looked over at him. He had his head in his hands, and I wondered if he was upset, but I caught the faintest of sobs and then he looked up at me, tears streaming down his face, and said in a whisper, "Thank you, Tommy. Thank you." He cleared his throat and wiped his face. He took a deep breath and said, "What kind of help do you need?" His voice was strong and resonant and reminded me of the Mister Ali who escorted me along the Nar Marratum.

I outlined my recent experience with the staff and then, for the first time, told him the story of my family's criminal legacy as my great grandfather had relayed it to me. I didn't spare his feelings, as he had clearly believed the false history of my family being the inheritors of the staff. He didn't interrupt me or seem surprised as I explained that my family had stolen the staff from his ancestors during the crusades. On some level, I don't think he was surprised.

"I'm not sure how much of that is relevant, but as I said the real problem is that the Staff no longer allows me to control it as I have in the past."

Mister Ali nodded as he stared into the distance. I could tell he was thinking, so I kept quiet while I waited for him to gather his thoughts. Eventually he spoke. "Your great grandfather was always dismissive of me and Declan, but he was also wise. I didn't understand how great his power was until you just explained it to me, but his connection to the staff was clearly deep and strong."

"So you believe his history?" Mister Ali nodded. "But it conflicts with yours. You always felt that my family were the stewards of the staff."

"Hand me the staff, Tommy."

I hesitated. Not because I didn't trust Mister Ali anymore, but because I feared it might hurt him, as it did my great grandfather. Still, Mister Ali had an idea, and this might help me, so I handed him the staff. It didn't shock him or hurt him. He lifted it up and looked at it. He held it firmly in his hand and squinted as he focused his attention on it. He handed it back to me.

"It is as dead to me as it always has been, and I think that is by design. I told you that the staff is its own master. I didn't have as deep a knowledge of this as your great grandfather and you, but I knew it, of course. There are many legends surrounding the staff. It would take me hours to go over them all with you, but I think I understand what has happened—the Persian people realized the nature of the staff and intended to contain it, perhaps even destroy it. The staff somehow understood this and fled into the irresponsible arms of the crusaders. Their own greed served the needs of the staff."

"And the staff is once again trying to control its own destiny?" That made sense to me.

"Perhaps, Tommy. Your great grandfather said my legends may provide you with guidance. Here are some relevant legends that may or may not be based on truth: The staff is one of three magical artifacts crafted by the legendary and mighty magician Jamshid, along with a cup and a coat." He leaned forward. "Jamshid used these artifacts to rule Persia. They were the keys to his power. Now I believe this to be only partially true. Jamshid was the greatest magician in history. This is a fact. I also believe he created the staff. But the Cup's powers are fanciful. The myth is that you could use it to see anywhere on Earth or even the future. Impossible. And the Coat? The Coat presumably made one invincible against any attack, physical or magical. Such a thing would not still be hidden after all these years."

"But how does that help me with the staff and its powers?"

Mister Ali leaned back and took a deep breath. "I'm not sure, but think about the legend. Jamshid created the staff. A mighty magician channels great power into an artifact—does that sound familiar?" I didn't reply, and Mister Ali shook his head. "Surely you can think of things that are not magical and yet do magical things?"

I shook my head.

"Think of the trains, Tommy!" Mister Ali shook a finger at me, and I had to smile. He was acting once again like my teacher. "The staff must have a magical creature trapped inside it! A very powerful magical creature. Jamshid enslaved an ancient power, and now that ancient power is perhaps trying to regain control over its prison."

As soon as I heard the words I knew they must be true. Non-magical people harnessing magic via an inanimate object. It was exactly like the trains!

The legacy of the staff wasn't only tarnished by how my family stole it from Persia, it was tarnished as a prison for a magical creature. The thought sickened me. I had spent months freeing magical creatures, and my own power was dependent on what I sought to end!

I closed my eyes and tried to talk with whatever it was. I focused on the staff and the way it was connected to me. Could I follow that connection to the source? I tried but felt nothing. It was not unlike when I met the Marids in the trains. I knew they were there but I couldn't see them, and while I would talk to them and use my voice to free them I could never sense them listening to me or responding until they broke free.

"Should I free the creature?" I asked.

Mister Ali shook his head. "We don't know enough. You don't know enough. Focus on the staff and see what you can learn. Besides, you don't even know if you have the power to free it."

I nodded. I couldn't free a train Marid unless I was the engineer. Maybe to free the creature in the staff I needed to do or be something special. "I don't want to use the staff any more knowing that it is the power of an enslaved creature that I may be using."

"That is not only kind but also probably wise. If the creature has started to gain control of its prison, you can't be sure of what it can do with you as the conduit of its power."

"My plan was to travel to Germany and free the Ifrit and other creatures in their iron works. I still want to do that, but without the staff I fear I won't have that power."

"Germany? That is the home of illusion. There are many accomplished illusionists there. You will need someone with the

Sight." Mister Ali slapped his hand on his thigh. "I will accompany you!"

"You are too old!" I replied. I wasn't sure what I'd face, and I knew Mister Ali was at least as old as my grandfather.

To my surprise Mister Ali smiled. "You do not know my power and history do you, Tommy?" I shook my head. "Did you ever wonder why Cain hates me so?"

"Because you helped me."

"No. He hated me well before that. He hates me because his illusions are useless against me. I have the Sight, Tommy. I can see through all illusions. They are useless against me."

I thought of the lenses that the quartermaster gave me. They were broken and useless now, but I had experienced how they allowed me to see through illusion. If Mister Ali was like that all the time, his was a powerful talent indeed.

"And Germany has illusionists?"

"Many, and there are more than a few that are almost as powerful as Cain."

That struck me as an exaggeration, but even if it was only partially true it was clear I'd need someone like Mister Ali to help. Mister Ali looked me in the eye and held my gaze. "Tommy. Let me do this as a penance for betraying you and your grandfather. I can help. Trust me."

I smiled. "It will be like old times."

"Yes, Tommy, yes it will." Mister Ali smiled widely. "But we will need arms. Without the staff and its magic you have no ability to defeat the Germans."

"Oh, I have magic."

Mister Ali raised an eyebrow. "You have some other magical artifact?"

"No. Even better—I have a Naomi." Of course I didn't know if she would help, but I didn't think she would turn me down. All I needed to do was find her.

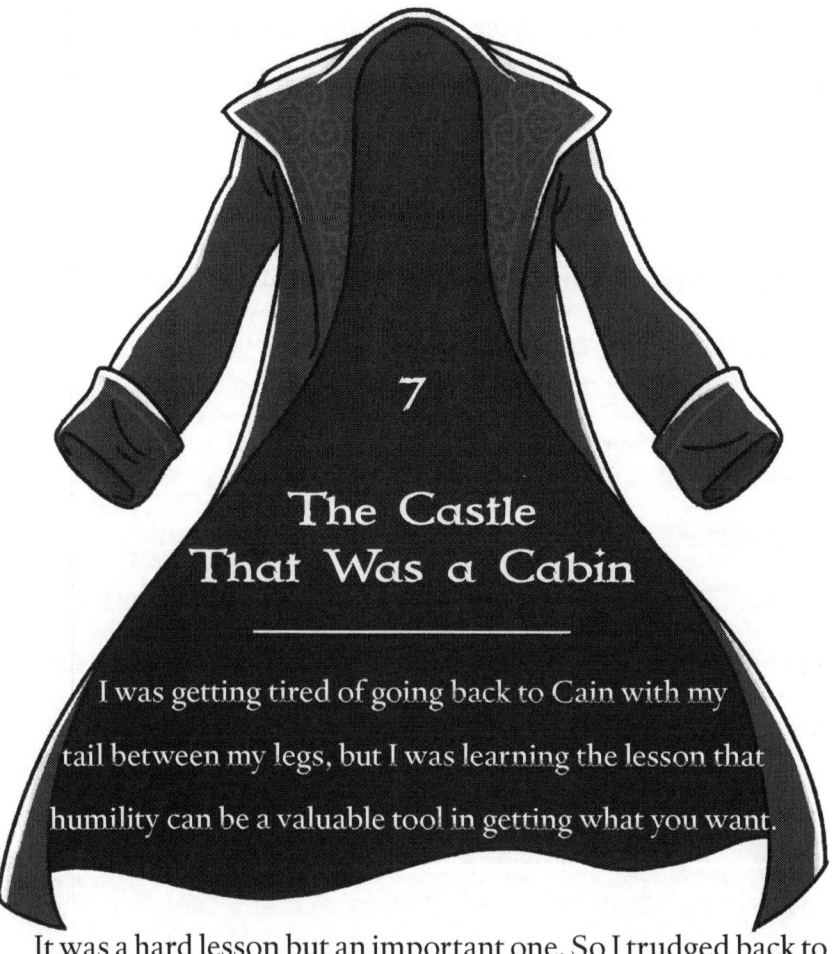

7

The Castle
That Was a Cabin

I was getting tired of going back to Cain with my
tail between my legs, but I was learning the lesson that
humility can be a valuable tool in getting what you want.

It was a hard lesson but an important one. So I trudged back to
Cain's office to ask him about Naomi.

Cain told us right away. We sat in his office, and he looked
like we had handed him a stack of presents. "She's in Scotland.
Please. Go retrieve her immediately. I've been trying to get her
to assist in the war effort for months." Cain leaned back in his
chair. "I may actually learn to like you, Black. You recruit a pow-

erful sorceress to the cause. You finally remove Ali from annoying me with his questions, and you, yourself, are going into the heart of Germany to wreak havoc. Next you'll be telling me that you've decided to give me the staff."

"I will never like or respect you, Cain." I stood up. "And you will never get the staff." Mister Ali stood up next to me but didn't say anything.

Shrugging, Cain added, "I can live with that." With a glance, Cain turned his desk into a replica of a rocky coastline. "See the house?" I nodded. There was a small cottage near an inlet not far from the sea. "It's along the coast north of Aberdeen. Naomi is there."

"Are you sure?"

Cain laughed. "Quite. She comes out, threatens my men, and then returns inside."

That sounds like her, I thought. "You're watching her?"

"Of course I'm watching her. She's a powerful magician. If she's not going to help England, I need to make sure she doesn't help anyone else." I smiled at Cain's admission that Naomi was a powerful magician. When she first visited the Citadel they had tried to teach her domestic magic.

"A magician worth watching from the likes of Cain is a powerful magician indeed," Mister Ali said to me, talking as if Cain wasn't even in the room. I knew he loathed Cain perhaps more than I did.

"Just aim her at the Germans, and I'll be happy." Cain smiled widely. "I'll get you transportation to Aberdeen and also have all three of you escorted to France."

I was grateful, even though Cain was clearly only helping us because it helped him. Still, transportation was a critical need for me with the country at war. "Thank you, Cain," I finally blurted out.

"Just don't die," he replied.

Naomi's cabin wasn't just north of Aberdeen, it was far north of Aberdeen. In fact, I doubted there was a living creature within a few miles of her seaside cottage. The car couldn't make it closer than a mile or so to the coast, and by then we didn't have access to horses or a wagon.

We trudged through grass, mud, and rocky land with the brightest part of the scenery being the gray clouds in a darker grey sky. I glanced at Mister Ali, who while strong and spry was still old.

"Should we rest?" I asked. He shook his head but didn't say anything. We continued on, sharing a grim determination.

Naomi's cottage was just across the mouth of the river Ythan, and by the time I saw her home I was cold, wet, and miserable. Still, the idea of seeing her for the first time in almost two full years brightened my mood.

Mister Ali stopped as we approached. I glanced over, and he looked stunned. "I had not heard of this magic castle," he said in a whisper.

I turned to look at her cabin. "I guess Naomi could consider that her castle, but, really, there's barely enough room for a kitchen in there, let alone a study or other space."

"You can't see through the illusion, Tommy."

"Illusion?" I looked back at Mister Ali, but he was still staring at the cottage.

"Yes. It is a very old, very mighty castle. Its walls start there—" He pointed at the shoreline, where I saw nothing but a rocky beach. "—And continue over to there, where they climb the hill." He swung his arm and pointed to what I saw as nothing more than sparse rocks, dirt, and grass leading inland. He turned and looked at me. "Where do you see the door?" I pointed to the wooden door of the cottage. "Yes. That's the entry to the castle. It is wood reinforced with iron."

"Wait, you can't see the cottage?" I knew Mister Ali could see through illusions, but wouldn't he also see the illusions, themselves?

"Alas, no, Tommy. It is perhaps a weakness of my strength. I have a very rare talent. Illusions have no effect on me, which is good, but as I am not aware of them I can't warn others."

"So we must act like a team. I tell you what I see, and you tell me if it is real?"

Mister Ali smiled widely, and it was as if we were back to where we were two years earlier. "Yes. That is exactly how your grandfather and I worked together for many years. We were a very close team. I saved his life countless times."

"I wish I had known that. Perhaps would have made me think of what was happening in a different light."

"Perhaps, Tommy, but he saved me countless more. You don't keep score when you're friends."

I thought of his comment and my own feelings. I badly wanted things to go back the way they were, and I felt I was doing a good job. But I still had some lingering mistrust, a small piece of resentment that he simply didn't trust my grandfather to do the right thing or, at least, to give him a chance. You don't keep score when you're friends. Maybe that's what I needed to do. Just accept the bad with the good. Not keep score. Just see Mister Ali as a friend.

"What do you see, Tommy?"

"A small cabin, almost a shack, there is a soft light glowing from inside, it looks like it may be from a fireplace or lantern. Mister Ali nodded. "Who do you think created the illusions?"

"I think Naomi has the help of a master level illusionist. This is a new illusion, very powerful. I can at least sense that. She is not alone. If Cain is right that she is training, she has someone training her or working with her." Mister Ali turned and looked at me. I looked down at his face, which was a mixture of curiosity and concern. "Can we trust her, Tommy? This may end up being more than we bargained for."

"I trust her with my life," I answered emphatically.

Mister Ali nodded. "Then let us go say hello."

As we approached the door, I remembered our parting. She had said something about the challenge I faced, and I said she had a similar one studying her magic. It was meant as a compliment, but she frowned and then we had an awkward goodbye. I had tried to contact her a few times, but she no longer lived at the address she had given me.

I had thought of her often, but it is embarrassing to admit that most of my thoughts were not of her magical talent but of her eyes, her sharp features, her golden hair, and her thoroughly enchanting and maddening character. But in light of Mister Ali's comment about power and trust I realized that I had dismissed something incredibly important. Naomi wasn't just a cute girl, she was a talented magician, perhaps a great magician. I was embarrassed at my shallowness. No wonder she didn't want to see me.

We stood in front of the door, and I looked at Mister Ali. He shrugged, so I knocked on it with my knuckles. It sounded like a normal door, and my raps sounded just like I was knocking on a piece of wood. "What does it sound like, Tommy?"

"Like I'm knocking on a wooden door."

He nodded. "Impressive. There aren't many illusionists in the world that could create this level of illusion. Perhaps Cain was involved."

I shook my head. "There is no way Naomi would accept Cain's help. You heard what he said." I knocked again, and the door opened a crack. A young man peered out. He had jet black hair and the stubble of a face in need of a shave. He looked a few years older than me and seemed quite handsome. He looked me up and down.

"Go away," he said, starting to close the door. His voice had an Eastern European accent. I tapped on it with the cane, stopping him immediately. He glanced at the staff and peered at me. "Archmage, this is unexpected." I tried to place his accent. Poland? Russia? I wasn't sure.

"I'm here to see my friend, Naomi."

"She doesn't accept visitors," he replied flatly.

"Don't be rude, young man. This is a friend of Naomi's," Mister Ali interjected, his voice booming.

The man's eyes went wide as he noticed Mister Ali behind me. "The Eye of the Archmage!" His voice was tinged with awe."

Clearly, this person was familiar with how Mister Ali and my grandfather had worked together. "What are you doing here?"

"I serve the Archmage, as I have my entire life." Mister Ali took a step forward. "Now let us in."

His eyes darting from me to Mister Ali, the young man replied, "I must ask her. Please wait." He closed the door.

"At least he was polite to you." I turned to Mister Ali. "Do you know him?"

Mister Ali looked grim. "No, but he's the illusionist that is maintaining the castle."

"How do you know that?"

Shrugging, Mister Ali replied, "Illusionists are always casting. It's easy to notice if you know what to look for."

"You mean to maintain their illusions?" Mister Ali nodded. "Even when they are asleep?"

"Yes. They train their body to make tiny movements without thinking. It takes years of training."

"He didn't look very old," I replied.

"Talent is a factor, as well."

I turned back to the door and tapped my foot, out of both impatience and nervousness. "I don't understand, Mister Ali. Why is he here with Naomi? I may not have seen her for a couple of years, but I know her well enough that she would never ask for help." I glanced at Mister Ali. "She is too proud."

Nodding, he replied, "I know not, Tommy. I imagine we'll find out soon enough."

I squinted all around as we waited. I looked for walls. I looked for high towers. I looked for anything that would remotely indicate that this was a castle. I couldn't see anything other than a small, shabby cottage. It made me grateful once again that Mister Ali was with me. I had known for a long time that my weakness was with illusions, but this was ridiculous. An entire castle that I couldn't see?

"I can't believe I can't see an entire castle," I muttered.

"No, Tommy. You can see it. The illusionist didn't make it invisible. That would require bending light around it. The illusionist makes you think it is smaller."

Something about Mister Ali's comment caught my attention but at that moment the door opened, and I pushed such distractions aside. It was the young illusionist. "She won't see you." And without further comment he slammed the door.

I looked at Mister Ali, who appeared puzzled. I was stunned. Naomi had always been a friend. We escaped the Citadel together. I saved her life! And now she wouldn't see me? I couldn't understand it.

"Perhaps we can find other help, Tommy," Mister Ali said, his voice subdued and respectful. He must have sensed my confused feelings.

"No." I rapped on the door with the head of the cane. "Something is wrong. I feel it." There was no response, so I rapped on the door harder. The door remained closed, and I started to get more concerned and angry.

"Perhaps she simply is focusing on her studies, Tommy." I ignored Mister Ali and banged the door with the cane loudly and with great force. "You strike too hard, Tommy. You may harm the staff."

I knew that harming the staff was impossible, so I ignored Mister Ali. By then I was convinced that Naomi was held captive or worse. The illusionist was Russian! Maybe he was trying to steal her knowledge.

These and other irrational thoughts filled my head as I pounded on the door. I knew I couldn't just walk through whatever magical shields protected the castle, so my goal was to simply get the Russian to answer the door again. I would use the staff to get past any defenses at that point.

With more desperation I pounded on the door, and to my shock the cane started to warm in my hand. With each impact I could feel an increasing vibration in the staff.

"Tommy, what are you doing?" Mister Ali looked up with alarm in his eyes. I slammed the cane against the door and heard a rumbling. I struck again. "You will bring the entire castle down if you keep that up!"

The door flew open, and the young Russian stood in front of me. He looked terrified. "Archmage, please. Do not destroy the castle. Please. I have a message from Naomi." I lowered the cane and leaned on it. The illusionist looked like he wanted to do anything but speak. He finally whispered, "Naomi wants me to tell you that—" he gulped. "—She finds your temper tantrum sad but predictable, and that 'When the streetlight learns how to be a friend he can ask me politely about a visit.'" I didn't move, but the young man added in a strained voice, "Please don't kill us."

I shook my head. "Kill you? Why would I kill you?" I turned to Mister Ali. "That certainly sounds like Naomi."

"Indeed. Did you offend her when you last saw her?" I thought back to our last meeting. It was awkward, and Naomi seemed upset, but I didn't think I said anything wrong. Did I misread something? It was certainly possible. I was an idiot with girls, let alone someone as headstrong as Naomi.

"I don't think so," I replied. I turned to the young Russian. "My name is Tommy Black. We can work this out with a conversation. Please let us in." He shook his head. "I said let us in." He went to close the door, and I shoved forward plowing into him, knocking him backward.

While I knew to expect the entry to a castle, when I entered it was still a huge shock seeing it. I had just been outside a cabin, and now I was stumbling into a stone entryway that was twice its size. The Russian gathered his balance, his face intense.

"He is a master of illusion, Tommy! Be wary!" Mister Ali yelled. I squeezed the cane to stop time, forgetting that the staff had decided to take that power from me.

"Last chance. Leave," he said. Presumably his fear of Naomi was greater than his fear of the Archmage. I looked around. I was helpless, and all I could do with the staff was the useless stuff I could do before. I considered creating darkness, but that just meant I'd have to stumble over to find Mister Ali, with the constant danger of discovery. I could have blinded the illusionist, but I really didn't want to hurt anyone. If only I could make him not see us without blinding him.

And at that point two random conversations came together in my mind—my great grandfather berating me for not being creative enough in my study of my powers with the staff, and Mister Ali outside the door talking about light bending around us. Of course. It didn't even require a thought. Light flowed around me.

"Where did he go?" I heard our host's strained voice. I was invisible, but the trouble was that I couldn't see either. That's when the final piece clicked into place. My own eyes need light to hit them so I could see. I allowed light to bend all around me with the exception of the center of my irises. I could see.

I walked over to the edge of the room.

The young Russian's eyes darted around. "What sorcery is this, Ali?" Mister Ali was smiling. "I have the Sight, and this is not an illusion. What is happening?"

"What is happening, young man, is that you are facing the most powerful Archmage in history." Mister Ali closed the door behind him, and walked over to the Russian, who was crouched in a defensive position. "What is your name?"

"Arkady," he replied.

"Well, Arkady, why don't you just go tell Miss Naomi that her rude friend Tommy did not take no for an answer." He looked around the room. "I see you have no chairs. It matters not. We do not mind standing while we wait."

Arkady nodded and backed out of the room. Once he was a few steps down the hall he breathed easier and increased his pace. He didn't know that I was following.

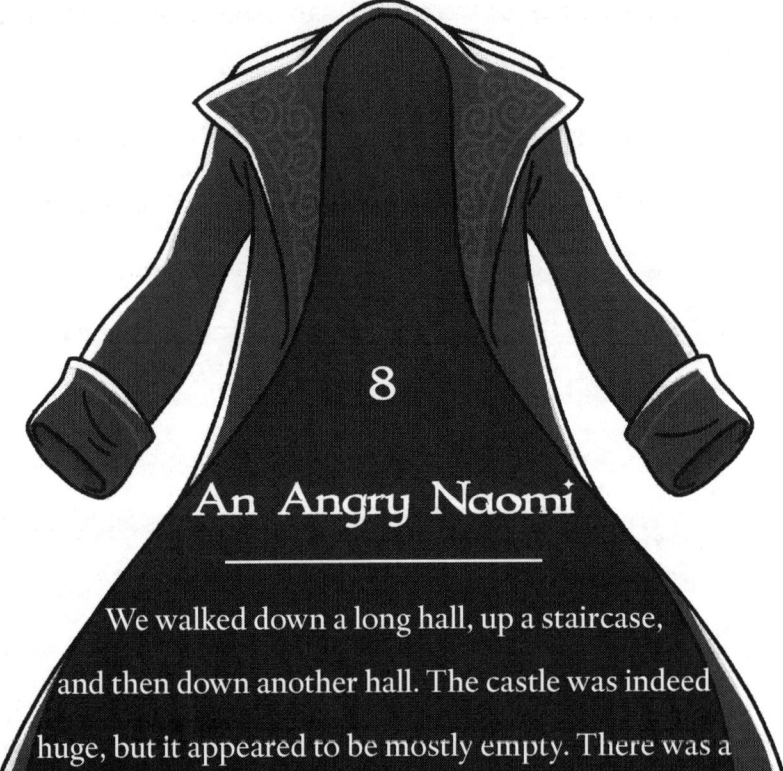

8

An Angry Naomi

We walked down a long hall, up a staircase, and then down another hall. The castle was indeed huge, but it appeared to be mostly empty. There was a library with a fire, and on the second floor there was a soft light coming from behind a partially closed door, but those were the only signs of life. Eventually, we climbed another staircase that ended at a single wooden door. Arkady knocked on it.

"Come in." It was Naomi.

I snuck past as Arkady closed the door and continued into the room. It was large and circular, with bookshelves full of books of all sizes filling the walls. Against the far wall was a large plush reading chair with books piled on a table next to it. A gas lantern filled the room with a diffused light.

Naomi looked up as Arkady approached, and my heart filled with a painful yearning, not necessarily of the romantic sort but of the type you feel when you finally see a dear friend that you have been parted from for many years. Standing across the room, alone and invisible, made things even worse.

I couldn't help but stare. Naomi looked thinner. Her face was drawn, and she seemed sad and tired. She smiled slightly as Arkady approached. "Did he leave?" He shook his head, which elicited a bigger smile from Naomi. "I didn't think he would. Did you get the door closed? Is he waiting outside? I should make him wait in the wet and cold for a few days before I see him. Teach him some humility." Arkady was shuffling his feet nervously, and Naomi noticed. "What's wrong? Did he stop time before you could get the door closed?"

The words came out in a jumble. "No. He didn't stop time at all. He forced his way into the foyer and turned himself invisible and I couldn't see him and you told me not to hurt him anyway and I wasn't sure what to do but he told me to come get you so here I am." Naomi frowned, and Arkady added, "I'm sorry." I couldn't tell if Arkady was afraid of Naomi or worried about disappointing her.

"It's okay." Her voice was warm as she talked to him, which made me jealous. I wanted her to talk to me that way. Naomi's brow furrowed. "Wait. He didn't stop time?" Not waiting for a response, Naomi stood up. "Something is wrong." She looked concerned as she placed a book on the table next to her. "I will handle this."

She walked past Arkady as he held up a hand. "One more thing."

Naomi stopped and waited. In her look I could see that she was simply waiting for Arkady to speak, to provide her knowledge, to interact with her on his own terms. And in that look I saw all the maturity that had developed over the past two years. She was obviously still rebellious and wouldn't listen to anyone, let alone me. She was just as intense as I remembered. Yet she was now willing to listen.

But then I considered something else. What if she was listening because Arkady was more than just a fellow magician? Were they alone in this castle? A handsome young man alone with her to share an interest in magic? Could they perhaps be girlfriend and boyfriend? My chest started to tighten as I pondered the possibilities.

As Naomi listened, Arkady stated, "Mister Ali is with him."

Her eyes went wide, and I saw what I thought was fear in them. "He is in trouble," was all she said before she rushed to the door. I ran to follow, doing my best to not make any noise or to give away that I was behind her. Luckily there were no closed doors between her study and the foyer, so as she rushed in, I quickly followed behind and moved over to be near Mister Ali, who stood like a statue, his arms crossed, and his eyes looking at the door we just entered through.

"Tommy?" Naomi's eyes darted around the room. I stopped light from bending around me. Ali jumped a bit in surprise, while Naomi's eyes went wide. I smiled.

"Isn't it neat?"

She marched over, a scowl on her face. The scowl somehow made her prettier, with her sharp cheekbones and blue eyes framed by furrowed brows and a gritted jaw. She was wearing a white cotton shirt and khaki pants, which was almost the same outfit I remembered her wearing when I had last seen her. But more than anything I was distracted by her straight blonde hair, which was fine and airy as it flew around her head with each step.

"How dare you!" she exclaimed, hitting me on the upper arm, punctuating each word with a punch. "You leave me for two years, forgetting all about me, and now you just show up with a smile and a neat trick?" She paused and stared at me, her chest heaving. I stepped back, thoroughly confused. In her office she seemed incredibly concerned about me, and yet now she was in a rage.

"Naomi—" Mister Ali said, which elicited a quick spin on her heels to face him.

"No, traitor. There is no Naomi from you." She turned back to me. Her eyes were glistening. "You have some nerve, Tommy. Tossing me aside and then forcing your way into my home." She emphasized the word home, and I was perhaps one of the only people in the world to know the force the word held for her. She had lost her home when her mother was killed defending us from an attack.

"Naomi, listen—"

"No, Streetlight. You listen to me. Yeah, I know. You went out and did all of these great deeds saving magical creatures. Believe it or not, I'm proud of you for doing that." She took a deep breath and added, "but you left me behind, Tommy. You left me behind."

I didn't reply. I was devastated. All of my feelings came rushing back as I watched her rage. I had seen her passionate anger again and again. It was one of the things I loved about her.

She looked at me while I looked at her. Finally, I replied, my voice a whisper, "I didn't know you wanted to come."

Her eyes went wide, and she hit me in the arm again. "You're an idiot. Why would you think I wouldn't want to come?"

"Because I'm an idiot?" I sensed the barest hints of a smile. I lowered my head. "You deserved more than to just run around with me, anyway. You needed more. And what about your magic? You were an amazing magician. You are an amazing magician. You wouldn't want to waste a chance at learning more just to watch me run around with this." I held up the cane.

"Well, thank you for being kind enough to decide for me how I should run my life, Mister Black. That's so very gallant of you."

"Wait, I didn't mean it that way!" She was mad again. I just didn't know how to talk to girls, most of all Naomi. Even when I tried to say something positive it came out all wrong.

"What did you mean then?" The hint of a smile was gone, and the rage was simmering.

"I- I don't know. I wanted you with me, but I was afraid. I don't know why. Maybe I thought you'd get hurt. Maybe I thought you'd get bored. Maybe I thought you were more interested in learning magic than being with me. I don't know. I really don't." I looked down at her face, which I couldn't read at all. "I wanted you with me, but the thought scared me. There. Are you happy?"

Naomi smiled. "Happy you finally told me the truth? Yes, I am." And like that the anger was gone. She turned and walked over to the door. "Follow me. There's a room with chairs down this hall." She glanced over at Mister Ali. "And the traitor can come, too."

I looked at Mister Ali, who shrugged.

9

Discussions
by Firelight

Not far down the hall there was an arch to the left that opened into the small study that I passed earlier. Naomi marched in, and the rest of us followed. To the right was a desk with chairs in front of it,

and to the left was a sofa against the wall with wingback reading chairs facing it. A large painting dominated the wall opposite the entry. It portrayed a mighty dragon falling from the sky from what looked like an attack from a Persian magician. Under the painting was a large fireplace, a crackling fire in its hearth. Gas lamps on sconces were interspersed along the walls. Unlike the Scottish weather, it was bright, warm, and comfortable.

Naomi sat in one of the wingback chairs. She leaned forward, her elbows on her thighs, and her hands folded between her legs. I sat in the other chair while Mister Ali sat on the couch.

She nodded toward Mister Ali. "What's with him?"

"You can call me Mister Ali, Naomi." He was clearly irked by her attitude, and it made me smile inside. Naomi drove everybody crazy. She ignored him and waited for me to reply.

I recounted my story, outlining how I visited Cain and how I was preparing to go to Germany when the staff somehow rebelled.

"I'm so sorry, Tommy. That must have been scary." I nodded. I hadn't exactly described it that way to the adults, but Naomi nailed it—it was scary, like suddenly losing your sense of hearing or sight.

"Mister Ali thinks that it must contain a magical creature, and that it may be trying to break free."

"Of course it contains a magical creature. Where did you possibly think the magic came from?" Naomi rolled her eyes.

"I don't know!" I replied, embarrassed at my own naïveté and ignorance. "It's a big question that I need to answer, but more importantly I'm trying to understand what this means for me and my control over the staff."

"I see. Nice to see your concern for enslaved magical creatures has a limit."

I stared at Naomi. "Is that what you think of me?" I stood up. "You really think that's how I feel?" I took a step toward her, preparing to yell, but I was too hurt to even do that. "Come on, Mister Ali. We don't need her help."

I strode toward the door wondering if I was making a huge mistake but too hurt to care.

"Tommy! I'm sorry!" I continued through the arch. I didn't care if Naomi or Mister Ali followed me. No one knew what was in my heart but me. I had spent two years alone, chased, and harassed. I could do it again. There were footsteps behind me, and a hand grabbed my shoulder.

"Tommy. Please." It was Naomi. I stopped and turned. Naomi's face was red, and she looked scared. "I sometimes say things that I don't mean. I don't know why I do it. I'm sorry."

"Yeah. You just say things that hurt others. I get it. It's your schtick. Ha ha. You don't know why. It's just a thing." I turned and started walking. "Well do your thing with someone else."

"Tommy!" She ran around me and planted herself in front of me. I had to stop so I didn't run into her. Holding out her hand, she spoke, her words coming out fast and clipped as tears started to fall down her cheeks. "I don't know why I do it. Maybe it's because I don't like people being close, but that's not right because I like you Tommy and having you around was one of the things I've really missed so maybe I am just afraid of that. Maybe I think you'll leave me like my dad did and my mother did and you did before and I just don't want that to happen to me again and maybe I've always felt that way because I've always been alone."

"So you are pushing me away because you're afraid I'll leave you?"

"I don't know." To my utter shock, Naomi walked forward and put her arms around me, hugging me tight. I lowered my hands onto her back and returned her hug as she whispered, "I really don't know anything."

"I don't either," I whispered.

"All I know is that you're really my only friend in the whole world." She pulled away and wiped her face with the sleeve of her shirt.

"You're my only real friend, too," I replied. "And I seem to have done a pretty good job of pushing you away in the past."

"Ha. We're a pair. Both of us do our best to drive away our friends, including each other." She grabbed my arm and tugged as she headed back toward the study. Mister Ali was near the archway, watching both of us. "I'm sorry I'm so difficult, Tommy."

"I'm sorry that I'm so clueless."

We sat down and Naomi's mocking attitude was gone. "So the staff is no longer working?"

"No. Some of it works. Just not the most powerful magic."

"So you've done magic with the staff since then?"

"Yes. I've created, removed, and focused light."

"What about the invisibility thing. What was that?"

"Oh, that's a new power I just discovered. I can bend light around things making them invisible. They exist, but they can't be seen because the light won't reflect off them back to our eyes."

"I did not know that, Tommy," Mister Ali finally spoke up. I glanced at him. He was rubbing his chin. "That's a powerful magic in and of itself."

"Yeah. I'd say being invisible is very powerful," Naomi said. "I could feign invisibility by creating an illusion that the person is something else, but that's sophisticated and would take a lot of preparation."

"You are that accomplished at illusion?" Mister Ali sounded stunned.

Naomi nodded and slid her hair behind her ears. "Okay, let's assume that the staff does contain a magical creature." She quickly turned to me. "I'm not saying that for certain, but I believe this highly likely."

"Mister Ali said as much," I replied, glancing at him as he nodded.

"So what does that tell us?" Absent-mindedly, Naomi moved her hands and an inky black swirling ball appeared in her hands.

"That's beautiful. What is it?" I asked. I had been used to her calming herself by creating detonations and other destructive magic. This was something entirely different.

Naomi squeezed a hand, and the ball disappeared. "It's the Hammer of Jamshid."

"Impossible!" Mister Ali replied. "That spell hasn't been cast in centuries. Only Jamshid himself mastered it."

She created the ball again. "Yeah, it's a tough one." Naomi shrugged. "But enough about this—" She squeezed her hand and the ball disappeared. "We were talking about the staff. So here's my thought: The creature that was imprisoned in the staff is really smart and really powerful. It has been probably thinking of every loophole to get out of his prison, and in that process he's figure out ways to limit the power of the staff. That it took this long tells me that you're probably safe for quite some time, but who knows?"

"Do you think it's coincidence that the creature was able to stop the single most powerful use of the staff?" I asked.

"No, Tommy." It was Mister Ali. "Something changed. I disagree with Miss Naomi. If there was a flaw in the imprisonment of the creature, it would have freed itself ages ago. Something about his prison has changed. Or at least its circumstances."

"But what could it be? Nothing has changed. Magic is even rarer in the world today than it ever has been. Are there even that many magicians left?" I replied, thinking of how the magicians in the Citadel of London had been replaced by soldiers.

"There is the appearance of the Angel of St. Petersburg." It was Arkady, leaning against the arch. With the stress of our entrance behind him, he looked calm, even amused. I didn't like his look. He was too handsome, with his black hair short but unkempt in the way of Hollywood adventure heroes. I finally noticed his outfit, which I wanted to call ridiculous but had to admit looked impressive—he wore a black trench coat that was buttoned all the way up and looked mysterious.

"Arkady! Please come in. Yes, perhaps you can be of help here with your perspective." Naomi seemed happy to see him, a contrast to their clipped and matter-of-fact conversation earlier. He walked in with long purposeful strides. Naomi turned to us. "Arkady is a master illusionist. His spells are very powerful and he casts them extraordinarily fast."

Arkady sat down next to Mister Ali. "The young lady exaggerates," he replied, bowing his head slightly. I looked from one to the other. Their attitude toward each other was completely different in the relaxed circumstances of the study. Naomi had moments earlier said I was her only friend, but I found doubt growing inside me. I may have been her friend, but was Arkady something more?

"We have met," I replied, trying to hide my bitterness.

"Indeed. I apologize for my mistrust. To be clear, I admire how you help the cause with your severing of magic and technology."

"The cause?" I asked.

Arkady glanced at Naomi. She paused before replying, "Yes, that. Oh well, I may as well explain what I've been doing for the past year." Naomi looked over at me and smiled. "Cain gave me this castle to preserve and rebuild magic in England."

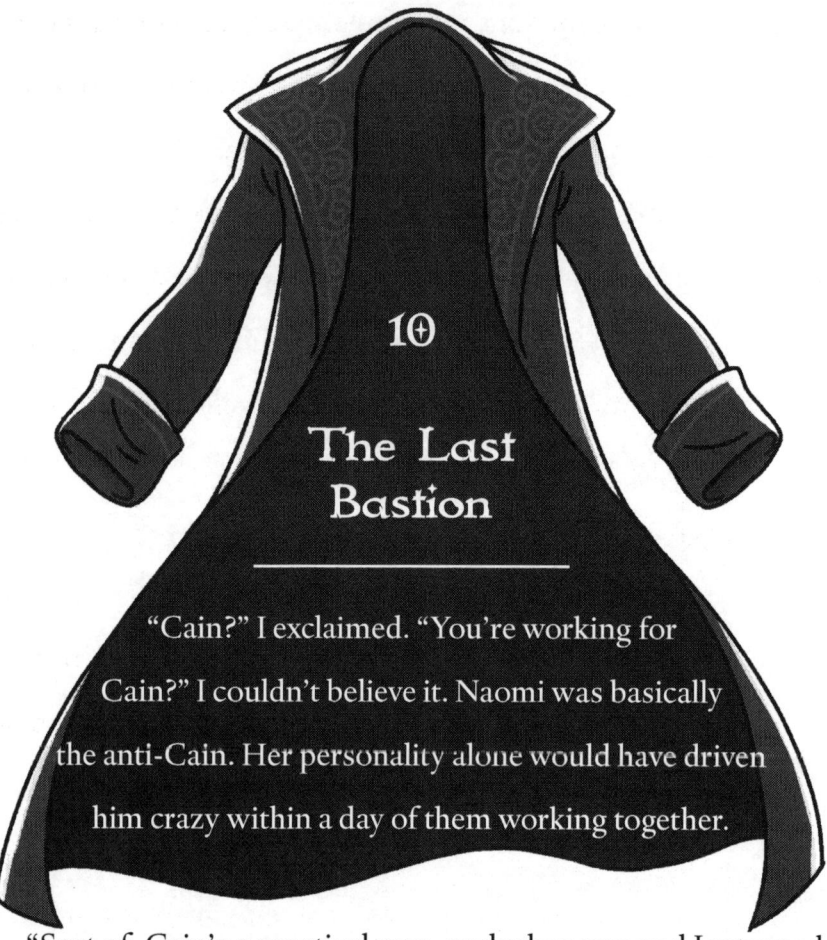

10

The Last Bastion

"Cain?" I exclaimed. "You're working for Cain?" I couldn't believe it. Naomi was basically the anti-Cain. Her personality alone would have driven him crazy within a day of them working together.

"Sort of. Cain's a practical man, and when you and I returned to England he kept tabs on both of us. Of course he sent magicians and others to try and stop you, but after you left me, he sent Master Behnam to me to discuss preserving and nurturing magic."

Mister Ali nodded. "Yes, that sounds like Cain. He is in a constant battle to keep magic relevant with the English government, if for no other reason than to maintain his power."

"It isn't about power for him. At least I don't think it is. He seems sincere. I've talked with him, and he badly would like to halt the slow death of magic. So he gave me Dunnotar Castle. He's relocated practically every magic book he could get his hands on to here." She waved her arm in a sweeping arc. "The magical knowledge in this castle is extraordinary."

Naomi sighed. "But unread books are just pieces of paper. He had me work with Master Behnam to recruit magicians to relocate here as both a place of study and a safe haven. It was a compelling idea with war raging. Still, there aren't many magicians left."

"How many are there here?" I asked, looking around and trying to imagine how many could live in the castle that seemed an impressive size and was full of millennia of magical knowledge.

"Two. Arkady and myself." My jaw dropped. I had expected two dozen, maybe ten if things were really bad. But two?

"There are only two magicians left in England? What happened to Behnam?"

Naomi laughed, but it was full of bitterness. "No, Tommy. Including Cain, there are three master level magicians left in the western part of the world. There were ten, but seven have been killed in the war, including Master Behnam." Naomi shook her head. "It was worse in Russia. Right, Arkady?"

He nodded. "Yes. The government was not happy with magicians. Magic was part of the Tsar's world, not for the people. We were hunted and killed. I escaped and am grateful for the home Cain has made for me here."

"Three?" I couldn't believe it. Magic really was dying in the world.

Naomi nodded at me as Mister Ali spoke up. "I'm sorry, Arkady. That sounds terrible," He looked at Naomi. "So what have you discovered in the past year?"

"Good question, traitor." I winced. On the one hand I was happy that Naomi was back to her normal teasing self, but I also knew that Mister Ali would take the insults personally. I hoped that Naomi would let up soon. "The answer is simple: It's a lost cause. Magic is dying." I was shocked at Naomi's comment, but even more so at the nonchalance in her voice. "Despite that,

I've spent the last two years dedicating my life to magic." She shrugged. "I don't even know why any more."

Before Mister Ali could reply, Arkady spoke up. "Naomi is modest. She will lead us into the future by example. She simply awaits the opportunity."

"What do you mean?" I asked.

"She is the heir of Jamshid. Her power can rule nations. When the time comes she will inspire the world to return to magic and away from machinery." His comment about my helping in their fight against technology was starting to make sense.

"Nonsense!" Mister Ali exclaimed. "Such arrogance. I remember the last person to claim such, and his name is Cain. He is a governmental bureaucrat now. To compare a girl to Jamshid? It would be offensive if it weren't so sad."

I tensed, because I saw the battle between Naomi and Mister Ali unfolding in front of my eyes, and I knew it would not end well. Naomi called him a traitor, and there was at least some truth to that. Mister Ali's attitude was one I couldn't understand. I was always disappointed in his outdated belief that women couldn't do magic. Had he not seen her spells up close? Still, I kept my mouth shut. Naomi could certainly handle herself.

"Listen, traitor. I would never compare myself to Jamshid. I've been telling Arkady to stop saying that about me. It's kind of tiresome actually. I have no interest in ruling nations or fighting battles for them. You can ask Cain. He's been practically begging me to join his battles." The idea of Cain begging anyone sounded preposterous, but it somehow seemed possible when involving Naomi. She created a spell in her hand. It was different, a luminescent ball of many colors. It was quite beautiful. Mister Ali's eyes went wide when he saw it. "All I want is to make magic. That's all."

"Is that Gate of Duzakh?" Mister Ali stared at Naomi's hands.

"No, this is the Key of Nar Marratum." Naomi closed her hand and the ball disappeared. "It is much simpler version of the Gate spell, which I haven't mastered yet." She looked at Arkady. "And I assure you that Jamshid mastered the Gate of Duzakh spell. So to be clear I am no Jamshid, nor his heir."

"The last magician to cast the Key of Nar Marratum was Merlin." Mister Ali shook his head.

"No. Although they were most likely contemporaries, Taliesin is the last magician to have cast the spell. In fact, his notes are where I found the critical missing piece to cast it."

"Impossible!" Mister Ali replied.

"No, really. He kept notes." Naomi laughed. "Okay, enough. Can we get back to Tommy's problem?"

"Tommy, I understand the need for a place like this, but I'm afraid they are hiding their failures with lies and exaggeration. We won't find help here." Mister Ali stood up.

"Please, Mister Ali." I held up my hand. Despite his apologies and humility, he was still the stubborn Mister Ali from my past. I couldn't think of anything else to say that wouldn't insult him or outright contradict him. Of course, Naomi didn't have any such reservations.

"You have some nerve to come into my home and call me a liar. Putting that aside, what is your goal here? I presume you are actually helping Tommy this time instead of betraying him."

Mister Ali clenched his fists and I could see the muscles in his jaw working. He eventually replied calmly, "I am Tommy's eyes. I can see through illusion, and I will be his guide through the illusionary perils that await him."

"Even this?" A snake slid out from under the couch Mister Ali was sitting on.

I jumped back, and Mister Ali looked at me. He frowned. "She cast some remarkable illusion, didn't she?" I nodded as the snake wrapped around his leg and climbed up his body.

"Interesting. You don't even see that, do you?" Naomi sounded excited.

"No. I have the gift of total sight."

Naomi nodded, and the snake disappeared. "That's valuable, for sure." She created the black ball again, almost without any attention to it at all. "So why did you betray Tommy and his grandfather?"

"I thought we were talking about helping Tommy?"

"Actually, we were talking about you doubting me, but we'll get back to that. I want to hear about your traitorous ways first."

Mister Ali sighed. "I saw the rise of technology. I knew that it would be a blessing for the magical creatures. They would no longer suffer at our hands if technology took their place. So I took it upon myself to hasten the disappearance of magic." He shrugged. "I was wrong. I have already apologized to the Archmage. I certainly did not intend for anyone to get hurt."

Naomi turned to me, and the sympathy and concern on her face surprised me. I expected her to push him even harder. "Is that good enough for you, Tommy?"

"Yes," I replied. "I trust Mister Ali. He had an idea, and it spun out of control. In hindsight I don't even know if it was a bad idea." I rubbed my thumb against one of the runes on the staff.

"Well, that's good enough for me." She snuffed out the spell and then cast it again. "Mister Ali. You are a friend of Tommy's, so I'll make this very simple for you. You don't have to believe I can cast the Key of Nar Marratum. The wonderful thing about magic is that even if you don't believe it, it still works. And you know what?" Mister Ali shook his head. "The fact that people don't believe in it is one of our greatest advantages."

Mister Ali didn't reply, so I saw my chance to take the chaotic and dangerous conversation to safer ground. "So, Arkady, you mentioned the Angel of St. Petersburg." Naomi and Mister Ali both turned toward him. Apparently this was new even to Naomi.

"It was but a rumor as I fled Russia. I left via ship through the Baltic Sea, departing from St. Petersburg. There was word of a woman who led a small group of White Army loyalists. They were well-armed and made significant progress within St. Petersburg, building it up as a beachhead against the Red Army, which was pre-occupied with the Germans."

"All of that didn't draw my attention, but as I was fleeing I did my best to look out for fellow magicians, and everyone spoke of the woman leading the White Army. They said she led the battles from the front, and that nothing could hurt her. There was rumor of her cackling laugh leaving her opponents in fear as the bullets bounced off her and the grenades caused her no harm. They called her the angel, as she protected those behind her.

"I tried to find her, but I had no time, as my ship to freedom left shortly after I arrived."

"What does this have to do with the staff? She could just be a master shield magician," I replied.

Mister Ali, Arkady, and Naomi all shook their heads. "No, Tommy," Naomi said. "Even the most powerful magical shields eventually fail, and they fail quicker when under sustained attack. As much as I hate to admit it, machine guns are very powerful against magical shields."

I was unconvinced. "So this is either a fanciful story or some kind of super powerful magical shield."

Arkady shrugged. "It could be but a story. The White Russians have been defeated for many years. Those that remain are desperate zealots."

Mister Ali's firm and commanding voice broke in. "No." I looked at him. He nodded his head and looked at me. "I am a fool, Tommy. I took it as a legend, but clearly it is not. The woman is wearing Babr-e Bayan, the great coat created by the legendary warrior Rostam. It was said to resist fire and blades. Our myths tell us that Jamshid took the coat and made it invulnerable to all attacks. This cannot be a coincidence—the appearance of a woman who is invulnerable to attack and the staff losing power."

Mister Ali looked at all of us, the firelight flickering in his eyes. "The second artifact of Jamshid has been found—the Coat of Invincibility."

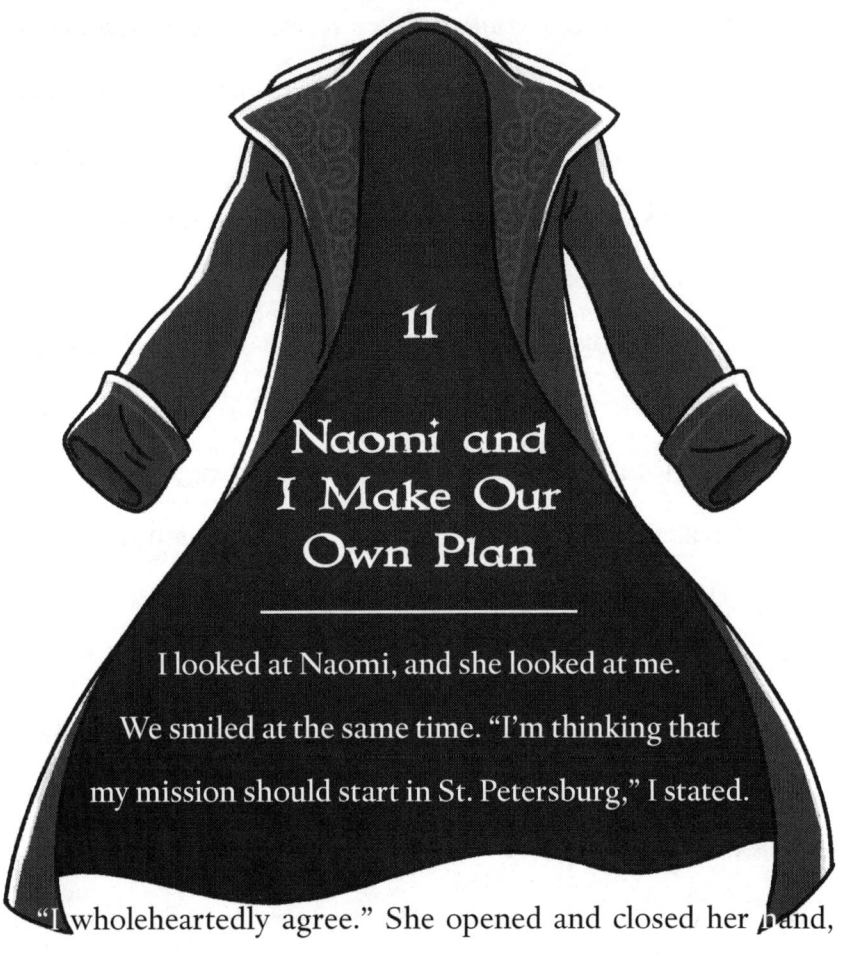

11

Naomi and I Make Our Own Plan

I looked at Naomi, and she looked at me.
We smiled at the same time. "I'm thinking that
my mission should start in St. Petersburg," I stated.

"I wholeheartedly agree." She opened and closed her hand, the glimmer of spells flickering through her fingers. Her excitement was palpable, and I knew why. She had been isolated for two years doing nothing but studying magic. She had progressed enough that others were calling her the Heir of Jamshid. Now it was her turn to actually utilize her powers. The thought both thrilled and frightened me.

As for me, I wanted to find answers about the Staff. We all embraced Mister Ali's theory without question. It made too much sense, and finding out more about Jamshid's artifacts became my goal—the Staff, the Coat, and the yet still hidden third artifact, the Cup.

At that moment the seed was planted, a seed I couldn't share with anyone: I wanted to wield all three artifacts. I certainly wasn't a magician like Jamshid, but if I could wield all three of his artifacts I was certain I could make a difference in the world, perhaps even bring worldwide peace.

And the first step was St. Petersburg.

"I think this is a wise decision, but it is risky. Artifacts are dangerous things." Mister Ali scratched his chin. "One of them alone has changed the nature of history in the West. Two or three? I fear the effect of such power. Plus, we must be aware that the other Archmage may want to do the same thing as us."

I stared at Mister Ali. He had zealously defended my title from those that would use it without respect, and here he was passing my title along to someone else. "Archmage?" I asked.

Mister Ali nodded. "Indeed, Tommy. I think it is clear. Wielding an artifact of Jamshid is no longer something you can claim as your own right. Plus, it provides us with the proper perspective. We are dealing with someone whose power is formidable—we cannot hurt her."

Naomi stood up. "It's late. There are rooms with warm beds down this hall. We can decide on a plan tomorrow." She mouthed the words we'll talk as she stood up and turned to lead everyone out.

My quarters were in a corner of the castle, and I could hear the wind howling against the stone on two sides of the room. The Scottish weather treated the walls as little more than conduits for its damp miserableness. Even the fire in the fireplace couldn't seem to catch into more than a flicker. I sat cross-legged on the floor in front of the fire, the only warm spot in the room.

There was a light knock on the door. "Come in," I said, and Naomi walked in. Her hair was pulled back in a pony tail, but otherwise she looked no different than she had earlier. I patted the floor next to me.

She sat down and crossed her legs. I watched as the flickering firelight illuminated her face, making it difficult to read. She rapped the floor with her knuckles. "Like the comfort of old times. The only thing missing is Djinn chasing us." She smiled without looking at me.

"Or magicians."

"We never had much trouble with them, did we?" I thought back to our escape from the train station in Persia.

"I guess not."

"So what's the plan?" She dropped the question with a suddenness that made it clear that it was all she really wanted to talk about. She was already thinking ahead. I had to smile. Naomi hadn't changed that much.

"I think that you, me, and Mister Ali should go to St. Petersburg and ta—" I stammered as I had almost said "take the Coat," but I wasn't ready to share with others that it was my goal, even Naomi. "—See if the Archmage with the Coat will join with us."

She looked at me, and the flickering light made her smile look almost sinister. "Yeah." She paused and then continued. "That was what I was thinking, see if this Angel of St. Petersburg will join us. That's a good plan." She put her hand on my arm and squeezed. "But do you trust Mister Ali, Tommy? I don't think I can ever forgive him for betraying you."

I nodded and looked at her. She was staring at me with her typical intensity. "Yes. I'm still not sure I understand his motivations, but I believe he has a good heart." Naomi didn't say anything, so I added. "I would trust him with my life. You weren't there with him when he escorted me from the attack in Manhattan. He was shaken, and I think even then he was wondering whether he had made some disastrous mistake."

Naomi let go of my arm but continued to peer at me. "Okay. That's good enough for me. His ability to see through illusions will be very helpful." She turned toward the fire and held out her hands to its warmth. "So the three of us go on a journey to Russia and have a little meeting with the Angel of St. Petersburg."

"Exactly."

Naomi stood up, and I scrambled to stand, too. It was funny how things had gone back to normal. Naomi rushing ahead, and me trying to keep up. "Sounds simple enough," I added.

"It also sounds fun." She smiled at me and turned. "We'll leave tomorrow," she said as she walked through the door, closing it behind her.

I buried myself under blankets and fell asleep thinking about the Angel of St. Petersburg. Who was she, and how did she get the Coat of Invincibility? I shivered, which I attributed to the cold.

The trip back south was tense, which was to be expected in such tight quarters. Mister Ali made the common sense recommendation to invite Arkady, as he was not only a master illusionist, he also spoke Russian, a skill that was obviously necessary with us traveling to Russia.

I was actually embarrassed with that oversight. If I was going to lead the group as the Archmage, I would have to think about more than how fun it would be to go on an adventure with Naomi. I dismissed the possibility that I had subconsciously wanted to keep her and Arkady apart.

We squeezed into the military sedan. I sat in the back seat in the middle, in between Naomi and Mister Ali. Arkady was in the front next to Rupert, my ever present escort. It was an uncomfortable seating arrangement for a trip that would take many hours.

We discussed the overall plan, which achieved a quick unanimity but bogged down when we started to discuss details. We were to take a ship to St. Petersburg, which Rupert rather gleefully explained would be absurdly dangerous, as the North Sea was an unpredictable battleground with death by German U-boat behind every wave.

Mister Ali took Rupert's warnings to heart and discussed a lengthy ground trip through Norway, Sweden, and Finland. I considered that reasonable, but Arkady laughed and said such a trip would take months. Naomi then jumped in and mocked Mister Ali, which made him call her an irresponsible child. To my surprise, Rupert saved the day by saying that the war would be over by the time we reached Leningrad via Mister Ali's route.

We next discussed what to do when we reached the city, which Rupert and Mister Ali stubbornly called Leningrad and everyone else called St. Petersburg. Once again we agreed on the strategy, which was to remain hidden and work in secret, while how to achieve our bigger aim led to disagreements. Mister Ali said he would work with Arkady while Naomi and I stayed hidden. Naomi said that she and Arkady would hunt the woman down. I objected, and she added me to the team, freezing out Mister Ali. I asked why we all couldn't work as a group, which only made everyone object, as a group of four would be suspicious. Frustrated, I finally asked why we couldn't just split up into groups when

Mister Ali replied, exasperation in his voice, "Because only one of us knows Russian!"

We shelved that discussion and then went over what to do when we finally met the other Archmage. I pretty much ignored everyone and demanded that I was the one to talk to her, Archmage to Archmage. Mister Ali felt that too risky, while Naomi liked the idea as long as she could be with me, which made Mister Ali even more adamant that I should stay behind.

By the end of the trip, we had agreed on only two things: We would travel by sea and we would look for the Angel of St. Petersburg while doing our best to remain unnoticed. We'd figure out the details later.

We stopped at the Citadel, and to my surprise Cain didn't even bother seeing us. Rupert met us after breakfast with the message that Cain didn't care where we went as long as we created problems for the Germans. He procured us transportation on a merchant liner that was being used as a bait ship to draw U-boats out for the English navy to attack. Rupert delivered the message with a smirk.

"Let me get this straight," I said. "The most powerful concentration of magic in the world is being placed on a ship that is being used as bait for German attacks?"

"You'll have major firepower as your escort. Remember: There's bait, but behind the bait is the hook." Rupert shrugged. "You should be fine."

I glanced at Naomi, but she looked bored as she repeatedly cast and snuffed out spells that hadn't been cast in centuries.

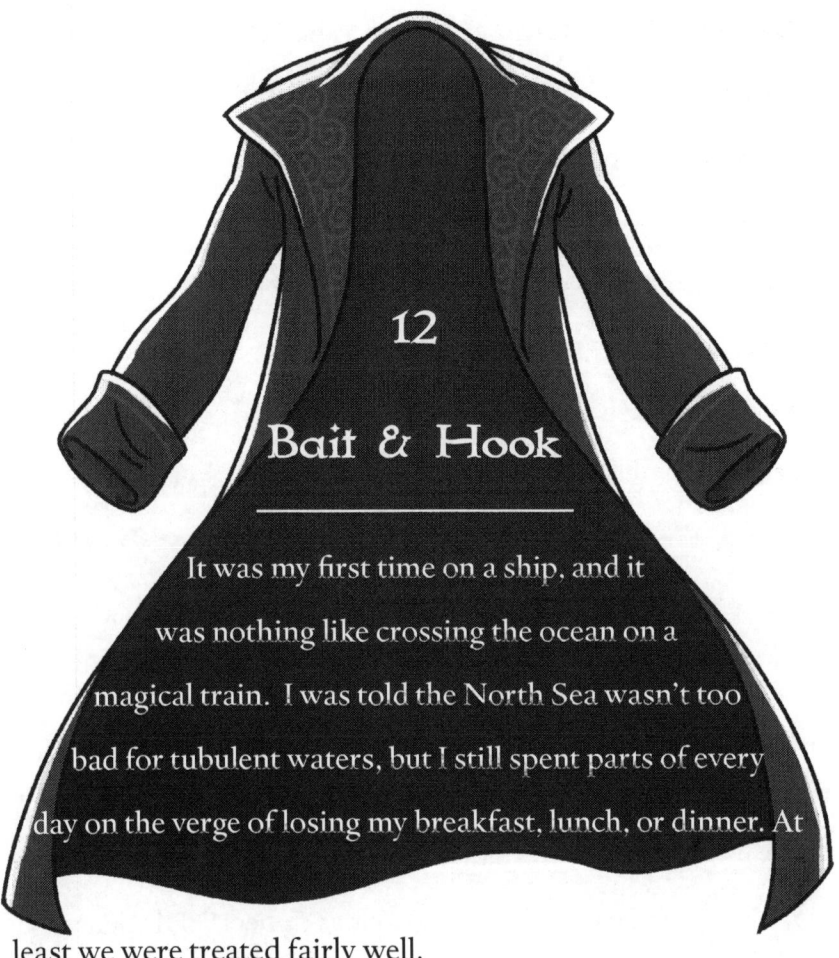

12

Bait & Hook

It was my first time on a ship, and it was nothing like crossing the ocean on a magical train. I was told the North Sea wasn't too bad for tubulent waters, but I still spent parts of every day on the verge of losing my breakfast, lunch, or dinner. At least we were treated fairly well.

When Cain said we'd be on a merchant ship, I half expected him to have us live in the hold or in some storage room. While we weren't living in luxury, we at least had bunkbeds. Naomi actually had it the worst. She was in her own room, but it was a recreation area, and she had to sleep on a couch that I wouldn't have sat on, let alone used as a bed.

The trip was to take three months. When I heard the travel time I nearly fell out of my chair. I had crossed the Atlantic Ocean in less than a day, and we were traveling through the North Sea over months? The captain scowled when I expressed frustration over the travel time. He apparently was proud of the speed of his ship, it being a smaller, faster type of merchant vessel. The moment the captain finished speaking I felt guilty, as it was an enslaved Marid that had powered the fast train voyage. So I accepted the length of the trip, but I feared that the Angel of St. Petersburg would be gone by the time we got to the city.

The most dangerous part of the trip would be a run through a strait called the Great Belt. We would be heading straight toward Germany before turning east toward Russia. When I asked the Captain about just how dangerous it was, he laughed and said, "Don't worry, I stocked each lifeboat with beer!" His demeanor didn't much help with my concern.

One unexpected benefit of the long trip was that I learned more about everyone, as we all shared our stories. I learned about the Communist revolution in Russia from Arkady, who couldn't discuss the topic without using curse words and angrily muttering long Russian phrases when describing Stalin and his policies. It wasn't just that the Communist leadership were hunting down magicians, they were apparently terrorizing the entire populace.

Naomi was very quiet and said little beyond stating that she grew up alone with her mother in the middle of nowhere and that all she could do to fill the time was learn magic. She noted that as she lived on a rail line, the engineers would often deliver her magical tomes from across the globe. "Those books saved my life," she said and then went quiet.

Mister Ali did the lion's share of the story-telling, outlining his many adventures with my grandfather. I was enthralled, never having heard them, as my grandfather never discussed his past with me.

The best part of the voyage, however, was when Naomi decided to teach me magic. "Look, I'll make it so dumb that even you'll be able to understand it," she replied when I had raised my hands and said I didn't want her to waste her time with me. I was hopeless with magic.

Naomi taught me as we stood next to the gunwale, the cold wind blowing from the sea and making us shiver. Everyone else stayed below deck.

"Magic is nothing more than using your body as a conduit for transferring energy. As the energy passes through, the magician shapes it via perfect forms. It's the combination of movement and form that direct spells." Naomi made a quick movement with her hand, and a small light glowed and then disappeared.

"Was that light?" I asked, knowing from Mister Ali's previous comments to me that creating light was one of the most difficult things for magicians to do. In fact, it was nearly impossible.

Naomi smiled. "Yes. I work on it every day. I doubt I'll ever be able to get it much brighter than that, but I hope to have it last for more than a fraction of a second some day." Naomi looked over at me. "It doesn't have much use, but it's how I calm myself."

"I thought you calmed yourself with that Hammer of Jamshid spell?" Naomi had always calmed herself by forming the most dangerous spells possible.

"No. That was practice." She created another tiny flicker of light. In a whisper, almost as if she hoped I wouldn't hear it, she added, "It's also been my little reminder of you."

I opened my mouth to say something clever, but I couldn't think of anything. Naomi looked away, her face turning red.

"Light is difficult because of what I said earlier. The magician is the conduit of magical energy. But first we need to tap into that energy. For some reason the energy that creates light is very difficult to harness. I've tried and tried, but it's like trying to change the flow of a mighty river with a leaky spoon. All you can do is collect a tiny bit of water and move it to a different location before it drains away."

"Whatever the source of the power in my staff is, it can move rivers," I replied.

Naomi nodded. "Yes. Its power is enormous." Things were quiet as we both pondered what kind of magical creature could harness that level of energy. Naomi soon broke the silence by holding up her hands. "Here, let me show you. She moved her fingers and manipulated her hand in a way that I couldn't fathom, and the inky black and blue ball appeared in her hand. "Did you see that?"

"Not really." I laughed.

"Well, I created a number of perfect shapes while calling forth the energy that is the part of all things."

"What do you mean by perfect forms?"

"Circles, parabolas, ovals—various motions that I make with my fingers that swirl the energy into a direction. And then I change it, refine it, and focus it." She then added, "It is very difficult." I nodded. "In fact, some magicians worry so much about losing their ability to replicate the motions that they do them often enough to develop tics and even spasms."

"Cain!" I said.

Nodding, Naomi continued. "I do the same thing, but I'm not maintaining permanent illusions so I don't have to be quite so crazy about it. But when you see me casting and dispelling spells? That's me practicing the forms."

"I thought they calmed you."

"That, too."

"So what's the hardest spell to cast? That Nar Marratum spell you know?"

"No. The spells that people think are hard like that one are difficult because the energy is difficult to gather, not because casting the spell is hard, although it can be that, too. The hardest spells to cast are implicit illusion spells."

"What are those?"

"Well, nearly every spell you cast is part of nature, part of the environment around us. I can cast a detonation at something, but it travels through the air, others can see it, and it's explosion affects everything it hits. Spells that interact with the environment as a whole are explicit spells. Merlin actually codified this in his notebook."

"Wow. You've read Merlin's notebook?"

Naomi shrugged. "It wasn't very helpful. Anyway, the other type of spells are implicit spells. These are the spells that are limited to a small piece of the environment, normally a single person. Casting an illusion that everyone can see? That's rather simple. In fact, you see it from street magicians all the time. Casting an illusion that only one person experiences? That's extremely difficult. I can cast implicit illusions, but they take so long that I don't even know if they have practical value." Rubbing her hands together, she continued, "So, here, let me teach you how to cast a Veil of Protection."

"What's that?"

"It's a really easy and not at all powerful shield spell. It may keep mosquitoes off you if you're lucky."

"I think my grandfather could cast it," I said, remembering the afternoon in the alley where his weak shield protected us from the rocks thrown by the Shadows.

Naomi spent an hour trying to teach me the spell, finally giving up and storming off to her couch, muttering "you're hopeless" into the misty air. I didn't mind. I knew I would never master magic, but watching Naomi explain and discuss her passion with such innocent excitement was something I cherished.

The next time I saw her she had a huge smile and we talked about a lot of things, but she never gave me another magic lesson.

We were heading toward the north end of Denmark, and Naomi and I took up our customary positions of standing along the gunwale of the ship, surrounded by water as far as we could see. We spent a lot of time next to each other staring out at sea while we talked. I used the staff to reflect light off the caps of waves, and Naomi did her best to follow the sparkling light with a detonation that would explode into the wave. It was both game and practice. I lit the target, and Naomi blew it up.

Her speed was extraordinary. I had seen master level magicians casting detonations when I had been attacked by Djinn at Kings Cross Station and marveled at their speed, but Naomi made them look slow. I finally stopped and looked at her. "How do you do that?"

"Do what?"

"Cast that spell so fast. You unleash them like a machine gun. I've never seen anything like it."

Naomi smiled. "Thank you, Tommy!" She opened her hand and looked at her palm. "But this spell is really simple. I've cast it so many times that I barely even think about it anymore." She looked around and then whispered in a conspiratorial voice. "Want to see a really powerful spell?" Before I answered she had already conjured the black ball that she had said was the Hammer of Jamshid.

"Please. Anything to break the monotony of this trip."

Naomi lifted her hands, glanced back at me, and winked. The ball in her hand started to expand, and there was a snapping and crackling sound. It became a bit hard to breathe as I felt a pressure against my chest. Naomi then extended her arms and the swirling black ball shot toward the horizon. She had aimed it very far off, and it skimmed across the water, appearing to get larger and larger as it flew far beyond where I could make it out.

A moment later a huge ball of shimmery light filled the horizon. Naomi turned back to me with a big smile on her face when a massive boom filled the air and I felt a whoosh of air push me back away from the gunwale. As I regained my balance a big wave slammed against the ship, knocking me off balance again. I had to hold onto the gunwale for support as the boat rocked violently as a succession of waves broke against the hull.

"That exploded about a mile from here!" Naomi exclaimed, barely able to contain her excitement.

"Wow. Exactly how powerful was that?" I asked, wondering if Naomi could flatten a city.

"That's the biggest one I've ever cast." Naomi looked sheepish as she smiled at me. "I didn't expect it to be that powerful. I guess I could flatten a large building or perhaps a city block, maybe more."

"That definitely would destroy more than a city block," I replied, which elicited more smiles from Naomi.

I was going to compliment Naomi again when there was the pounding sound of footsteps, and the angry voice of Mister Ali. "What was that?!"

Naomi shrugged. "The Hammer of Jamshid. I think I probably killed some fish. Sorry." She didn't sound very sorry.

"You foolish girl! Do you not understand that these seas are teaming with U-Boats and German ships? You will get us killed!" Naomi shrugged.

"I thought we were bait," I replied.

"Tommy, use your head. Just because we are bait doesn't mean we want to be eaten by a fish." Mister Ali looked at me and then Naomi and then back at me. Not seeing the response he wanted, he shook his head.

He pointed out to sea and was about to say something when his eyes went wide. "We are under attack!"

I spun around and looked out to where he was pointing. Naomi did, as well. "I don't see anything," I said.

"Just some seagulls," Naomi added.

"They must be using illusions. There!" He pointed to his left. "Is a cruiser. There!" He pointed a little further to the right. "Is a smaller gunship." He turned to us. "We are in grave danger. They will radio for U-Boats, and they may fire at any moment." He looked at Naomi. "Can you cast a shield?"

Naomi glanced back out to sea, looking skeptical. "Against cannon fire and shielding a ship this size? That would require the Wall of Jericho, and it would take me an hour to cast that." She faced the sea and called up the Hammer of Jamshid spell. The ball of destruction hovered in her hand.

There was a clanging in the distance, and Mister Ali stared out at something I couldn't see. "We are in luck. Your spell must have scared them or put them on the defensive." Mister Ali looked at me. "Can you make us invisible, Tommy?"

Of course! I squeezed the staff and smiled at Mister Ali. "Yes! I can bend light around us, and then you can guide Naomi's attack spells."

"That's a great idea, Tommy!" Naomi said. I beamed as I held the staff up for effect. I didn't really have to do that, but I found that using the staff that way intimidated and impressed people. With a thought I bent light around the ship.

"Are we hidden?" Mister Ali asked. I looked at the staff. It was dead in my hand. Light was not bending around the ship. I hadn't affected light at all.

The staff had failed me again.

I looked at Naomi, and I don't know how I appeared to her, but she looked frightened. "It didn't work?" she asked. I shook my head. Naomi clenched her teeth and turned toward the sea. "Mister Ali, tell me where the biggest ship is." Her voice was all business.

"Look out straight from the ship. No. Turn to the right a bit. That's good. Now. Look about forty-five degrees to your left. Yes, there you go. Almost to the horizon is a cruiser. You said you saw seagulls. That is the illusion hiding the ship. If you aim for the seagulls you will hit it."

Naomi made a few motions, and I again felt my whole body compress, as if the energy of the spell was pushing against everything around it. Naomi extended her hands, and the ball once again flew across the caps of the waves. I watched as it let loose its energy near the seagulls. There was the loud boom of an explosion, and I knew a huge wave was going to hit us, as this was a lot closer than the previous casting of the spell.

"Very good, Naomi! Your spell clipped the rear of the ship, and it is sinking!" The sound of boots filled the air, as the crew poured out of the door leading below decks. "Get out of here, you fools! We are under attack. You must tell the captain to go to maximum speed and to notify our escort!"

At that moment two sounds competed for my attention—the sound of machine gun fire from somewhere out at sea, and the sound of bullets hitting and ricocheting off the metal of the ship. Men scattered everywhere, while Mister Ali and I dove for the deck.

Naomi, however, stood tall. I glanced up at her and she waved her right arm back and forth in a wide arc, as if she were a bull fighter, and the bullets were bulls. "I can handle bullets," she said. The sharp clang of bullets hitting the ship turned into a soft thudding sound from right beyond the ship.

"There," Naomi said, looking down at us. "That shield will protect us for about ninety seconds." She reached down and offered Mister Ali her hand. "Get up and show me where the other ships are. I need to destroy them within the next minute or so."

Mister Ali took Naomi's hand and stood up. He scanned the horizon. "Straight ahead and speeding toward us is a smaller boat, it is zig zagging but mostly approaching us."

Naomi nodded, as she squeezed her hands into fists. She opened them again, and both palms held the bright light of a detonation spell. "I'm going to cast constantly. I'll need you to tell me directions to hit the target like 'closer,' 'further,' 'left,' or 'right.' Okay?"

Mister Ali nodded. "Of course."

Without any further delay, Naomi launched detonations at a speed that was otherworldly. I watched as both hands moved forward and back, balls of explosive light shooting out in a constant stream, each one a destructive spell that exploded in the distance. She cast them in a straight line, giving Mister Ali time to let her know how to adjust.

"Quite a bit closer. Left. Further left. No. A little right." With each direction from Mister Ali came a stream of spells. I stared in awe at how quickly the spells flew from Naomi's hands. "It is moving too fast for us to hit." Naomi cursed, and then Mister Ali added, "They must fear your spells, they are turning away from us."

Naomi shook her head. "Hold on." With her left hand she made a series of movements. An orange light flickered and then she held her hand up above her head.

"Is that?" Mister Ali asked, his voice full of awe.

"Yes." Naomi looked at me with her arm still extended above her head. "Tommy, can you at least blind them?"

I didn't even bother to respond. I connected with the staff. It was there. It was part of me. Its light shone within me. I could have cried out in joy at its return. The understanding between us was total. I filled the entire ocean, from horizon to horizon, with the blinding light of a thousand suns, shielding only those of us on the merchant ship.

Naomi and Mister Ali were blinking their eyes. "Wow," Naomi said, before turning to Mister Ali. "Guide me." With her left hand in the air, she cast detonation spells with her right.

"This is impossible. You cannot be maintaining the illusion while casting another spell." Mister Ali stared at Naomi. "It is impossible."

"Guide me!" Naomi looked annoyed.

"They are not dodging but moving straight to the left away from us. You are too far to the right." Naomi moved and started shooting spells to the left, adjusting her fire after every few casts.

While each detonation ended in an explosion, I could tell from the different sound of the last one that Naomi had hit her mark. "You did it!" Mister Ali exclaimed.

Naomi looked around. "What about the third ship? You said there was another one."

"It fled."

Naomi dropped her hand and turned to look at me. I was shocked. Her hair was tousled mess, with strands sticking against her forehead and cheek, which were wet with perspiration. There were deep circles under her eyes. She started to sway, and I ran over and grabbed her arm.

"Not bad for a girl," she said before fainting into my arms.

I held her while frantically looking around for a soft place to lay her. "Help!" I cried out. Mister Ali walked over and put his hand on my shoulder.

"She'll be fine, Tommy." I held Naomi against me, her head resting on my chest. She felt much lighter than I expected, and she smelled of sea and sun and the faint fragrance of ancient books. I was frightened, as the last time I held her like this she had been teetering on the edge of death. "The magic she just performed—" Mister Ali shook his head. "—It was beyond exhausting."

Mister Ali put his arm around Naomi's shoulder, and we carried her back to the door leading into the ship. "What was the spell with the orange light?" I asked.

"It was the Mirror of Anahita. Do you remember the never-ending hallway in the Citadel of London?" I nodded my head. The hall in the quarters where I stayed had an illusion on it that made it look endless. "That is the same illusion. The viewer sees a mirror of some aspect of the environment. In that hallway it mirrored the end to make it look endless. I can only assume that Naomi hid our ship by mirroring the sea and making it look endless to the men on the boat."

"Ah, that was smart," I replied.

Mister Ali stopped, and I looked at him with Naomi unconscious between us. His normally joyful face was intense and serious. "Tommy, I don't believe you understand. That spell would take Cain at least a few minutes to cast with total concentration. Naomi cast it in mere seconds and then maintained it while casting other spells."

Naomi was a better illusionist than Cain? That seemed impossible. In fact, she herself had said she wasn't as good an illusionist as Arkady, let alone Cain.

Mister Ali nodded at my dawning comprehension. "Arkady didn't create the illusions around that castle, Tommy. Naomi did."

"Wow," was all I could say, and it didn't seem remotely adequate.

"She is the heir of Jamshid, Tommy. There can be no doubt." Mister Ali started walking again, and said nothing more as we carried Naomi down to her quarters so she could regain her strength.

I watched her as she dozed, quiet and beautiful, even as she looked drawn and weary. She had spent two years doing nothing but studying and practicing magic, the last year in a remote Scottish castle. With her extraordinary talent and dedication, she was now the most powerful magician in the world, possibly one of the most powerful of all time.

I looked at my cane. I could not only no longer stop time, I couldn't even bend light. Naomi had grown into the heir of Jamshid, while I was no no more than a streetlight.

PART II

St. Petersburg

13

We Arrive in St. Petersburg

Naomi quickly recovered her strength, and seemed more upset that she had fainted than proud over the fact that she had just achieved one of the greatest displays of magic in centuries. Mister Ali practically fawned

over her, which annoyed me. He was supposed to be the Eyes of the Archmage, not the Eyes of the Magician.

I was heartened by the fact that Naomi didn't seem to care much more for the Mister Ali that respected her than the Mister Ali who disregarded her as just a girl. What she did say was that he was good to have around, as his ability to see through illusions was "extraordinary."

My feelings for Mister Ali continued to be complex. He was my mentor, the one who betrayed me and my family, the one who asked forgiveness, the one who insulted Naomi's abilities, and the one who declared her a great magician. In the end I had to trust my instincts, which were that Mister Ali was a good man, but one I couldn't quite figure out.

The rest of the ship's voyage was spent with me mostly working alone in my room below deck. Mister Ali joined Naomi on deck scanning the horizon and alerting her to possible threats. Her preferred response was to work with Arkady in casting some illusion or another that would let the ship pass through unnoticed.

I had to laugh—we were supposed to be bait, but the one time we were attacked, Naomi had laid waste to the threat before our escort could even get close enough to assist. Now we were so well-hidden that we couldn't even be considered bait at all.

For what must have been the hundredth time that hour I ran my fingers over the runes on the cane. It was like running my fingers through my hair or feeling my ribs. The staff was still part of me. I could feel the immense energy inside waiting to be tapped. I still knew how to bring forth that energy to manipulate light.

As I did all the things that were about seeing light it was as natural as breathing. Yet when I thought of more complex things like bending light or stopping it, I failed.

After days of depressing trial and error, I reached a point where I simply gave up. Instead of focusing on manipulating the flow of light, I decided to be creative. I projected light and created forms on the wall, shadow puppets I controlled with my mind. I became good enough that I felt that I could actually scare those with knowledge of the magical world by imitating Shadows. I noted this as a possible weapon and felt glad that my own creativity had provided me with something useful.

The remainder of the trip alternated between frustrating and fun. I realized that I could filter light by color. It was an epiphany that led me to creating more lifelike shadow creatures, with colorful clothing and realistic skin tones. Yet it seemed so pointless. How valuable was art like this when there were motion pictures that were infinitely more complex and exciting?

It suddenly struck me that I could finally understand what had driven Naomi her whole life—even her most powerful magic paled in comparison to the current weapons of war. Her illusions were pointless when Hollywood was creating entire worlds. Naomi's pursuit of magic had become a noble pursuit of preserving a dying art.

I looked at the staff. Was that all I had become—someone preserving an ancient artifact that was slowly losing its power? I created a scene on the wall—the stony beach near Dunnotar Castle. I made the waves move and shimmer, while the dull gray of the rocks stood unmoving as I crashed wave after wave at them.

After a few minutes I tossed the staff on my bed. It was a pretty scene, but what use was it in the end?

We disembarked in a port that was empty with the exception of the crowds on the docks waiting for our ship to unload its cargo. While we were considered bait for the Germans and the goal for our small group was simply to get to St. Petersburg, the ship did contain goods and supplies. Thanks to Naomi, we were one of the few allied ships that had actually made it through to the city. As a result, we were surrounded by longshoreman and merchants that wanted first crack at unloading and distributing its goods.

As a native Russian, Arkady took charge of our small group, ignoring the chaos around us as he led us down a gangplank to the dock. I followed behind next to Naomi, while Mister Ali brought up the rear. Arkady set a brisk pace, and we didn't pause until we were a few blocks closer to the center of the city.

He turned and looked at us. "We will need lodgings."

Mister Ali stepped forward. "Yes. We need a base of operations, a place where we can both hide and plan our search." He turned and looked at me. "Remember, the goal here is simple: We are to find this Russian Archmage and confront her about her artifact. We can then see if it has some bearing on what is happening with the staff."

I nodded, but Naomi shook her head. "I say we just take it and give it to Tommy. He'll have two artifacts and will be that much stronger. That may even spark the staff into working again." I could have hugged Naomi, as that was exactly what I wanted to do.

"That may be what we eventually decide to do, but it may be too dangerous. We need to take care. These are artifacts, not books." Mister Ali peered at Naomi, who shrugged.

"Tommy knows what he's doing." She turned to me. "Don't you, Streetlight?"

I couldn't help but smile. "Yes. I don't foresee any problems with another artifact. I understand the power and the nature of connecting with it."

Before Mister Ali could say anything, Arkady interrupted. "We can discuss the details later. First we need to find lodgings. May I remind everyone it is war time?" He nodded toward the distance, and I turned to see a group of Russian soldiers carrying machine guns scanning the street as they walked toward us.

Everyone nodded, and Arkady led us away from the soldiers and down a side street. He eventually pointed out a decrepit old building with a sign out front that I couldn't read. Not only was it written in Russian, some of its letters were missing. It dangled from a corner, swaying sadly in the wind.

We walked in and after a hushed conversation between Arkady and the old man behind the desk, we were ensconced on the third floor. The three men shared a room, but we at least had our own place to sleep. Mister Ali and I each had a full-sized bed, while Arkady took a couch. Naomi had her own room, which was smaller than ours, but appeared to be more luxurious, if you could use that word for a room with peeling wallpaper and a torn carpet.

As I fell asleep I wondered if we would even get a chance to meet the Angel of St. Petersburg, let alone convince her to give me the Coat. She could have been anywhere in Russia by then. I finally drifted off, with the thought that I'd have to trust Arkady.

After a few days everone was getting frustrated with the lack of progress. Naomi had to be practically restrained from just walking out into the streets shouting, "Angel, Angel, where are you?!" Arkady would walk in after a long day of searching and asking questions, shake his head at us, and then have a chat with Mister Ali. Eventually, I walked over and asked, "What's going on?"

Arkady sighed. "She is here, but she chooses not to be found."

"What does that mean?" I asked.

"She is avoiding the Reds as she re-arms her militia."

I sat down on the couch next to Arkady as Mister Ali paced. Naomi was working on some arcane spell, repeating the complex movements and cursing as she occasionally got it wrong.

"But she's an Archmage. Why does she need a militia? She should use her own power. Doesn't she have magicians to help her?"

Mister Ali paused. "Her artifact protects her, Tommy. She needs others to overcome opponents. I doubt there are any magicians in Russia left who can help her." Arkady nodded. "So she enlists help from those that believe in her cause, and she has to find ways of arming them."

"It sounds like she is a revolutionary."

Arkady chuckled. "She is an anti-revolutionary. She wants to bring back the former Russia, the Russia defeated by the October Revolution."

I ran my fingers through my hair. "So she is in hiding waiting for help?" Arkady and Mister Ali nodded. "Why don't we offer to help?" I looked at Arkady. "You're a magician. Everyone knows the Soviets are killing magicians. So all you do is cast an illusion, tell someone that you want to join her, and they'll know you that you'll provide a valuable contribution."

"That's brilliant, Streetlight." I looked over at Naomi, who was grinning. I hadn't even realized she was eavesdropping.

Arkady tapped his chin with a finger. "That is actually a very good idea."

"No. It is too dangerous." Mister Ali shook his head as he talked. "You are putting Arkady's life at risk, and there is no guarantee that he would be able to get a message back to us."

I looked at Naomi, but she seemed more concerned with her spell. Did she not care about Arkady? After all the time on the ship I still couldn't get a handle on their relationship. They constantly talked magic. They laughed together. They spent as much time together as she and I did. Were they friends? Colleagues? More? I couldn't tell.

"It is a good plan." Arkady stood up and put his hand on Mister Ali's shoulder. "My life was at risk the moment I stepped off the ship, Ali." Arkady walked over and grabbed his coat. "I've stumbled upon a bar. It is a place where foreigners and those critical of the government gather. Very quiet discussions there. I believe that if I were to lower my guard and do some magic I may find someone to take my offer of help to the Angel." Arkady slipped his coat on and walked toward the door. "This may take a few days. Don't worry about me."

He walked out the door without a debate or even a goodbye.

Three days later Naomi was ready to march through the streets herself looking for Arkady. Mister Ali begged her to be patient, and just when it seemed he wouldn't be able to stop her, Arkady walked through the hotel room door.

Naomi and I were playing cards, while Mister Ali was reading a book. I looked up and immediately knew Arkady had some good news. Naomi tossed her cards on the table and stood up.

"Where were you? I was worried about you!" As Arkady smiled, Naomi added, "Did you find her?"

He walked over and fell into a chair. "I have not heard much. There is word of magicians that have entered the city and are staying in the north."

"Is it her?" Naomi asked.

"Who else it could be?" Arkady asked. "The Reds have rounded up every magician of note, and the rest have either fled or are so frightened they have given up magic. I did a few illusions, and the contact I made asked to see us."

"Us?" Mister Ali's brow furrowed. "What did you tell him about us?"

"Don't worry, Ali. I simply said that a group of my friends and I were looking to join with the Angel. He asked a few questions, but all I said is that we were powerful and a meeting would be worth having."

"I don't like it," Mister Ali said. Naomi rolled her eyes behind his back.

"We have nothing to lose," I replied.

"So what's the plan?" Naomi said, pretending that Mister Ali's concerns didn't exist.

Arkady replied, "They are a good ways off. They gave me a location to meet them tomorrow afternoon. We should get transport tomorrow morning to take us there and then come up with a plan for separating the Archmage from any defenses she may have."

There was quick agreement. Mister Ali begrudgingly approved the plan, just noting his concerns that we should be extremely careful. "We don't even know if she'll be there," he noted. "What do we do if she is not? We aren't Russian, and the rest of us will never be trusted as allies."

"That's your biggest problem, Mister Ali." Naomi said the words loudly. Everyone turned to look at her. "You plan for failure. Success is an accident in your hands."

Mister Ali's face went red. "Young lady, I was succeeding in countless battles before you were even born. The reason I succeeded with the Pehlivan was due to my ability to see." He tapped his forehead with his finger. "I don't plan for failure. I anticipate things that can lead to failure."

Naomi shrugged and turned to me. "Card game?"

I nodded but had trouble focusing on the cards and lost game after game. We finally had a lead on finding the other Archmage. All I could think of was that I would be wearing the Coat of Invincibility in a few days. I had no doubt it would not only restore my missing abilities with the staff, but that it would make me powerful enough to perhaps defeat the Nazis all by myself.

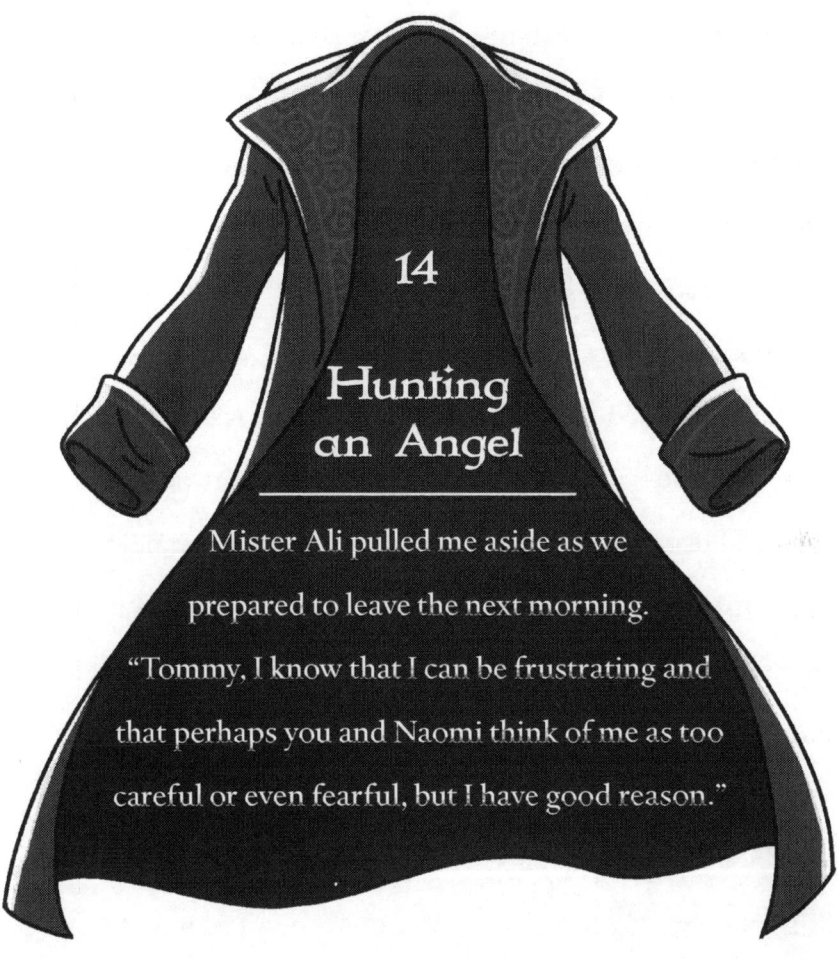

14

Hunting
an Angel

Mister Ali pulled me aside as we
prepared to leave the next morning.
"Tommy, I know that I can be frustrating and
that perhaps you and Naomi think of me as too
careful or even fearful, but I have good reason."

He kept his voice low, so I knew that the message was only for
me. "You have seen a lot and done so much, but you still don't
know what kind of things that people are capable of or the forces
that are arrayed against you." He put his arm on my shoulder and
squeezed. "I just worry about you."

I nodded. "I understand, but we'll be okay. You've seen how powerful Naomi is, and while the staff is limited, I can still surprise people with it." I tapped the cane on the floor. Mister Ali didn't say anything, so I added, "I'll be careful."

At that he let go of my shoulder and patted me on my back. "That's all I'm asking."

As we shuffled into a sedan that was to drive us to the magicians and the Angel of St. Petersburg, I thought of Mister Ali's history. He had been the "eyes" for my grandfather, pointing out illusions and risks as they fought during the Great War. He saw risk and danger where others did not. No wonder he was worried about me and my friends.

I watched Mister Ali as the car rumbled over roads pitted with holes and rocks. His eyes constantly darted left and right. His brows would furrow and he would squint as if he perceived something we could not, but then he would move on and look elsewhere. It suddenly struck me that perhaps I had not paid as much attention to Mister Ali as I should have. If he saw threats where others didn't, what kind of life would that be? One full of stress, fear, and concern.

Maybe I was finally starting to understand Mister Ali. He just looked at the world differently.

The city of Leningrad was beautiful but torn with the wounds of war. I knew that it had been a major part of the Soviet revolution, and it appeared to be preparing for the onslaught of the Germans. Troops were everywhere, and a trip that Arkady said would normally not have taken long took us hours, as we had to drive around streets with tanks, checkpoints, and lines of soldiers.

Arkady sat up front with the driver that we had found at the hotel. The man looked nervous, but seemed intent on getting us where we were going. Mister Ali and Naomi sat on either side of me, neither seeming much interested in the other.

A few hours after we left, Arkady looked over his shoulder and said, "There is a warehouse nearby. We are to meet at the front and then, hopefully, we will be taken to the Angel."

The comment increased Mister Ali's irritation. "And then what do we do? Tell this woman to just give us her artifact? May I remind you that we cannot harm her?" Mister Ali shook his head. "I've lived this with Declan time and time again. March in without any kind of plan, destroy anything that looks suspicious, and then hope it all works out."

"That's my kind of plan. I like it," Naomi replied.

Arkady was shaking his head. "No. That is not the plan. It's just that there are too many unknowns. How can we plan when we don't know what we are facing? We need to be nimble and prepared for anything."

I had to admit that Arkady seemed to know what he was doing. I didn't necessarily like that Naomi often paid more attention to him than me, but in terms of us needing a mission leader, he was the best thing we had.

"I'm ready," Naomi said, and in response she opened her palm and started casting the small light spell she showed me earlier, the she said calmed herself.

"I can't disagree with your logic, Arkady," Mister Ali said. "But let us at least agree to go slow and be observant. We should also have a plan for retreat." Mr. Ali looked at the driver. Arkady turned to him and said some words in Russian. The driver shook his head and said, "Nyet."

No one said anything, but I didn't need a translator to know that there wasn't going to be any escape plan. I looked at Mister

Ali who seemed pained, and then at Arkady who actually looked unhappy, as well. Naomi was ignoring everyone as she pushed her blonde hair behind her ears, cracked her knuckles, and began casting the light spell again.

The car made a sharp turn to the right, and the tires crunched over gravel. Up ahead were three large buildings with metal walls that looked like flimsily constructed warehouses. The walls were bent in spots, exposing a dark interior, and the second floor was lined with large windows, many of which were covered with plywood.

We drove up to the middle warehouse, which had a huge set of closed doors facing the road. As the car stopped, the driver looked around nervously and then said something in Russian.

"We're here," Arkady said, opening his door. Naomi opened her door and practically leaped out of the car. Before I had even slid out of the car she was making movements with her left hand. I walked up, and the four of us stood facing the warehouse.

Behind us the car backed up and turned to drive away. "So, what next?" I asked.

"They are to meet us here," Arkady replied, looking around.

"Are we early?" Mister Ali said.

"They didn't provide a time. They said just to be here in the afternoon. I was under the impression that this was a base for their operations and that they had someone here all the time."

Mister Ali turned to me, "Tell me what you see."

"There is a large two story warehouse in front of us."

"Yes. That is not an illusion."

"To the left is a road leading between another warehouse that is behind us and to the left. It is paired with another warehouse behind us and to the right. There is a parking lot with a few small trucks to the right beside the warehouse in front of us. Behind it is a fence."

Mister Ali breathed out. "Good. There are no illusions. That is a good sign."

A horrible screech filled the air, and the large sliding doors in front of us parted. There was nothing but darkness behind them, but I could make out a group of men walking out. They were in plain grey uniforms without any markings. One of the men pointed at us.

"I don't like this," Mister Ali said, a moment before the men crouched down, and with dizzying speed unleashed a flurry of detonations at us. I dove to the ground instinctively as Mister Ali flinched.

I heard a few thuds followed by Naomi shaking her head, her hair flying in a mist of yellow around her head. "Did those idiots not think the first thing I would do is cast a shield?" Holding up her hand, she launched a detonation at the group of men, who couldn't seem to understand how we were still standing. They scattered as the spell flew toward them. It exploded on the ground, tossing a few of them backward and in the air.

"No shield spell? This won't be a challenge at all." Naomi looked positively giddy. There were about ten men that I could see, several of whom ran back to the warehouse, while the rest moved to surround us. Two of them were casting what looked to be shield spells.

"They're casting shields," I said as I walked next to Naomi. She was looking around, presumably picking her next target. She had the same kind of smile on her face that I saw on my grandfather during the attack on the Persian Garden restaurant.

"It won't help them." Naomi said it as a statement of fact, and there wasn't a bit of pride in her voice.

"Arkady, we could use a quick illusion," Mister Ali said, as his eyes darted around.

The Russian was already focused on the movements of his body. He wasn't remotely as precise or fast as Naomi. I thought of using the staff, but what could I do? Even putting everything in darkness seemed to be more problematic than helpful. We needed to see what we faced.

There was a rumble, and I looked over to see a tank approaching from the road to the left. "A tank!" I yelled.

Naomi turned and launched her spell at it. There was a whoosh, and then a large explosion. It wasn't the Hammer of Jamshid. In fact, I didn't know what spell it was, but it appeared to be a more powerful version of the detonation spell.

"That was an illusion!" Mister Ali exclaimed. "They are trying to distract us!" Mister Ali pointed. The magicians in gray had fled back into the warehouse.

"Where are you, Angel?" Naomi yelled out. "Come out and play!"

"Hush, Naomi. We need to know what we are facing." We all looked around. I had turned my head for an instant, but in that time Naomi had started walking toward the warehouse. "Naomi, no! We need to work together."

She turned. "Stay there. You are protected by a good shield. I'll find this woman myself."

"Naomi—" I said, but I knew that there was nothing I could say that would change her mind. She walked straight ahead.

A whistling sound came from the left, and then a huge explosion shook the ground. I was thrown back along with Arkady and Mister Ali. The wind was knocked out of me, and as I struggled for breath I looked over to Naomi. The ground she stood on was unharmed, while the ground around her was charred, with a deep hole to her left. Naomi was coughing and brushing dust off her pants. It looked like she was bleeding from her forehead.

"Naomi, are you okay?" I yelled.

She turned to me, a grim smile on her face. "I hate technology," she said. She lifted her left arm, brought her right arm around, and then extended them to the warehouse to our left. A massive column of flame shot out and filled the entire front of the building.

"Arkady, are you okay?" Mister Ali said. I turned to see how everyone was. Mister Ali was covered in dust but seemed otherwise fine. I looked at Arkady, who was kneeling with his head down. I couldn't tell if he was hurt.

He said something that made no sense. I was concerned that he was dazed and took a step toward him. He looked up. "I held the illusion. We are butterflies."

"Butterflies?" I looked at Arkady and then Mister Ali. They looked a little shaken up but otherwise okay.

"It is an illusion, Tommy. We appear to be butterflies to those looking at us. We will hopefully be small enough that others won't notice us."

"But what about Naomi?" I asked. She had walked around the crater that the projectile had blown in the ground and was marching toward the left warehouse.

"We are not strong enough, Tommy."

"Is she?" I asked. Mister Ali didn't reply, as Naomi brought forth a series of detonations and blew holes in the warehouse.

"Angel, I know this won't hurt you. But you don't want me to hurt your men, do you?" Naomi shouted as she cast some detonations at the roof of the warehouse, and it started to cave in.

I was in awe. She was an Angel of Destruction. The warehouse was being obliterated by her barrage of spells. There was a whoosh from the right, and I turned in alarm. The men in grey had returned and were casting powerful offensive spells at Naomi. She didn't even look back at them. She pushed the palm of her hand toward the men, and they all flew backward, falling and then skidding across the ground away from her.

"The Djinn's Breath!" Mister Ali exclaimed. "That spell was lost to history. Very few know it even existed!"

A howl of buckling metal filled the air, and the warehouse collapsed. Naomi stopped in the middle of the road. I watched her from behind. Her hands moved in a blur, the energy pushed back on her hair, each strand flickering behind her head. No one emerged from warehouse. One of the metal walls twisted and fell inward.

Naomi turned and faced us and then looked to her left and then to the original warehouse. She was standing in the middle of the road that led off between and then behind the warehouses. "Now don't you prefer to have us on your side, Angel?" Naomi yelled out, looking around. "You don't want us against you!"

Glancing over at us, she shook her head. "I am guessing that the attack from this warehouse was a diversion." She nodded over her shoulder at the warehouse she had just destroyed.

She pulled up the black ball of energy that I knew was the mighty Hammer of Jamshid. "I wonder if I should just explode that one—" She motioned toward the center warehouse. "—And see if we can extract her and the Coat from the rubble."

She had an intense look on her face as she stared at the warehouse, with her eyes glinting in the sunlight. She looked amazing—beautiful and powerful. I had even forgotten how powerless I was. I didn't need to be the Archmage. I just wanted to fight next to her.

"Naomi, look out for the truck!" Mister Ali shouted. Naomi was about twenty yards from us, and as I looked around I couldn't see a truck. My eye caught a rather sad and bedraggled dog limping toward her along the road, but there was no truck. Naomi looked around, confused. Not seeing anything, she focused on the original warehouse, calling forth the Hammer of Jamshid.

Mister Ali took off running toward her. "There is a large truck coming toward you! It is too big. Your shield won't protect you!" He shouted between breaths as he ran toward her and the dog. Naomi appeared to be so focused on her spell that she didn't even notice Mister Ali calling to her.

I knew exactly what was happening, even though I couldn't perceive it. We were all fooled by the illusion of a dog, but Mister Ali saw the the reality. "Naomi! Move!" I screamed. She turned to me, looking like she didn't understand why I interrupted her. Alarmed, Naomi braced herself for the collision as she noticed Mister Ali barreling toward her.

He reached her a few seconds before the dog, knocking into her with the full force of his compact and muscular body. Naomi flew backward while the unseen truck slowed as it ran into her shield. Mister Ali struggled to get to his feet as the limping dog appeared to almost grind its way forward, tearing through Naomi's shield.

"No!" I cried as the air shimmered, and Mister Ali was knocked backward by the small dog. Some element of reality must have disrupted the magic. And as I looked at Mister Ali lying on the ground, the illusion of the dog was replaced by the reality of a transport truck with huge wheels heading toward Arkady and me. The shield had slowed it down, and we were able to dodge the truck. It passed us and then made as if to turn for another attempt.

A series of explosions to my left knocked me to the ground. I pulled myself up to my arms and knees to see the truck not just a mangled mess but actually melting under the intense heat from the flame emanating from Naomi's hands. I scrambled up and ran to Mister Ali, Arkady right next to me.

By the time we got to him, Naomi was already on her knees leaning over him. I looked down to see Mister Ali's neck twisted in a way it shouldn't. I couldn't breath. I closed my eyes and tried to focus, but all I could picture was the a small dog and then a truck and then Mister Ali's broken body. I tried to speak, but no words came out.

"Don't move. I have a strong shield around you." It was Naomi. I looked up, but couldn't see much through the tears that blurred my vision. I saw her blonde hair, a shimmer of light, and then she strode off behind me.

Before I could turn to see what she was doing, I felt the pressure of Jamshid's Hammer being cast press against my chest. The spell hit the warehouse in front of us, and the metal exploded into shards.

"Where are you?!" Naomi screamed. "Show yourself!" She shot detonations at the pile of rubble and metal just to underscore her point. They exploded into clouds of dust.

"Naomi!" Arkady yelled. "Stop!"

She ignored him and looked at the third warehouse, the one that hadn't had any activity. She called forth Jamshid's Hammer again. "Naomi!" She cast the spell and again the entire warehouse exploded in front of us. The force knocked me backward, leaving me coughing and a little dizzy. "She is not here, Naomi!" Naomi finally looked at Arkady. Her face was red and wet with tears. Her hair was wild and covered half her face.

"What?" she replied, her voice barely above a whisper.

"These were Germans, Naomi. Nazis." I looked at the wreckage all around us. This was a trap set by Germans? How did they know we were here? What did they want with us?

"Germans?" Naomi asked, dropping her hands to her side.

"Yes. We must go. The army will be here soon. It may already be too late." Arkady looked back down the gravel road that led to the warehouse complex.

I looked down at Mister Ali again. His eyes were closed, and through a tear in his robe I could see his chain armor. The image struck me so hard I fell to my knees.

I finally understood him.

He hid it from nearly everyone, but he had committed his life to protecting others—my grandfather, magical creatures, me, and… Naomi. He had never chose the path that would help himself, only the one that would help others.

I started to sob and couldn't stop. Arkady pulled on my arm. "Tommy, there will be time to mourn later. I will hide us with an illusion, but we must go. We don't know if they will have someone with the Eye.

And with the mention of someone with Mister Ali's talent to see through illusion I felt myself just go numb. I pushed away Arkady's assistance and stumbled forward, using the cane to support me.

We passed troops and vehicles rushing toward the warehouse complex. I didn't know which illusion hid us, and I didn't care. I didn't know where we were going, and I didn't care about that either. At some point we stopped, and Arkady led us to a shed behind a large house.

"We'll rest here. We can decide on our next move tomorrow."

As Arkady looked around for something for us to sleep on, Naomi walked over and touched my arm. I looked up at her face. Her eyes were drawn and bloodshot. She looked exhausted. I was going to tell her to rest after casting so many spells, but she pressed her finger against my lips and shook her head.

"I'm so sorry, Tommy." She threw her arms around my neck and started to sob into my shoulder. I held her, feeling her body shake with each sob. "I'm sorry. So sorry," she whispered over and over. I didn't know what to say, so I just held her.

Eventually she pulled back and turned away from me, saying nothing else. She ignored the various rugs and tarps that Arkady was laying out for us to sleep on and curled up on the cement in the corner.

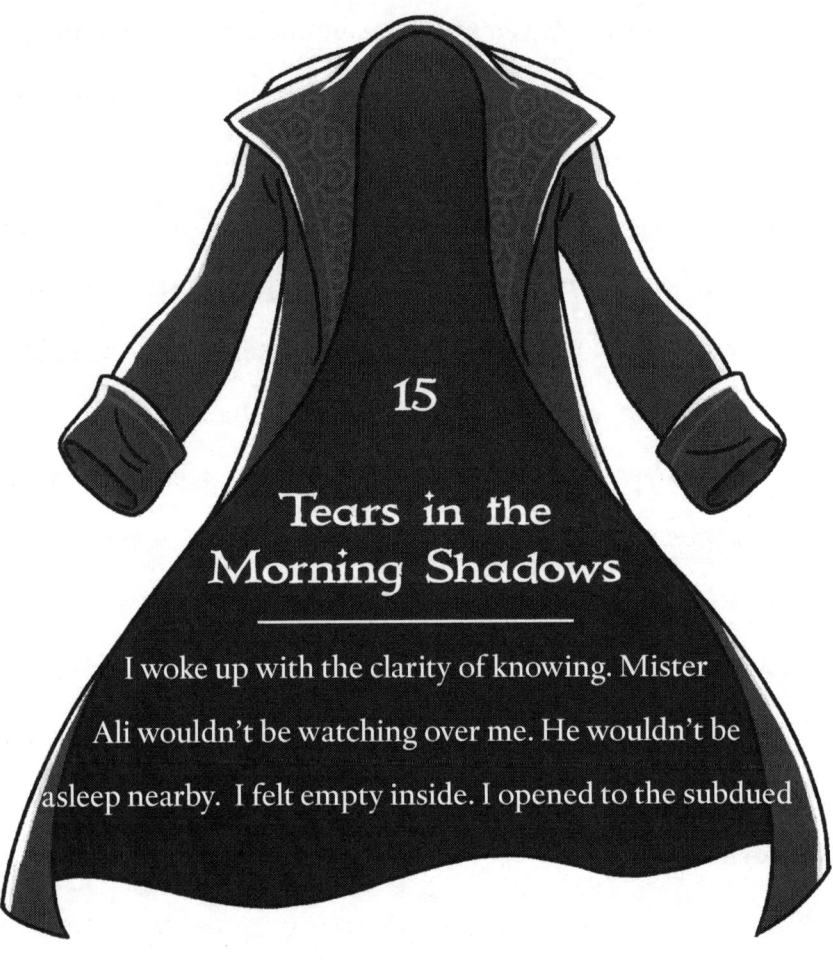

15

Tears in the Morning Shadows

I woke up with the clarity of knowing. Mister Ali wouldn't be watching over me. He wouldn't be asleep nearby. I felt empty inside. I opened to the subdued

lighting of the sun bleeding in from cracks in the shed door and Arkady and Naomi sitting on the floor whispering. As I glanced at them, the lines from the shadows looked like streaks of tears on their faces.

They both were eating what looked like bread and apples. I watched them, frozen by the normalcy of the scene. I was broken inside, and felt like I didn't belong with them.

Naomi glanced at me and must have noticed my eyes were open. "Tommy! Are you okay?" Naomi said, concern on her face. Her hair was tucked behind her ears, and she looked like she hadn't slept well.

"Kind of numb." She nodded as I stood up, stretched, and then walked over and sat on an upside down pail. Arkady held an apple out to me. I accepted it and took a bite.

"I will destroy them, Tommy. I promise you, I will." Naomi swallowed hard and formed the Hammer of Jamshid spell in her palm.

I took a deep breath. I wanted nothing more than to seek vengeance on the Germans, but we didn't have the Coat and we didn't know where to find it. We seemed powerless to do anything at that point.

Arkady spoke up. "We have two problems. The Archmage is deep in hiding, and the Germans are aware of our presence and apparently want us dead."

"Yeah. I guess vengeance will have to wait." Naomi didn't say anything. "How did the Germans find us, anyway?" I asked.

"We were just discussing that," Naomi said. "They obviously knew we had powerful magicians on the ship. They may have been unable to attack us at sea, but they got glimpses of us during our journey. It's not surprising that they knew we were coming to St. Petersburg."

"Knowing powerful magicians were coming to St. Petersburg, they sent people to track us down." Arkady violently ripped a piece of bread apart. "Bragging about us being powerful magicians! I can't believe I alerted them to us, saying the exact wrong thing to the exact wrong person at the bar. I led us right into a trap!" Arkady handed me the shredded bread.

"It's not your fault, Arkady. How could you know? We had so few options and it was our only lead." Naomi spoke while I ate. None of us mentioned Mister Ali, which was a blessing as I didn't want to think about it, but at the same time it also seemed wrong. We lost a friend and important ally. Shouldn't we be mourning him?

"Regardless, we have no options now." Arkady lowered his head. I thought over the past week, and a plan formed in my mind.

"What about the man you talked to at the bar? The one that led you to our ambush. Do you think he is still there? He may assume that we have fled. We could grab him and see if we could get information out of him."

Naomi's face lit up. "Oh, I can get information out of him." She opened her palm and a spell filled the space. It was then that I noticed that she hadn't cast a single spell since I had woken. "Do you think he's still there?" We both looked at Arkady, who shrugged.

"It's possible. He seemed to be a regular. He is probably a German spy, and that is his base of operations."

"Can we return to the hotel? Are we safe there?"

Arkady nodded. "I believe so. At least I believe our money makes us safe there."

"Got it," I replied. "So how do we grab the man without drawing attention to ourselves?'

"I have an idea," Naomi said. The spell in her hand crackled loudly.

After a long walk through a series of alleys and neighborhoods, we took hailed a taxi back to the hotel. We still had plenty of money, which was the one thing that Cain didn't seem to begrudge our mission. Naomi did her best to disguise us with illusions. The beards and rough hair seemed fine to me, but Naomi cursed every time she looked at us. "I wish I had Cain's talent for detail," she said.

"Nonsense," Arkady replied. "You are more powerful than he is already, and he has practiced for decades."

"Argh. I give up!" Naomi shook her head. "We'll just have to deal with it when the illusions dissipate. I can't move and maintain three illusions with so much detail at the same time." As we continued onward, I heard her mutter, "I guess I'll just blow up anyone that causes trouble."

The illusions were gone by the time we hailed a taxi. The driver seemed innocent enough, although I could see Naomi staring at him, flexing her fingers while she did. Arkady did all the talking, and we had little trouble navigating the various checkpoints. At one of them a soldier pointed at us and asked a question. Arkady replied, and the soldier smiled. He nodded and pointed at us again, saying something in Russian. Arkady looked over his shoulder and whispered, "Kiss each other."

I was about to object when I felt Naomi's right hand touch my cheek and then her left hand pull my head to hers. She kissed me lightly on the lips, then turned toward the guard and blew him a kiss. The guard laughed and waved us on, but I barely noticed. All I could think about was how soft Naomi's lips were, how nice it felt to kiss them, and how I swore that I felt a shock when she touched me and then another one when our lips touched. More than anything I was thinking how confused I was. She was my friend. I shouldn't like kissing her, especially a kiss that was clearly an illusion to get us past a checkpoint.

"He wanted to interview you both, but I told him that he didn't want to interrupt a young couple on the morning after their wedding. He mentioned that you two looked too miserable to be newlyweds." Arkady looked embarrassed. "I figured a kiss was the only way to prove him wrong."

"It was a good idea," I said, hoping the confidence in my voice covered the nervousness in my heart. I could picture Naomi wanting to wipe her mouth with her sleeve but being too polite to do so.

"It wasn't entirely disgusting," Naomi replied.

"No?" I asked, at that point pretty sure the confidence in my voice was gone.

Naomi turned away and replied, "Still disgusting, though." I waited for her to give me a playful nudge with her arm or to add something signifying that she was just kidding, but all she did was stare out the window.

We arrived at the hotel and Arkady once again checked us in. The manager said something and Arkady snapped at him. The manager didn't say anything else and handed over three keys. As we walked up the stairs to our room, Arkady explained what had happened.

"He asked where the fourth member of our group was. I told him it was none of his business." The reminder of Mister Ali filled the stairway with gloom, and we were all silent during the rest of the walk to our rooms.

Arkady and I had single rooms that shared a door between them, while Naomi's room was across the hall. We gathered in my room, Arkady taking a chair, while Naomi and I sat on the edge of the bed.

I looked at Naomi. "I think Arkady should check and see if our German spy is still around. Then we can trap him tomorrow."

"No way," Naomi replied. "If he sees Arkady we'll never get another chance. I want to get him tonight." I could see Naomi clenching and unclenching her teeth. "I will get him tonight." She stared at me, as if daring me to cross her. "I have a plan." I looked at Arkady, but he just shrugged.

I liked Naomi's plan, but it did seem dangerous. Naomi was going to cast an implicit illusion, making it seem to the spy that the room was full of Russian military and that they were there to escort him away for questioning. No one else would see the illusion, so it would appear that the man was just walking out with Arkady.

Arkady declared that the plan seemed sound. Naomi would sit in the corner and focus on the illusion, while Arkady would cover himself in the illusion of being a Russian colonel. He would be the one to escort the spy out.

"Are you ready?" I asked Arkady. "You're doing an implicit illusion, too. Are you sure about it?" I didn't want to question Arkady's abilities, but Naomi had told me how difficult the implicit illusions were. I just wanted to make sure he wasn't concerned.

Arkady nodded. "I'm not Naomi, but I'm still a master." I couldn't help but be amazed at how things had changed. When

Naomi and I first came to England, she was insulted and sent to work on domestic magic. Now everyone treated her with the utmost respect. It made me happy.

"How about you?" I asked Naomi.

Arkady jumped in before Naomi could answer. "Yes. Do you have the energy for this illusion?" Naomi stared daggers at him. "The illusion alone would be impossible if we were talking about anyone else, and even then I would think you would need to be thoroughly rested."

"I already have the forms worked out." Naomi continued to glare at Arkady. "You just get him outside."

Arkady nodded. "Get some rest. We'll leave in a few hours."

"Fine," Naomi replied. She stood up and walked to her room, not saying anything else.

"She is a very angry young woman, Tommy," Arkady said, shaking his head.

"She watched her mother die. She just watched Mister Ali die. And she almost died at the hands of an Ifrit," I answered. "I think some anger is justified."

Arkady's eyes went wide. "An Ifrit? How did she survive an Ifrit?"

"I saved her." Arkady glanced at the staff and then at me, nodding. "It's one of the reasons she's angry," I added with a frown.

Arkady laughed and stood up. "Women. They are the same no matter where you come from." He started toward his room. "Get some rest yourself, Tommy. A bed is better than concrete."

I closed the door behind him. I badly wanted to help, but I was relegated to keeping an eye out and not getting in the way. I was to stay out of danger.

The thought made me think of Mister Ali. He looked out for me. He protected me. He warned me of danger. But he was gone, and now I had to look out for myself, and with a staff that no longer worked, I felt powerless to do so.

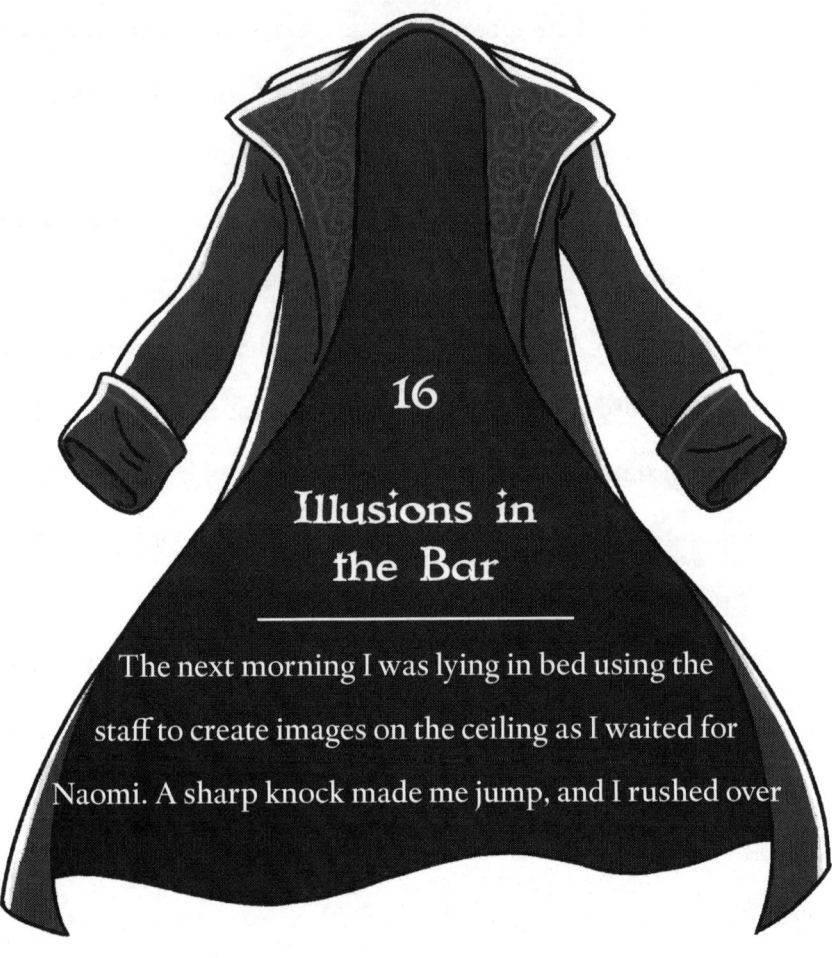

16

Illusions in the Bar

The next morning I was lying in bed using the staff to create images on the ceiling as I waited for Naomi. A sharp knock made me jump, and I rushed over

to the door. I opened it to find Naomi with her hair pulle back in a pony tail, something I had only seen her do once before—the moment in her castle when she came to talk to me in my room. It highlighted her face, especially her cheekbones.

"It's time," she said, smiling. When she smiled, her dimples made an appearance, and it changed her entire look from hard and serious to light and beautiful.

"Sometimes I think you're only happy when you're causing trouble," I said, matching her smile.

"That's not true," she replied, as I moved out of the way and let her into the room. "I'm only happy when I'm doing magic," she added over her shoulder. "And this is going to be some really challenging magic." She knocked on the door that connected my room to Arkady's. "Time to go."

Arkady opened the door. I had never seen him so focused. He said something in Russian but then quickly added, "I'm sorry. Just concentrating. I'm ready."

I led the two magicians down the stairs and outside. We had paid a driver to take us to the bar and then wait for us for the return trip. Leningrad was entirely consumed with preparing for war. Troops were everywhere, and order in the face of impending violence was paramount. In such circumstances often the only way for practical business to take place was to bribe people to look the other way so that you could operate outside the tight controls. That's what we did for transportation.

The driver was a bearded jolly man, who happily took our money and spoke in a torrent of Russian to Arkady. "He doesn't want to know anything," Arkady noted. Despite his desire, the driver kept up a steady conversation with Arkady during the whole trip, waving with his arms at traffic stops and laughing heartily at even the most succinct reply.

When we finally stepped out of the car a block from the bar, I turned to Arkady. "What was that all about?"

"He knows we're up to something, so he trusts us and decided to spend the trip complaining about the Soviets." Arkady shrugged. "At least it made me feel better about trusting him."

We walked slowly toward the bar. I was nervous as we passed a few groups of young men, but they paid us no mind. I had a thick coat with a wide collar that I pulled up around my face. Everyone near the bar seemed secretive. I glanced over at Naomi. She looked like she was in a trance, her eyes nearly motionless as they stared ahead. Her hands made barely perceptible movements that were so complicated that they didn't look quite real.

Arkady was just as focused. When we got to the front door, Naomi whispered, "Take my arm and lead me in, Tommy. Please don't let anything hit my hands. Then go to a safe corner." I took her arm and opened the door, ushering her through. She continued to stare straight ahead, as if she wasn't even aware of the physical world around her. I guided her in and held the door for Arkady.

The bar was dimly lit, with booths around the back and right walls. The rest was full of bar tables with stools. A long wooden bar ran the length of the left wall, with two bartenders behind it. The room was full of men of various ages, all of them rough-looking, with grim, weathered faces.

There weren't any free seats, so I stood to the left of the bar, close enough to look like I belonged, but far enough out of the way that no one would bother me. Naomi crouched in the middle of the room, making a series of movements. It was like watching a ballerina who is forced to dance a complicated ballet without moving her feet. Despite the fact that she was lightly clothed in the cold weather, no one paid any attention to her. Tapping the staff on the floor out of nervousness, I wondered if she was camouflaged by some illusion.

Arkady walked up to a large man and grabbed him by the shoulder. The man turned around with scowl on his face. He looked at Arkady and his eyes went wide. Arkady said something and pointed in Naomi's direction. The man then looked back at Arkady, nodded, and stood up.

I was excited at how well things were going. The man was going to walk right out of the bar and follow us to the car without so much as an objection. The spy was about five feet from Naomi when he sprinted ahead, knocking directly into her and sending her sprawling on the ground.

I had only one chance. I ran over and intercepted him just as he reached the door. I swung the cane with all the force I could muster and brought it down on the back of his head. He stumbled forward and instead of opening the door slammed into it. He slid to the ground dazed but still conscious.

It was a mess inside the bar. Men were gathering around Naomi, who was slowly getting up. Arkady was fighting through men to help her, and as he did so men were pushing him away. One started to yell at him in Russian and pulled his arm back, as if to punch him.

"Arkady, bring her this way!" I held up the staff and filled the room with a blinding light. It did not affect Naomi and Arkady, but everyone else was shielding their eyes. "Hurry!"

Arkady lifted Naomi, who was unsteady in his arms, and helped her over to the door. "Take the spy," I said. "I'll help her." I put my arms around Naomi, and as I helped her stand I was shocked. She was extremely thin and light, mere skin and bones, even lighter than when I held her on the ship.

Arkady grabbed the groggy spy and pushed him through the door. "I can handle myself," Naomi said through clenched teeth. She tossed her hand back, and there was a crash. I glanced backward, and the room looked like a giant bowling ball had rolled through, with men and tables tossed all over the floor.

Naomi pushed on the door and stumbled. I put my arm around her again. "No more magic. You're too weak." I walked out to the street, where Arkady was dragging the man toward the car. Naomi pulled herself from my arms and marched forward.

She ran in front of Arkady, stopping him in his tracks. "Do you see this?" Naomi held up her right hand, and a deep red ball appeared. Unlike much of her magic, this didn't glow or crackle with energy. It hovered above her hand.

I ran up to her and Arkady. "Naomi!"

"No, Tommy." She held up a finger from her left hand. "He has the Sight. There's no other way he would have seen through my illusion." She poked her finger against the spy's forehead a few times, making him cringe and close his eyes. "You know what this is, don't you?" She held up the red ball, and the man cowered.

"Naomi, we just need to question him." I glanced over my shoulder, and noticed some men leaving the bar and looking our way. "Also, we have company."

"I already cast an illusion. They see an empty street." She turned back to the spy. I glanced back at the bar again, and the men were looking up and down the street and pointing in various directions. "The only reason you aren't dead is that you have value." The man didn't reply. "Arkady, please translate."

Arkady spoke some words in Russian, and the man nodded his head. I stared at Naomi. Some of her hair had fallen out of her ponytail, and rather than look cute, it made her look almost crazed. Her eyes were blazing, and her mouth had the sneer of someone looking for the slightest excuse to unleash violence.

"Now you will tell me where the Germans are."

Before Arkady could translate, I interrupted, "Naomi, we don't need to know that. We're looking for the Archmage."

Naomi turned to me, her eyes brimming with tears. "Mister Ali died saving me because of them. We can get the Coat later."

She turned to face the spy and moved the red spell closer to his face. The man cried out. "First we have to take care of the Nazis."

"Naomi—"

Something caught Naomi's eye, and she looked up. "Oh for crying out loud." I looked up and a few men must have heard us and were heading our way. Naomi raised her hand to cast her spell at them.

"No!" I cried out and pushed her arm, the spell shot out and struck a motorcycle that was parked on the other side of the street. It started to glow and then burst into flame for a moment before falling to the ground in a pile of ashes.

"Sheesh, Naomi. We're not murderers!" I said. "Arkady, let's get to the car. We can interrogate the spy back at the hotel."

"Is that wise?"

"Well, we don't have time to do it here, unless you're okay with Naomi going on a murderous rampage." Naomi glared at me as Arkady nodded.

Naomi avoided my gaze as we walked back to the car. The driver looked at the half-conscious man in Arkady's arms, shook his head, but didn't say anything as we loaded him into the back seat between me and Arkady.

Naomi sat in the front seat. She was quiet during the drive back to the hotel, resting her head against the glass of the window. After all the spells she had cast, she must have been exhausted.

We arrived at the hotel, and after Arkady and I had climbed out with the spy, I looked back. Naomi was sitting with her face in her hands. I couldn't tell if she had collapsed in exhaustion or was so angry that she didn't want to look at me. I walked over.

I opened the door, and she looked up at me. Her face was red. "Tommy, I'm really weak. Can you help me?" Nodding, I reached in and lifted her up. We walked to our rooms, Naomi leaning on me for support.

I escorted her into her room, where she fell on top of the bed. She rolled over, and looked away from me. There was a quilt at the base of the bed, which I pulled up to cover her. I turned off the lamp and turned to leave when I heard Naomi whisper, "I'm sorry, Tommy. I can't do anything right."

I turned to tell her that everything was all right, that I understood her anger. I didn't really think she was a murderer, and more than anything I was also wracked with pain over Mister Ali. Before I could speak, however, I heard a small snore. I turned away and left, closing the door behind me.

17

Answers

I walked through the door
that linked my room to Arkady's and
found him standing in front of the spy, who
was sitting on the chair. He looked alert and was
rubbing the back of his head. The man said something in
Russian, nearly spitting out the words.

"He says that he won't tell us anything."

The spy was sneering, and the look on his face was full of arrogance. I thought of Mister Ali's crumpled body and that this was the man who had led us into the trap that caused his death. The rage that I had suppressed started to well up inside of me. I walked over to him.

I tapped the cane on the hardwood floor during the few steps it took to reach the man. I stopped in front of him. The sneer remained on his face as I drew the sword that was hidden inside the cane. I held the point an inch from his heart. He quivered a bit, but didn't say anything.

I turned to the nightstand that stood next to him. It had a candle and an ashtray on it, setting on a small decorative cover of embroidered material. I raised the sword and in a single swift motion brought it down. The wood of the nightstand put so little resistance on the sword that it looked and felt like I was slicing through air.

The nightstand stood for a moment and then fell into two halves. I had seen the sword do similar feats of slicing in the past. The artifact was so powerful that things split before they even struck the edge of the blade, as if their very touch were an insult.

I turned back to the spy and held the sword above his head. "Arkady," I said, my voice flat and emotionless. "Ask him if he would like to know what it feels like to be split in two."

Arkady spoke, and the spy's mouth dropped open. The fear on his face was palpable. "Please tell him he has three seconds to tell me who he is with and what their intentions are." Arkady repeated the words in Russian.

As Arkady spoke, I said, "One."

"Uhdeen." The spy looked at me, then at Arkady, and then back at me.

"Two."

"Dva." I raised the sword a couple inches, as if preparing for a killing stroke, and the spy's eyes went wide in terror.

"Zhdat!" the spy exclaimed. I looked at Arkady, who nodded at me. I pulled the sword away and sheathed it in the cane. The moment the sword clicked in place, the spy started speaking quickly.

Arkady translated in pieces as the man talked. "He is a spy for the Germans. They are looking for two things… An artifact and… Powerful magicians… just arrived in Leningrad."

"Well, he found an artifact, just not the right one," I replied grimly. "Ask him what the interest is in the magicians."

They exchanged words, and Arkady said, "He doesn't know. They were considered dangerous is all he was told. He was to lead them to an out-of-the-way place to be taken care of."

To be taken care of. I felt sick, and the rage started to cloud my vision. All I wanted to do was to do to this man what he did to

Mister Ali—leave him in a crumpled heap. I took a deep breath. "Ask him about the Angel."

Arkady spoke and then translated the answer. "They want her artifact... But they haven't found her... She is well hidden."

"Why does he want the Angel's artifact," I asked, but I could assume the answer—something that would protect one from real harm had value in a war.

"He says he won't answer," Arkady looked at me and shrugged. I unsheathed the sword again, but the spy just shook his head and said something in Russian.

"He says death is preferable over what would happen to him if he revealed more than he has already."

I had an idea. "Does he know magic, Arkady?"

"Absolutely. Naomi immediately understood what happened in the bar. This man is like Mister Ali. He can see through illusions and is very knowledgable about magic. I'm sure it makes him very effective at trailing and finding magical targets."

I sheathed the sword and smiled. I dropped the brass tip to the floor and leaned on it. "Ask him if death would be preferable to being absorbed by a Shadow."

"I'm not sure an empty threat will work, Tommy. He is knowledgable in magic and knows that Shadows can't be slaves or servants. Even if I were to create an illusion of a Shadow he would see through it."

"Just ask him."

Arkady said the words, but the spy didn't reply and his face was emotionless. I shook my head and motioned with the staff toward the wall. I used what I had learned on the ship during our journey to create the inky black outline of a Shadow by manipulating the rays of light. It emerged from a small shadow next to the bed, and oozed up the wall into the rough outline of a human-like shape that was blacker than black.

"My God," Arkady said, stepping back away from the Shadow.

"I am glad you could be here, my friend," I said, not knowing if the spy could actually understand English. "You can have this one." I motioned toward the spy with the staff, and then manipulated the light so that it appeared the Shadow was dripping down the wall and moving toward the spy.

"Arkady, tell him that the perpetual cold of a Shadow is about to consume him if he doesn't tell us more. He won't die. At least not immediately. But he'll wish he had." The black oozed past the tips of my shoes toward the spy.

Arkady spoke, and the man's face filled with abject terror. He scrambled back in the chair, trying to get away from the Shadow. I motioned with the staff and the movement of the Shadow paused.

"Uhdeen," I said, echoing Arkady's Russian. Not even waiting for a response, I said, "Dva."

"Zhdat! Zhdat!" the spy screamed. He then let loose another torrent of Russian.

"You can dismiss your Shadow friend, Tommy. The spy is telling us everything." I nodded and used the power of the staff to move the Shadow under the bed, after which I ended the magic.

"The Fuhror is gathering all of the magic artifacts in the world," Arkady translated. "He has men in Egypt, Persia, and even the Far East looking for them. He is especially interested in the artifacts of Jamshid, and he has his top magicians in Russia looking for the Coat. They are also looking for the staff but they know that it is in England."

As the spy finished, he turned to me, a look of pleading on his face. "Please," he said in English, and then added a few sentences in Russian.

"He asks that you release him," Arkady translated. "He promises not to say anything more about you." The spy looked at me, and then, in a hushed tone, spoke again. Arkady nodded as if agreeing with the Russian words. "Someone who can call forth and control Shadows is a magician of such great power that they will go down in history. It would be foolish for him to cross us."

I walked over to Arkady. "Do you trust him?" Arkady shook his head, and I nodded. "I don't want to kill him. We're not monsters."

"We should just hand him to the Soviets. They would be happy to have him, I'm sure." At first I liked Arkady's idea, but then as I was about to say it was good I thought harder about what would happen. I was nearly positive that they would execute him, and I was wondering if that would make me a party to his death.

As I thought over our options, a new idea struck me. One that used Arkady's idea but would help us find the Angel of St. Petersburg. "How about this?" I tapped the cane on the floor. "We'll use him as bait for the Angel's men. Tell her that we have the spy that was the source of those hunting her. When we arrange to give him to her, we use that as an opportunity to grab the coat."

Arkady was quiet as he tapped a finger on his chin. He then replied, "It's a good idea, Tommy, but how will we know where to find the Angel's men?"

I grinned. "We ask him." I pointed to the spy.

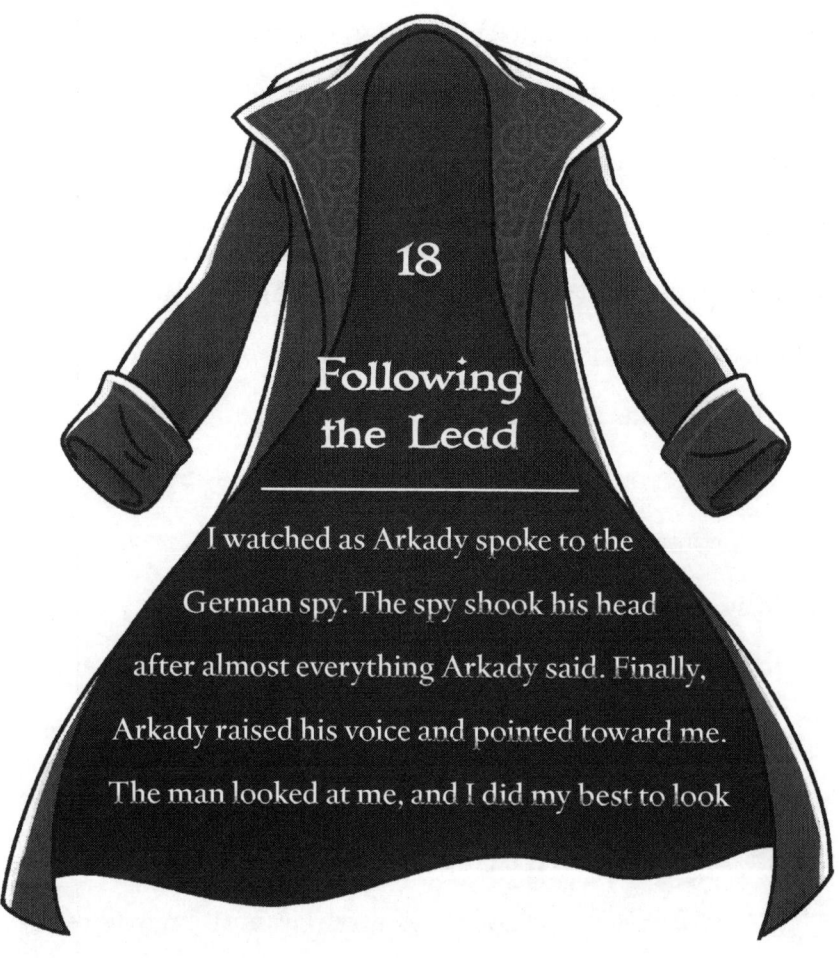

18

Following the Lead

I watched as Arkady spoke to the
German spy. The spy shook his head
after almost everything Arkady said. Finally,
Arkady raised his voice and pointed toward me.
The man looked at me, and I did my best to look

intimidating. He lowered his head and finally said, "Da." What
followed was a hesitant stream of words in Russian.

When he finished he lowered his head into his hands, looking
utterly defeated. "He said he'll do it, Tommy. But we are to give
him a chance to escape during the transfer. He believes we'll kill
him and if we actually hand him to the White Russians that they

will kill him, so he said that since we won't need him once we find the Coat that we should let him escape. He will do everything he can to help us, but we must let him go once we meet the Angel."

I ran my hand through my hair and looked at the man. He seemed helpless, but I didn't want to let appearances fool me. "What do you think, Arkady?"

"I think he has no option, so we can trust him solely because this is the best outcome for him." Arkady looked at me. "He truly believes you will feed him to your Shadow friend."

"Okay, let's do it. Find out what he knows."

Their conversation went on much longer than I expected. I thought the spy would say something like, "We last saw her to the east of the city," but he clearly had detailed knowledge of her. Finally, the spy stopped talking and Arkady turned to me.

"He knows her people, but he doubts that she is anywhere near them. They are very secretive and not very trusting. She is being hunted constantly by the Soviets."

"So he can lead us to people who will pass a message along to her?"

Arkady nodded. "He knows people who are close to her."

"Can he take us to them?"

"Yes. We can leave tomorrow. They are far out in the country-side, and he doesn't know how many people there are between his contact and the Angel, but he can at least get us to that first step."

"I want details. I don't trust him." And I didn't. He had knowledge of magic and was a good enough German spy to go undetected in the heart of Leningrad.

Arkady spoke with him. At moments Arkady would raise his voice and at others he would cajole the spy. In the end he looked at me with a smile on his face. "I trust him. He told me everything he knows, and it makes sense to me."

"Could he be lying?" I still didn't trust him.

"I don't believe so. We'll be taking him there tomorrow, and if it isn't the way we expect, he thinks we will kill him."

"Yeah, death is a good motivator." I looked over at the spy. "What do we do with him until tomorrow?"

"I'll get some rope, tie him up, and then keep watch."

"Make sure the knots are strong, and wake me up before it gets too late. You need your rest, too."

Arkady assured me that he would, and I left for my room and some much needed sleep. I was exhausted just from the stress. I couldn't imagine how Naomi felt after casting so many spells. I fell asleep with the knowledge that at least she was getting some rest and we were one step closer to retrieving the Coat of Invincibility.

I awoke to the sound of a crash nearby. It was still dark out, but the staff lit the room as I grabbed it from its place next to me. I rolled out of bed and ran to the door to Arkady's room. As I opened it I could see the door to the hall standing open, Arkady holding his hand to his head. Blood was dripping through his fingers.

"Are you okay?" I asked running over to him.

He nodded his head. "I was watching him but must have fallen asleep. He untied his hands, but he made some noise as he was tugging his legs out of the ropes. It woke me, and I ran to stop him, but he hit me in the head. I'm afraid it knocked me backward, and then he ran out the door."

I poked my head out of the door and looked down the hallway. The spy was long gone. I glance back at Arkady. "Your head is still bleeding."

"It's okay. I've been hurt worse." He walked slowly back into the room and grabbed a sheet off the bed. Rolling it up, he held it against his head. As he sat down he looked at me. "What are we to do?"

"He'll warn the Germans and tell them where we are." Arkady nodded. "We should find a new hiding place and lay low," I added.

"They'll hunt for us, like they are hunting the Angel."

I sat down next to Arkady and rubbed my eyes. "So what are our options?"

"We can go directly after the Angel before the Germans can find us. We can flee and hide somewhere distant, coming back when things quiet down." He paused and then looked at me. "Or we can head back to England."

"That's not an option," I said firmly.

"Then we flee or we fight."

"Naomi won't let us flee," I replied.

"No. She won't."

"Do you know where the Angel's people are?"

"Yes. I asked the spy for details."

"We can just go after her, grab the Coat, and then leave." I waved my hands around as I talked, as if the movement of my hands could clear away any doubts.

"I don't think it will be that easy," Arkady said.

"When has any of this been easy?" I asked, shaking my head.

We wanted to give Naomi as much rest as we could, but in the end we needed to leave. The spy had probably already contacted the Nazis. I knocked on her door. She didn't answer, so I knocked louder. After knocking again, she finally opened the door, her eyes glazed over and her hair a mess around her face.

"We have a problem," I said. At that Naomi opened her eyes wide and waved me in.

I walked over and fell into her reading chair. "Arkady is packing our supplies. We need to leave immediately." I then outlined to her what happened while she was sleeping.

She rubbed her eyes and slid her hair behind her ears. "So we're going to go after the Angel?"

I nodded. "Assuming we can find her."

"Good. We'll find her." Naomi stretched her arms above her head and then cracked her knuckles. "What time is it?"

"Almost dawn. Did you get enough rest?"

"Yeah. I'll be fine."

I walked over, and sat down next to her on the bed. "You look so skinny and weak. What's wrong? Are you okay? Is the magic draining you?"

Naomi grinned. "No. It doesn't steal my life energy or any of those old wives tales. But—" Naomi yawned. "It takes enormous physical energy and concentration. It does drain you. Did you ever take a close look at the masters or Cain?" I nodded but wasn't quite sure I was entirely truthful. Cain was a mess of tics and muscle spasms. The masters looked normal, if a bit gaunt, but they all hid behind suits that hid their actual bodies.

"Isn't there anything that can stop it?" Naomi was doing a lot of magic, and I pictured her eventually collapsing in a pile of nothing more than thin skin and bones. She was already close to that.

Chuckling, she replied, "Food. Rest. Exercise. You know, all those things that I ignore. I'm not exactly known for living smart."

"Didn't you have food in your castle?" Arkady walked in with a couple carpetbags.

"Oh, I had plenty of food. I just didn't have time to eat." She nodded toward Arkady. "Ask him. Arkady, what did I do all day?"

"Study and practice."

"So you didn't eat enough?" When Naomi nodded, I replied, "Well that's just stupid."

"We must go," Arkady said, interrupting my scolding. Naomi stood up. She looked fine, but for the first time I looked at her without being intimidated by her power and beauty. She was thin, some would say dangerously so. I knew that Naomi would never let me take care of her, but I promised myself to nudge her toward taking care of herself.

Our driver from the previous day was nowhere to be found, and the taxis refused to take us where we wanted to go, which was a small city called Toksovo. It was to the northeast and one step closer to the Arctic cold. The look on their faces when we mentioned the city seemed to indicate that very bad things happened there. We tramped back into the hotel, and Arkady spoke with the clerk.

Arkady would say a few words, and the clerk would shake his head. At one point, Arkady pulled out his wallet and laid a long string of bills on the counter top. It looked like the remainder of our money. He tapped the money with his forefinger and then said some words in Russian. The clerk, who looked to be about the same age as Arkady, nodded his head, grabbed the money, and then started walking around the counter to join us.

As the clerk led us to a car, Arkady explained what happened. "He can drive but doesn't have a car. He is borrowing the owner's car, which will certainly get him fired. So I had to give him an inducement to help us."

"I'm guessing that inducement was quite a bit of money," I said.

"I paid him about six months wages for him."

We turned the corner from the front of the hotel, and there was a new black sedan parked next to the side entrance to the hotel. "It looks like we don't have much money left," Naomi noted.

"Well, we don't have many more options after this. We either find the Angel and leave with the Coat or we don't find her and leave without it. Either way we are leaving."

"True enough," I added as the clerk crawled into the driver's seat. Once again Arkady sat in front while Naomi and I sat in the back. Naomi had talked about attempting to disguise us again with an illusion, but I told her that we'd need her energy for the confrontation with the Angel's men. She nodded, and we all were quiet for what turned out to be a long drive into a wild but beautiful countryside.

19

The Angel

I heard a shrill whistle and immediately knew what it was, a train powered by an Ifrit or Marid. The howl of pain was unmistakable. It eminded me of my original mission—to free the magical creatures in Europe like I did in England. The thought only hardened my resolve—I would retrieve the Coat of Invincibility, walk into Germany, and free the slaves.

But first I had to retrieve the artifact, and that was looking to be a difficult task. We were being knocked around as we bounced over rutted dirt roads, trying to get to some location where we would find someone who hopefully would lead us to the mysterious Angel of St. Petersburg.

"What was that spell you threatened the spy with?" I asked Naomi, thinking of the solid deep red ball that she held in front of the spy's face.

"Zahhak's Rage," Naomi replied. Almost absent-mindedly creating it in her hand as we talked. "It penetrates whatever it hits and then burns it or them up from the inside. The heat is so intense that all it usually leaves is a pile of ash."

"Wow. No wonder it scared him."

Naomi closed her hand, and the spell snuffed out. She brushed her hair behind her ears and looked at me like she wanted to tell me something but didn't quite know if she should.

"What is it?" I asked.

"Nothing." Naomi turned away, once again staring out the window. She sighed and then said, "Zahhak was the last great dragon that terrorized the world. Jamshid defeated him, and rumor has it that he created this horrible spell to both honor the battle and remind us all of the horror that was Zahhak."

"Neat," I replied.

"Yeah. Neat."

Naomi didn't seem to be in the mood to talk, so I focused on the scenery outside the window. It was desolate and gorgeous.

Wherever we were going was isolated and beautiful and dangerous. It seemed appropriate.

We stopped for food at a farmer's stall outside of a tiny town. I had to practically force Naomi to eat, but she did. I asked Arkady what we should expect. "How much do we know?"

Crunching on a sweet onion, Arkady replied between mouthfuls, "There is a farmhouse in Toksovo. I have detailed directions. The farmer who owns it is the contact for the Angel. We will need to convince him to take us to her."

"Nothing else?" It seemed like minimal information to me.

Arkady shrugged. "We have a name and a location. Hopefully that is enough."

We piled back into the sedan and closed in on Toksovo. The trip took much longer than it should have as the roads were horrible—full of ruts and holes. Naomi was smiling over a particularly rough patch that tossed us all over the back seat.

"What's so funny?" I asked.

"This is good practice."

"For what?"

"Casting a spell while moving. It's very difficult even when still, but when being tossed around like this?" She squinted her eyes as she closed and opened her hand. "It's practically impossible."

"Why do I always think that when you hear 'impossible' your immediate thought is to see it as your next challenge?"

Naomi looked at me and smiled, "Why, Tommy, it's like you finally understand me."

The driver said something and pulled to the side of the road. Arkady handed him a large wad of Russian money, which the driver kissed and then shoved in his pocket. We all climbed out. My door wasn't even completely shut before the car started to pull away. It turned sharply, passed us, and began the trip back to Leningrad.

"Arkady, we don't seem to have a way to return to the city."

"Don't focus so much on the negative," Naomi said. I glanced at her, and she was practically bouncing on the balls of her feet. She seemed completely wired with nervous energy. "Where's the guy who will lead us to the Angel?"

Arkady pointed to a dirt road that was even smaller and more derelict than the one we were on. Twisting to the right, my gaze followed it to the horizon, where I thought I could see a group of buildings, although it was far enough away that I couldn't be sure.

"Let's get us a coat," Naomi said, starting forward. Arkady carried our bags, and I used the cane as a walking stick.

"We have to be careful. None of us are particularly good at seeing through illusions."

Naomi nodded, but Arkady spoke up from behind, "It should not be a concern, Tommy. The spy told me that they are solely an armed group. The Angel carries a machine gun and uses regular armed troops. She does not believe in the power of magic."

"Oh, I really want to take her down now," Naomi muttered.

"But she's an Archmage," I replied.

Arkady shrugged. "She only uses the Coat for protection. It is just a tool, not an artifact to her."

"The spy said this?" Naomi asked. She seemed skeptical.

"Yes. He contrasted the goals of his country, which is to utilize the magical artifacts and magicians to help achieve their goal, with the goals of the Angel, which is to simply destroy the Soviet Union and bring back the Russian monarchy."

"Good luck with that," Naomi replied. "All the royals are dead."

With each step I could feel a change in the staff. It was almost as if it was buzzing with excitement from the inside. It wasn't a physical feeling of vibration so much as a psychic connection of excitement, as if the staff couldn't wait to get to our destination. I had never felt anything like it before with the staff, and I took it as a good sign. Perhaps I would be able to bend light or stop time again.

"I see it," Arkady said. I squinted and could just make out a farmstead in the distance.

"It isn't exactly a fortress, assuming they aren't hiding anything with an illusion," I noted.

"Yes, but it's on a hilltop. No one could get within miles of there without being seen first." Naomi started moving her hands. "Which reminds me, I'll cover us with a shield, but we should be ready for anything." No one had to reply. We all knew this would be dangerous.

It was eerily quiet. There was the normal sound of insects and birds and the wind blowing through grass and trees, but there were no sounds of human life—cars, voices, or doors banging open or shut.

As we finally reached the house, I was tense and on edge. The staff was vibrating so hard I didn't know if I could retain my grip, yet as I looked down I saw that it wasn't moving at all. It was all in my head, thanks to my connection to the staff.

Scanning the surroundings, I couldn't see anything out-of-the-ordinary. There was a field to the right with some cows, and a barn straight ahead with big closed doors. The farmhouse was to the left. To the right beyond the barn was a smaller barn that looked like it held livestock.

The farmhouse was surrounded by a rickety fence, and a broken gate opened to a path leading to the front door. I squinted as I looked at the house, but it was still and quiet.

"Is there even anyone here?" I whispered.

"We should knock on the front door," Naomi answered.

I looked at Arkady, who shrugged. I opened the gate and the three of us walked to the front door. With no other option, I reached out and knocked. There was no answer, so I knocked louder. I turned and looked at Naomi and Arkady.

"Do you think we were misled by the spy?"

Before anyone could answer, the doors of the barn squealed open. A man in coveralls walked out wiping his hands on a cloth. He was dirty, and looked exactly like you would expect a farmer to look after fixing a tractor.

As he slid the cloth into his pants pocket, he closed the distance between us. Arkady waved and greeted him in Russian. The man seemed pleasant enough and smiled as he talked. They exchanged a few words, with the man shaking his head after every question from Arkady.

Arkady held up a finger to the man and turned to us. "He said he doesn't know anything about an Angel of St. Petersburg or a Coat or anything like that."

For the barest of moments my heart fell as I considered that we were misled, but that feeling was overwhelmed by a rush of insight from the staff itself. I gripped it tight, and closed my eyes. I had never been so connected to it. It wasn't just a part of me, it was almost controlling me. For the first time since touching the staff I felt frightened.

"Tommy!" I opened my eyes to Naomi looking at me strangely. "Are you okay?" she added.

I ignored her question and turned toward the house. "The Archmage is inside. She awaits with the Coat."

As soon as I said the words, the farmer squinted at me and then reached into his pocket. I ran forward and knocked him to the ground with my shoulder. Naomi and Arkady stared at me. "Open the door!" I exclaimed.

I couldn't quite explain my urgency, but I had to get in and get the Coat. As the farmer tried to get up, I reached into his pocket and found a pistol. I pulled it out. He raised his hands even though I hadn't even aimed the gun at him.

"Stand back," Naomi said. She faced the door, and Arkady and I retreated a few steps behind her. With the barest of motions, a detonation flew from her hand and exploded against the house, leaving a hole where the door used to be.

She looked over her shoulder and shrugged, a smile on her face. "Maybe that was overkill." Without a care for her own personal safety, she walked right through the hole, which seemed big enough to weaken the structure of the house. Arkady followed her in, while I motioned with the pistol to the farmer.

"You seem to know what's up," Naomi said, as we stood in the living room and looked around. "So, where is she?"

"I don't know. She is close, though." I didn't know it; the staff did.

"Maybe I should just blow up the house. She can't be harmed, so we'll just dig her out of the rubble."

I was about to object when the sound of a woman came from a hallway on the other side of the living room. "That will not be necessary, miss." A woman entered wearing a thick velvet coat that flowed out behind her. It was almost impossibly black. Under the coat she wore an elegant maroon dress. Her hair was up, but not in a pony tail, rather it was arranged in an elegant formal style.

It took me a moment before I realized that she had spoken English, although with a Russian accent. "The Angel of St. Petersburg," I said as she walked up to Naomi.

"I fear I haven't done much to protect my beloved city lately, so the title is perhaps undeserved at this point."

Arkady appeared to be in shock, while Naomi stared at the woman, a spell poised at the ready in her palm. The woman seemed completely unconcerned as she walked around Naomi.

"A young woman shooting detonations. Have we sunk so far that women are all that's left to defend our friends?" As if illustrating the Angel's comment, the farmer inched over to her side.

She turned to me and crossed her arms. "I've heard of you. They call you the Archmage." I stared at her but didn't say anything. She looked middle-aged or older, and had a roundish face. She didn't look cruel, but she didn't appear kind either. More than anything she seemed serious and determined.

I leaned on the cane. "It is a title that was given to my family ages ago."

She looked at my cane and then back at my face. "I know something of titles." She spun around. "But let us talk over tea. Enough of destroying things. Perhaps we can work together on rebuilding lost legacies." She walked into a room to the right that looked like a rustic but comfortable dining room.

Naomi looked at me, and I shrugged. Arkady had already started to follow her.

The Angel snapped her fingers, and the farmer hurried into the kitchen to retrieve a teapot. Naomi sat at the table, and I sat next to her, across from Arkady. I placed the pistol on the table. With the Angel wearing the coat I knew I couldn't hurt her.

She walked around the table and poured tea into a cup that she had placed in front of me. "How much do you know about me, Archmage?"

"Nothing, really." She moved on to Naomi.

"How much do you know of the artifacts of Jamshid?"

I looked at Arkady but he couldn't seem to stop staring at the Angel, his brows furrowed as if he was concentrating on something. I wondered if she had used some kind of magic to affect his mind.

"That there are three. And two of them are in this room." The Angel moved on to her cup and filled it.

"Nothing more?" I looked at Naomi and she gave a slight shake to her head. She wanted me to play ignorant, which wasn't too hard as I really didn't know much more anyway.

"I'm afraid not. Up until recently I didn't even know there were three artifacts."

She sat down. "Oh my, I have been rude, asking you questions without even introducing myself." She nodded her head toward me. "My name is Ana. I bear the Coat of Babr-e Bayan."

"I am Tommy Black." I paused, not even knowing which artifact I held in my hand. It was embarrassing. I sputtered, "I bear the Staff."

She nodded. "The Staff of Darius. The most powerful of the artifacts."

I motioned to Naomi. "This is Naomi, a legendary magician."

"Legendary, you say?" Ana looked at Naomi and then turned away dismissively. "I have not heard of you."

Before Naomi lost her temper I waved a hand toward Arkady. "And this is Arkady, a master illusionist."

Ana said something to him in Russian, and his eyes went wide. She smiled kindly and nodded her head. Arkady stood up so quickly that his chair fell backward. He bowed. "Your majesty!"

I was confused. Majesty? She just said her name was Ana. As she spoke again to Arkady in Russian, I remembered something from my incomplete education. "Wait," I blurted out. "You're Princess Anastasia?" Just as she did to Arkady, Ana nodded to me. "But she was assassinated with her family."

Ana rubbed the fabric of her coat between her fingers. "Before he died, Rasputin passed the Coat on to me. Someone who cannot be harmed cannot be assassinated."

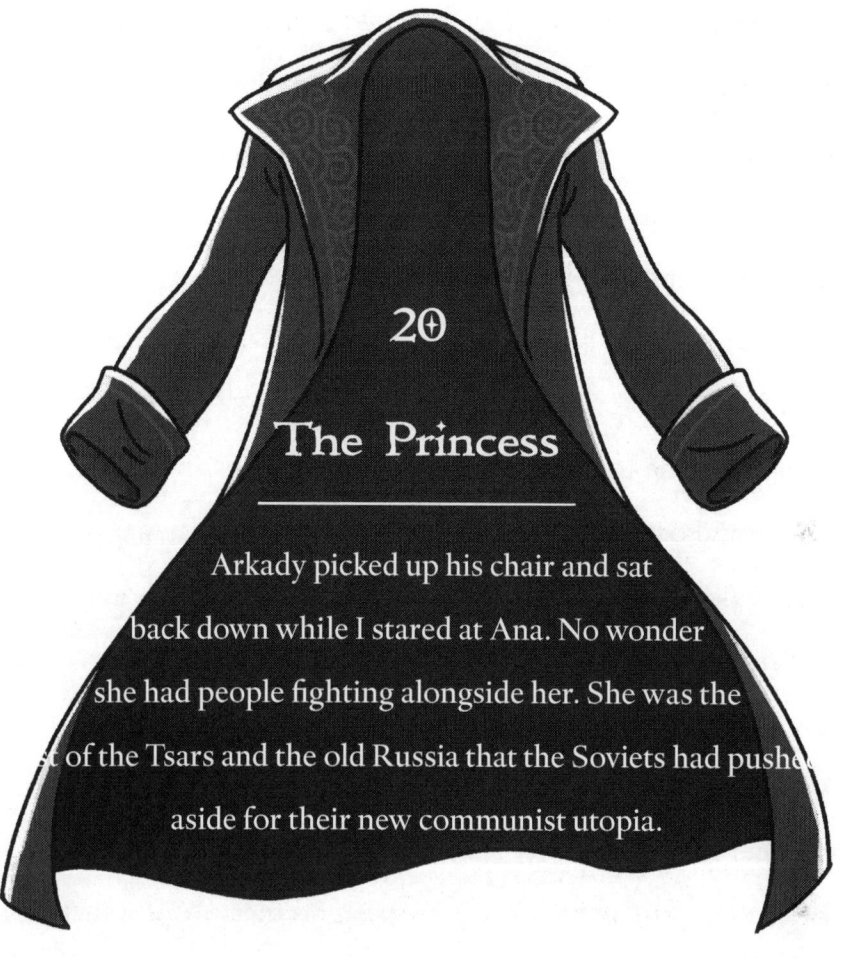

20

The Princess

Arkady picked up his chair and sat back down while I stared at Ana. No wonder she had people fighting alongside her. She was the ... of the Tsars and the old Russia that the Soviets had pushed aside for their new communist utopia.

Ana laughed. "Everyone is so quiet. Yes, I am Princess Anastasia. My mentor was the great magician Rasputin. He bore the Coat for decades, in service to my family. He knew he would die in handing it to me, just as he knew it would save me." Ana lowered her head. "He was a great man."

I rubbed my eyes, and Ana turned to me. "You feel it, don't you? The artifacts. They need to be reunited."

I didn't answer, but the pull toward Ana was enormous. I can't say that I felt compelled to hand her the staff so much as I felt that the staff wanted to be joined with the Coat, however that happened. There was no reason for me to deny it. "Yes. They belong together."

Ana breathed out. "Oh, I'm so glad you understand. I was afraid you would demand the Coat. As the heir to the Russian throne, it is obvious that I am the rightful heir of Jamshid. I should wield the artifacts."

At a certain level I knew that bringing the artifacts together was the important thing, and it didn't matter who had them, but another part of me knew that I should be the one to wield the artifacts. A very small part of me—perhaps the only part that was still me—screamed out that every option was full of unknown danger.

In my mind the battle for the artifacts had begun. To that end I knew I needed the Coat. What had Ana done? She had fought and killed Russians. What had I done? I had saved the Shadows, freed Marids and Ifrit. Perhaps I was simply providing reasons to support the urge I had to control the artifacts, but that didn't mean the reasons weren't real.

I looked over at Naomi, and it was then that I realized she was only being quiet on my behalf. I had not expected that from her. It was a humbling surprise that she was letting me handle this important conversation without interrupting. But it was clearly tough on her—her jaw was clenched, and I could see that her palms were ready to launch an attack on Ana at any moment. But for what purpose? We couldn't hurt her. It was then that I knew I had to somehow do two things: Get more information out of Ana and stall while finding a way to get the Coat.

"What about the third Artifact?" I asked.

Ana stared at me for a bit and then took a sip of her tea. "The Cup of Jamshid is in the hands of the Germans. That is going to be a real challenge for us, Tommy." Ana continued to talk as if we were on the same side, which made me relax. I knew it was inevitable that we would fight over the artifacts at some point, but I wanted that fight to be on my terms.

"How so?"

Ana laughed. "Well, beyond the fact that it is in Germany, the bearer of the Cup can see all. All he has to do is look into the Cup and he would know when we were approaching."

"If it sees all, why haven't the Germans found you yet?" Naomi finally spoke, and her question seemed to stun Ana. It looked as though she had never thought of that possibility before.

"Because—" she stammered. Before she could say anything else, she was interrupted by a shout and the sound of men running through gravel. With the front of the house blown open, it was easy to hear.

Ana looked toward the front of the house, which was visible from her seat at the head of the table. A man ran through the hole. He was panting as he ran up to Ana and bowed. He stammered some words in Russian. Ana rubbed her chin thoughtfully, not seeming concerned.

"The Germans are approaching," Arkady whispered to me and Naomi. I immediately thought of the spy.

Ana overheard Arkady and frowned. "You appear to have led the Germans to me."

"More like the Germans led us to you," I replied without explanation.

Ana stood up. "Hand me the staff. I'll take care of this." I had never been closer to having no control over my actions than at that point. Nearly every part of my body compelled me to hand her the staff. My eyes rolled up in my head as I clung to the few things that meant so much to me—the pride of my grandfather, the confidence and trust of my great grandfather, and the faith that Mister Ali had in me, a faith he betrayed and made up for with his life.

"Tommy, are you okay?" I opened my eyes to Naomi shaking my shoulder.

I took a deep breath and looked at Ana. "You will not be able to master it so quickly. I will wield it to fight the Germans." And at that moment I had an inspiration. "Give me the Coat. I will be able to handle them easily with the Coat protecting me."

At that moment I knew with certainty that the Coat and Staff didn't care who bore them. They just wanted to be together. As I looked at Ana, I saw her stumble back a bit as her hands reached for the front of the Coat. Her eyes fluttered, and her hands shook. I thought I heard the lightly whispered word "no" come from her mouth.

There was an explosion, followed by the sound of machine guns ringing out. Everything sounded much closer than I had expected. I stood up quickly, and Naomi did the same, drawing a detonation into her hand. By then Ana had recovered and was yelling out in Russian.

In a scene that reminded me of the assault on the Persian Garden restaurant two years earlier, men that I hadn't seen emerged from the rear of the house, carrying rifles. One of them ran up and handed Ana a wicked looking machine gun. She looked at me and Naomi.

"One of the things you will learn, Tommy, is that with technology eradicating magic, the difference will be those magical artifacts that technology cannot replicate. Nothing else matters in the face of cannons and bullets."

She marched toward the front of the house, paused, and looked back at us. There was a grin on her face that reminded me of my grandfather—as if the violence she was about to embrace was the only thing she enjoyed in life. Without saying a word, she turned and strode out of the house.

I looked at Naomi, but she had already started after Ana, bouncing on the balls of her feet like some kind of predator approaching its prey.

I followed her outside to a scene that boggled the mind. Far in the distance along the same road we used to approach the farm, numerous trucks approached. There must have been about a dozen of them. The first few had already pulled to the side of the road, and small groups of men approached, none of whom were in uniform. They bore machine guns and the first few had already started shooting in our direction.

Men in grey emerged from the second truck, and I knew instinctively that they were magicians. The Germans definitely considered magic a valuable tool, but a quick glance at the first truck and the rat-a-tat of the machine guns made it clear that it wasn't their only tool.

"We don't have much time, Tommy, my shields cannot withstand a constant barrage of bullets for long." Naomi was standing on the porch watching the Angel's men firing on the Germans from entrenched positions. The Germans were clearly protected by magical shields, while the Russians were protected by things

I hadn't noticed before—trenches and tractors that were there as cover and not for plowing fields.

"I don't think we'll need to worry about bullets being aimed at us," I replied as I pointed toward Ana. She simply strode toward the Germans, firing her large machine gun at them. It was an absurd and frightening scene. Her brown hair blew out behind her in the face of a slight breeze, while the entire might of the German weaponry focused on her.

The power of the artifact was clear. Bullets simply stopped as they approached and fell to the ground. I walked forward, and Naomi grabbed my arm. "What are you doing? We should just wait and let her take care of things."

"We don't know what the Germans have in mind. We may have a chance to grab the Coat. We should stay close." I couldn't bear to tell Naomi how weak I truly was. The truth was that the staff was telling me to stay close to Ana. It had nothing to do with me at all.

Naomi nodded. "Dangerous, but opportunistic. I like it." She let go of my arm, and we started toward Ana. "I'll let you know if my shield starts to give out. At that point it will be a good idea to get away from the force of the attack."

I nodded, but I wasn't really paying attention to Naomi. All of my energy was focused on the Coat.

We were about twenty yards behind Ana, who walked toward the Germans as if she was having her morning stroll. She was spraying the trucks with gunfire, and she looked like she wanted to do nothing more than to kill every single German, but she did it with a slow and steady determination.

There was a whizzing sound and then a huge explosion blew Ana, Naomi, and me backward. Naomi's shield saved us, but while it absorbed the bulk of the impact a whistle of shrapnel past my ear told me that it was shredded by the percussion of what I assumed was a mortar.

I pulled myself to my feet and ran over to Naomi, who was lying on her side. She was dazed but unhurt as I gently pulled her up. As I lifted her to a sitting position, she opened her eyes wide and pushed me away.

"I'm fine," Naomi grumbled as she looked back toward the Germans. Ana had been tossed off to the side, but she appeared annoyed and not harmed. There was a crater where she was standing.

"It did nothing," I said, impressed.

"No, Tommy. Can't you see? It may not have hurt her but it knocked her off her feet. Perhaps if someone were close enough they could take the Coat from her when she is off balance." Naomi stood up and grabbed my arm again. "We need to get to safety. My shields are a one shot deal against something as powerful as mortars, and I can't just keep casting them and have energy for anything else."

Ana had tossed away her weapon, which appeared to have been damaged by the explosion. She was much closer to the Germans but had turned around and was marching toward us, calling out something in Russian.

There was another whizzing sound, and Naomi threw her arm out while spreading her fingers. The whizzing snuffed out, and somewhere between us and the Germans there was an explosion.

"Wow," I said. She had somehow redirected a mortar.

"Let's go," she replied, running back toward the farmhouse.

I couldn't move. The staff refused to let me leave the Coat. "What are you doing?!" Naomi exclaimed. "Come on!" She ran back to me and grabbed my arm.

"I— Can't," I said.

"The Staff." Naomi spoke the words as a statement of fact, not a question. She seemed to know exactly what was happening. She grabbed my arm and pulled hard. I held my ground.

"I will be okay," I said. "I'll stay near Ana. The Coat will protect me."

Naomi turned me around to face her and put her hands on the upper part of my arms, holding me as she stared in my eyes. "No, Tommy. The staff will kill you, and then Ana will take it." She pulled me hard, and I stumbled toward her.

She continued to pull, and her willpower must have affected me, as I became more like myself and started to walk and then run with her. There was another explosion behind us. I felt the impact, but it was far enough away that Naomi and I remained unharmed.

I glanced over my shoulder and Princess Anastasia, the Angel of St. Petersburg, was armed with a machine gun in each hand, walking toward the Germans once again, laughing as impotent destruction rained down upon her.

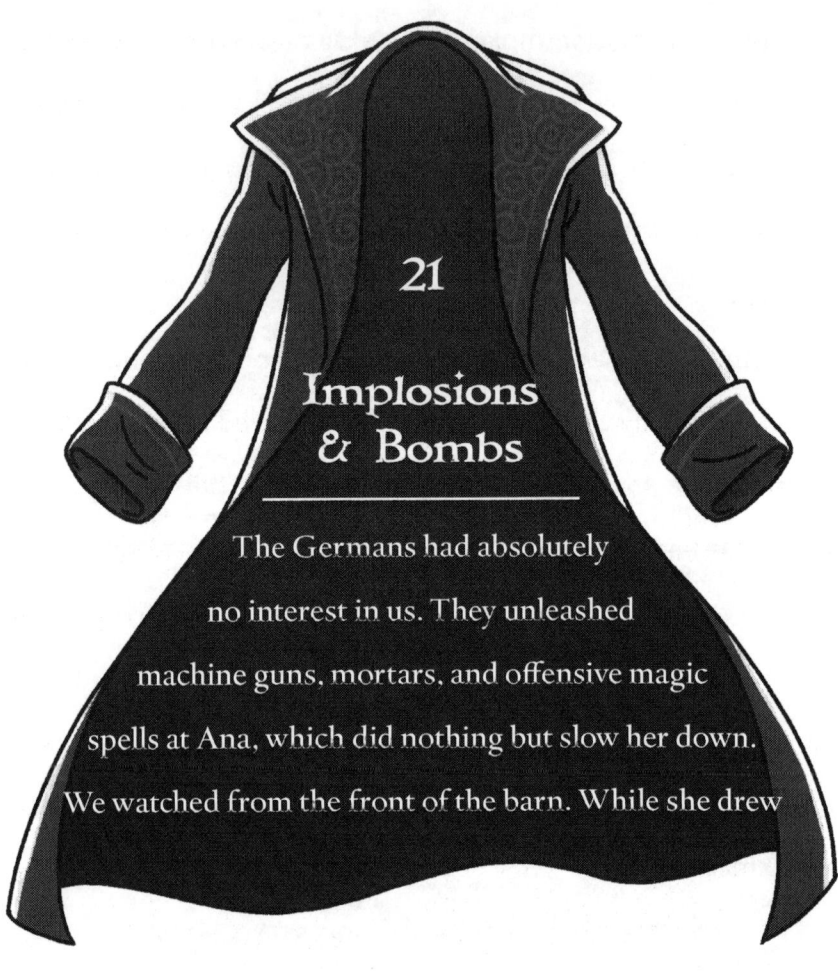

21

Implosions
& Bombs

The Germans had absolutely
no interest in us. They unleashed
machine guns, mortars, and offensive magic
spells at Ana, which did nothing but slow her down.
We watched from the front of the barn. While she drew

the brunt of the attack, the rest of her small force inched forward
and attacked the German troops at the trucks. The topography
gave the Germans very little cover, so they split their forces and
sent some to deal with the Russians fighting alongside Ana.

Naomi shook her head. "This is getting boring."

"What do you mean?"

"This!" she replied, holding out her palm with an iridescent mass of energy that indicated yet another spell I had never seen. She closed her eyes, made some motions, brought her hands together, and then opened her eyes again. She tossed her hands out toward the row of trucks.

A shimmery light skimmed across the grass until it hit one of the rear trucks. A light flashed, and then I saw one of the oddest things in my life. The truck expanded out as if it was a balloon and then imploded into a pile of dust. Everything within a thirty to fifty yard circle of the truck had been pulled into the implosion and ended up as part of the pile of dust.

Naomi turned to me and smiled. "I figure if I do that to Ana, she'll be knocked to the ground and perhaps even lose her breath. We could then swoop in and take the coat."

"That's a good plan!"

"Let me take care of the Germans, and then we can focus on her."

At that moment, an odd kind of screeching filled the air. At first I thought that we were about to see a sky full of Djinn, just as Naomi and I had experienced in that horrible day when her mom had died, but as I looked up I saw that it was an airplane. Right behind it was another one

"This can't be good," I said. As if in response, an entire row of German trucks were obliterated in a row of explosions. I looked up to see even more bombers screaming through the air. They were turning around and heading back.

"Do you think they're just here for the Germans?" I asked.

As if in reply, the bombers came through again, dropping bombs in the fields around the farmhouse. We sprinted toward the barn, but that gave precious little cover. As we ran, Naomi moved with a series of pauses and sprints. I was about to grab her arm and pull her toward me when a flash burned my eyes.

I felt like someone had punched me in the chest and then, after knocking me to the ground, knelt down on my ribs, pushing all the air out of my lungs. The light faded and I gasped for breath.

As I sat up, Naomi was already on her feet looking around. Her hair was wild, and, as she spun, I could see her face she. She looked more frightened than I had ever seen her.

"They're flattening the farm, Tommy!" I struggled to my feet. "That was a really powerful shield, and it barely protected us."

"I don't know. I feel pretty good," I replied, trying to lighten her mood.

She spun around and marched over to me. She grabbed my shirt in her fists and practically yelled in my face. "We're dead, Tommy. Dead! The bombers are coming around, and I won't be able to shield us next time. I spent a long time on that spell while we were talking. That wasn't even a direct hit and it obliterated my shield." She let go of my shirt, and in a whisper added, "I hate technology."

I looked to the horizon and saw three bombers approaching. I glanced around, and it suddenly hit me. They had already destroyed the farm house. The barn was half gone, and there were craters in the fields. Naomi was right—they were planning on flattening everything in their attempt to get to Ana.

"It's the Soviets," I said, and Naomi nodded.

"They want Ana. They may not even realize the Germans are here."

"Oh, they know. I'm guessing that we pushed our little spy into upsetting a house of cards that had been hiding her from the Germans and the Russians."

Naomi looked off at the approaching bombers. "I don't think they realize that she can withstand this." The planes were getting closer. "I wonder if I could shoot them out of the air," Naomi added. She bent her knees and brought forth a detonation. She sent it toward the planes.

As the spell flew, I squeezed my staff. I was so helpless! I had gone from the Archmage back to a streetlight. It was killing me. As I thought about the staff, I was once again drawn to moving closer to Ana and getting the coat.

I closed my eyes as I heard Naomi curse and say, "It is so hard judging distance with something so far in the sky." I tuned her out and let the staff speak to me. It's voice was clear even though no words were spoken: Unite me with the Coat.

The urgency to do it was impossible to resist, and as I started to walk in the direction the Staff told me to go, I felt Naomi's hand on my arm. A voice, barely a whisper, said, "I guess I'll die next to you after all."

The words were like an early morning dive into a cold lake. No. I cannot let this happen. As I turned my attention to stopping the bombs from killing us, I realized that my power with the staff had returned. Perhaps it was the proximity of the Coat. Perhaps it was my being so perilously close to being a slave to the staff itself, but whatever it was I knew that I had healed.

I opened my eyes, and looked at Naomi. As she glanced at me with utter defeat in her eyes, I lifted the staff, smiled, and stopped time.

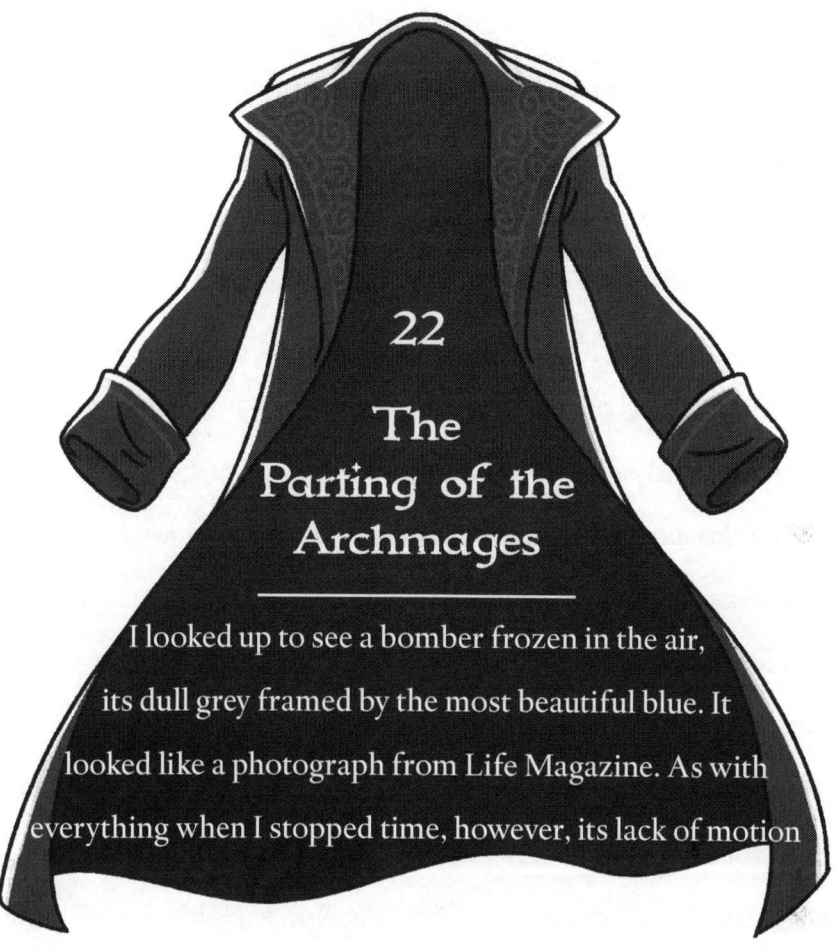

22

The Parting of the Archmages

I looked up to see a bomber frozen in the air, its dull grey framed by the most beautiful blue. It looked like a photograph from Life Magazine. As with everything when I stopped time, however, its lack of motion while I moved made it look unreal.

The still scene, however, wasn't as unsettling as the hunk of metal that was hovering high above our heads. It was a bomb that would have destroyed everything in the area, including Naomi and me. In the distance another bomb was in the midst of exploding in a field. Dirt sprayed out from a forming crater. It was held in place by the stoppage of time and looked like a crown.

"You did it!" Naomi ran over and hugged me. I wrapped my arms around her and hugged her back, the top of the cane rapping the back of her head.

"Sorry!" I said, letting her go and backing away. I didn't think I'd ever be able to get within a few feet of her without doing something stupid.

Smiling, Naomi said, "Hey, if that's the price I have to pay for a celebratory hug over our lives being saved, I'm okay with that." She glanced around. "This is spooky."

It suddenly hit me—Naomi had never experienced me stopping time. She was unconscious when I had first learned of it and used the staff to stop time to save her, and we parted soon after. She walked over and ran her hand through a cloud of smoke that was suspended in the air. The smoke didn't move, and she left a clearly defined hand-shaped tunnel through it.

"What next?" I asked.

Naomi couldn't stop smiling. "Does it matter?" She ran her hands through her hair and then tucked it behind her ears.

"What about Ana?" At the mention of the Angel's name, Naomi's eyes went wide.

"Tommy! You stopped time. We can just go over and grab the coat right off her back." She looked off to where we had last seen Ana.

As I looked around, all I could see was dirt, smoke, and the devastation of the initial bombing. "She was over there," I said, pointing toward the field that was between us and where the German trucks had parked.

Naomi nodded, and started jogging in that direction. I followed.

We hadn't gone more than twenty yards when Ana appeared from a crater. It looked like the Russians had scored a bullseye, dropping a bomb right on her head. She was, of course, unharmed. Her biggest struggle was climbing over the shattered ground.

"Uh, Naomi. She's walking toward us." Her pace was measured but sure. Naomi and I stood our ground, watching as she got closer. When I finally got a good look at her face, it was clear that she was angry. She was carrying a machine gun but didn't seem at all interested in using it.

She didn't say a word until she was standing directly in front of Naomi and me. She nodded toward me. "You have used the staff to stop time."

"Yes. It is one of its powers."

Ana squinted as she stared at me. Finally she spoke, her voice matter-of-fact and even. "You are not going to give me the staff, are you?" I shook my head, even though I felt a surge from the staff to my soul to do just that.

"And you're not going to give me the Coat."

Ana laughed. "It will be a sad day indeed when a Queen gives up her birthright to a foreign commoner, and a child at that." But even as she said the words her face twisted a bit, and I knew she was feeling the same surge that I felt.

"Tommy is not a child." Naomi's voice dripped with suppressed anger.

"So says another child." Before I could say anything to calm Naomi, Ana held up her hand. "Regardless—" She turned to me. "I assume at some point you will return time to its normal passing."

"Of course."

"Then we will need to flee first." Ana brushed the coat with her hand, even though it looked pristine. Not only could it not be damaged, it looked like it couldn't get dirty either. "I cannot be harmed while I wear the Coat, but that does not mean the Soviets can't make things difficult for me."

"We can't part," I said. Ana looked at me, her face emotionless. "You feel it." I was referring to the power that lived within the Coat and Staff, and Ana had experienced the same thing I did. I knew it. "One of us needs to give up our artifact."

Ana laughed. "I see you are not volunteering." Before I could reply, Ana waved a hand and continued, "It matters not. We will need to settle this another time. Debating while we are chased by both the Germans and Russians is not wise." She looked around and then back at me. "Besides, it may not even be our decision to make." I knew exactly what she meant. The force inside the artifacts was exerting some kind of control. "Things have changed. I am not safe here, and there are more urgent goals than rallying the country around the rightful monarchy." She tossed her machine gun to the ground. "Tommy Black, I still have my resources. Meet me in Paris, and we will find a resolution to our… problem."

"Paris?" I said, not sure what was happening.

"It is neutral ground. I have allies there. As do you. We can meet and decide who will wield the artifacts." She noticed my uncertainty. "Like civilized people," she added, as if teaching a peasant how to properly curtsy.

She didn't even wait for a reply. She started through the field to the north. I looked at Naomi, who just shrugged. "How do we get to Paris?" I finally asked.

Naomi ran her fingers through her hair. "I have an idea." She looked a little nervous and then added, "but you won't like it."

23

The Way Station

"How long can you keep time frozen?"
Naomi still appeared amazed as she
looked around.

"I don't know. I never bothered testing it."

"It's so quiet. Did you ever notice that?"

"Yes. I don't like it. It's not natural." As I said the words I realized that I wanted to return time to normal. The powerful influence of the staff made me nervous, and using its power made me worry that I would be less able to resist its power over me. "What's your plan?"

"Did you notice the train tracks on our way here?"

I spun around and faced her. "No way!"

"Tommy, it's the only way we'll get to safety."

"I am not going to use a slave to free myself." I thought of the Marids I freed in England. Every one left with a scream of triumph but echoing behind that triumph was the undeniable sound of sadness and pain.

"Think of how we left England for Persia." Naomi poked me in the chest with her finger. "Has your pride made you forget those moments when you needed help?" She looked like she was getting angry.

"No! I remember." I thought back. We had taken a train from England to Persia to look for my grandfather. I had freed the Marid when we arrived. But before we left I had argued with Naomi. She had considered magical creatures as nothing more than animals, not even slaves. I was disappointed with her, and it was probably one of the reasons that led to our leaving each other on such awkward terms.

"You used a train then, and that was after you knew that they were slaves. So don't play all high and mighty now." She put her hands on her hips. A wisp of her hair fell over her eyes, but she didn't flinch. It would have been cute if she wasn't so intimidating when angry.

"Look, I know you think magical creatures are just that—creatures. But I don't agree with you, and just so you know, I didn't tell the Marid to take us to Persia, I asked him to. That he agreed should tell you all you need to know about them. He didn't have to help us, but he did out of gratitude."

Naomi just stared at me.

"What?"

She shook her head. "Listen, Streetlight, you cannot possibly be this oblivious. Have you not been paying attention? I said I was proud of you for freeing the Marids. Or did you miss that? I agree with you. I want you to free them. I joined you in this stupid adventure so you could free them."

I felt like an idiot. She had said all those things. I had just missed them. She had changed so much, all for the better, and I was just the same old Tommy. Heck, I was worse. I was proud of what I was doing, and that probably clouded my thinking.

"I could ask the Marid to take us to Paris."

Naomi smiled. "What a great idea, genius. Oh, and I have another idea. Why don't you free it from its slavery, too? I bet it would really appreciate that."

I lowered my head, turned, and started walking down the scarred and pitted road. "Yeah, that's a good idea," I muttered.

Naomi ran up to me and put her hand on my arm. "Tommy, I'm sorry. I shouldn't lose my temper like that, especially with you." She looked around. "Especially as we're all alone. It's just you and me."

It suddenly hit me that we had lost Arkady. "Arkady! Have you seen him?"

"He stayed behind with the old hag, but I don't know what happened. I don't think he could have survived this bombing. I mean maybe, but he would have had to have gotten out of here pretty fast. Let's just move on."

"Maybe he's safe but hiding somewhere." Naomi shrugged. "Should we go back for him?"

Naomi was silent, and when I looked over at her she appeared pale. Of course. Arkady's loss had to be hard on her, especially with her blaming herself for Mister Ali's death. Before I could say anything, however, she replied, "He saw me, but he left with her. You happy? Can we now leave it at that?"

An awkward silence followed. I remembered thinking that Arkady had been her boyfriend, but over time I had dismissed its likelihood. However, based on Naomi's behavior, it again seemed possible. Although with her pride, it could be that she felt that he had betrayed us, and she blamed herself.

"Illusionists aren't right in the head."

Naomi turned to me, a small smile on her face. "Streetlight, sometimes you say just the right thing." She marched forward before I could reply.

I knew we weren't far from the railroad tracks, which had run parallel to the road for the bulk of our trip. The only question was whether the station the tracks led to would have a magical train or not. If not, we would be in a very tough spot.

Naomi added, "Yeah. I can't wait until you get the coat from her. Then she can go back to reminiscing about the good old days while sipping tea by the fire, with some servant named Sven waiting on her."

"I don't think Sven is a Russian name."

"Whatever." She increased the pace.

Neither Naomi or I spoke much during the walk to the rail line. It almost felt wrong to be living while time was stopped. We would pass animals that were frozen mid-stride. Rather than be sources of joy, they looked like they were posed in a museum display. It all appeared cold and lifeless.

We had walked for a few hours through the stillness of a world without time, and I couldn't take it anymore. "I'm restoring time. I think we need to listen for a train whistle."

I almost kicked myself for such a stupid explanation. We were heading to a rail line and then the station. There was no need to listen for a train whistle. However, Naomi quickly agreed. "Oh yeah. That's a good idea. You should unfreeze time."

I restored time, and the air felt fresher. Everything seemed just a bit more vibrant and beautiful. We stood still and listened. It was almost as quiet as when time had been stopped, but some-how the silence felt calming, not ominous. I looked at Naomi. Her eyes were closed as she took a deep breath.

She opened her eyes, and I quickly looked away, hoping she didn't notice me staring at her. "Let's just find the tracks and then head toward town," she said. I nodded, and we started walking again. I looked up and watched as the clouds slowly rolled across the sky. The beauty took my breath away.

We walked through a few farms where we grabbed some vegetables to eat. Again, I had to practically force Naomi to take even a single carrot.

"You do know that you won't be much of a magician if you die of starvation." I handed her another carrot, which she accepted.

"It's not that I don't want to eat. It's just that I'm never hungry." She shrugged and took a bite.

It was dark by the time we reached the station, which was in the middle of town. We had to take great care as there were people everywhere, even with it being night.

"What's with all the people? This town isn't even that big." Naomi said, looking around.

"There are a lot of soldiers. Maybe there's a base nearby."

"There are a lot of civilians, too. More than you would expect for a town this size. It is very strange."

"Well, it is war time." Naomi nodded as we hid in the shadow of a building that was about fifty yards from the train station.

The station itself was of a bit bigger than the surrounding buildings. It was brick and not quite two stories high. It was certainly big enough that it looked like it handled a lot of traffic.

"Good news, Tommy," Naomi whispered. "That is definitely a Way Station." A Way Station was the kind of train station that handled magical trains. Naomi would know as she had lived in one for almost her entire life.

"Yeah, but I'm not sure we can get to an engineer. We're not exactly dressed like the locals." I looked at Naomi, whose khakis and dirty white cotton blouse made her look like an archaeologist portrayed in Hollywood movies. "Plus, even if we find the engineer, how can I convince him to take us where we want to go? Neither of us speak Russian."

"Great. So we have to sneak into the station without drawing anyone's attention, where we then find an engineer, and then we convince him to take the train to Paris, while you free the Marid and beg him to power the train. All the while doing so without knowing how to speak Russian."

"More or less."

"This may require you to stop time again."

"I was thinking the same thing." I took a deep breath and stopped time.

"Any second now," Naomi said.

"What do you mean?"

"Stopping time. We're close enough to the station. You should probably stop time now."

"I did!"

Naomi looked around. "No, you didn't."

It was true. I could hear the sounds of the town, and there was activity in the distance. "Oh no," I said.

"It didn't work?" I nodded. "Do you think it has to do with the Coat?"

"I don't know what else it can be. The staff lost its power before, but it regained it when we were close to Ana. Maybe now that the Coat is moving further away from me I've lost the power again."

Naomi grabbed my arm. "Do you think the staff is punishing you for not going after the Coat? Maybe if you aren't staying near the coat it will take away its own powers!"

I had been thinking something similar, but Naomi's explanation was clearer. "Yeah. The Staff and Coat belong together. Distance or even decisions that take them further apart appear to affect their power."

"So what do we do? We need to get into the station without being seen, and we need to sneak up on the engineer."

"Could you cast an illusion to make us look like Russian peasants?"

"Yes, but it's complicated. I'll need to maintain it while we walk, and it won't be perfect. You're going to have to deal with all the people and tracking down the engineer yourself."

"I can do that."

"Okay, let me get things ready." Naomi stood still, and I watched as she made what appeared to be random movements. Her hands, though, spun and wove and elegantly twisted in a dizzying array of forms. I caught a circle, a triangle, and more intricate patterns. After about five minutes I assumed she would be close to done. The amount of detailed movement and concentration was extraordinary.

Twenty minutes later, sweat started to drip down her face, but she continued her movements. At one point I thought she was going to faint as her body swayed, but it was apparently part of the spell she was casting. After forty-five minutes she slowly lowered her hands to her side and swayed slightly.

I ran up to support her, but she shook her head. "I'm okay." She took a deep breath and whispered through clenched teeth. "I'm a young peasant girl, and you're one my one of my girl friends." A hint of smile snuck onto her lips.

"A girl?"

"Don't worry, you look cute." I looked down and couldn't see anything different about me. "Now stop bothering me and guide me toward the station. We have a lot of work to do, and I won't be able to help. I'm channeling the energy right now. Just moving is going to take intense concentration." She closed her eyes for a a few minutes and then whispered, "Let's go."

I took her elbow and led us to the station.

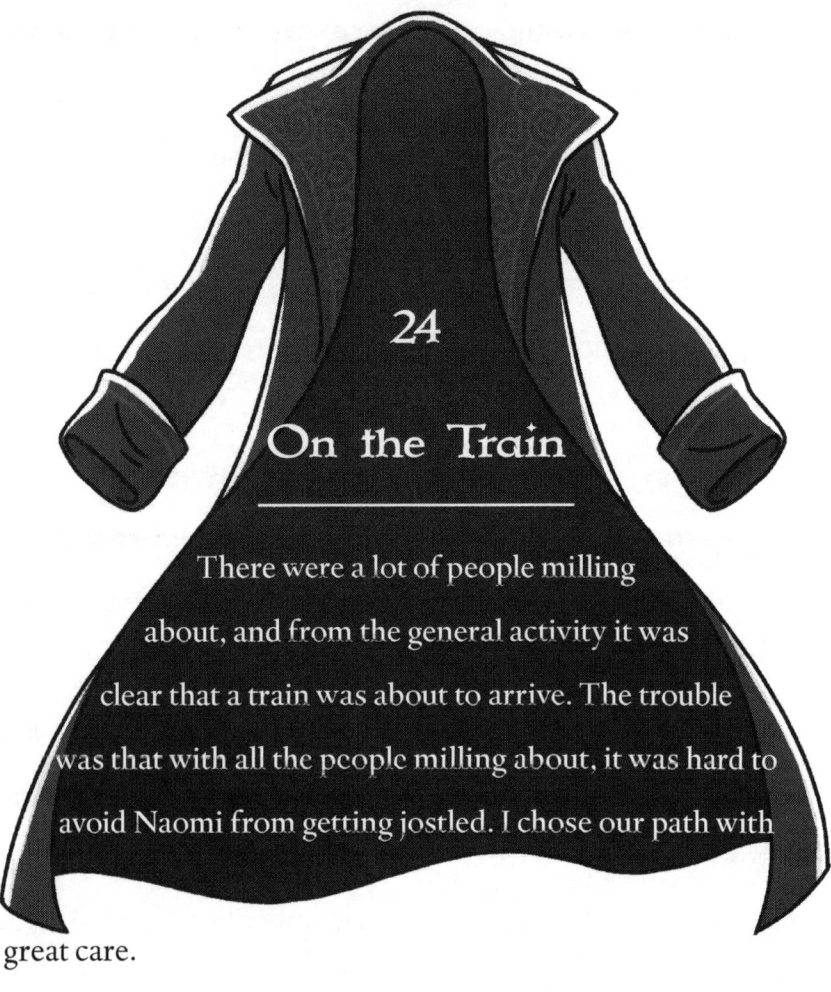

24

On the Train

There were a lot of people milling about, and from the general activity it was clear that a train was about to arrive. The trouble was that with all the people milling about, it was hard to avoid Naomi from getting jostled. I chose our path with great care.

The inside of the station was similar to the station near the Citadel in England. It was one big room, with a ticket window, benches, and a room behind a counter for package pick up. Facing the tracks was a large set of double doors.

I slowly walked Naomi over to an empty bench and sat down facing the doors. "Let's wait here for the train to arrive." Naomi almost imperceptibly nodded her head.

It wasn't long before I heard the distant screech of a whistle, and I shuddered. I had heard it dozens of times. What others heard as a mundane everyday noise, I heard as the helpless screams of a magical being bound in slavery.

I glanced over at Naomi. Her face was glistening with sweat, her hair wet and stuck against her cheeks. She looked like she had just run a marathon. "Not long now," I whispered. Naomi didn't move.

The train arrived, and I waited for the mass of people to exit through the door. The last thing I wanted was for someone to jostle Naomi while she was holding the illusion. Finally, I touched her elbow, and she stood up. Her eyes were closed, and she was shaking a bit.

I guided her lightly as we walked to the door. A soldier with a rifle guarded the door but looked bored and inattentive. Just as we were walking through the open doors, an older man rushed past us, shoving Naomi into me as he pushed through the door. Naomi's eyes opened and went wide.

She looked at me and shook her head. "It's gone," she said, her voice strained.

I looked up and the soldier stared at us. He shook his head, looked at me, looked at Naomi, and then back again. Shouting something loudly in Russian, he started to raise his rifle. With no other option I took two steps and brought the cane down on his arm. There was a scream of pain, and I grabbed Naomi and pulled her into the station, half running and half dragging her along the wall. I was hoping to escape out the front door, but soldiers appeared there.

I was so mad at myself. Why didn't I flee out to the train?

"Tommy, I'm too weak to cast a shield. You have to do something. Make us invisible. Stop time. Something." Naomi sounded scared and desperate. She was shaking, and if I had ever wondered what it was like to see her powerless, this was it. I hated it. Didn't she know that things had changed. I needed her.

I willed the staff to bend light around us, hiding us from sight, but, like before, I knew that something was broken, and I couldn't do it.

The soldiers approached us slowly. Luckily, they didn't seem afraid of us and appeared to want to take us into custody, not kill us. I considered summoning the fake Shadow, but, with magic dying, they probably wouldn't even know what a Shadow was. I was running out of ideas as they closed in.

I knew I could blind them with light, but with all the people around I would undoubtedly blind some innocent people. Also, the place was crawling with soldiers. More would come, and I'd have to blind them, too. In the end, they would send more, and I would be captured before I could blind everyone.

Filling the room with darkness wouldn't work, as I had yet to figure out how to make it so that only I could see. So if I went the darkness route, I'd have to surround Naomi and me with light, and in such close quarters we'd undoubtedly run into soldiers.

Clearly being a streetlight wasn't the solution. What had I learned on the ship? I could manipulate colors and create pretty pictures. That seemed less than helpful. We needed to blend into the background or something.

And then it hit me.

It was complex. It involved pieces of light, not just brightness and darkness but color and motion. It would need to constantly adapt as we moved. It sounded impossible.

But I knew I could do it. The staff told me so.

I put my arm around Naomi and said, "Just walk with me. Don't worry."

Then I let the staff take control. It would do the impossible and reflect only the light that matched the colors behind us. We wouldn't turn invisible by bending light around us; we would turn invisible by making the light look like the background colors behind us.

I turned us into chameleons.

And it worked. The moment I thought it, the staff made it so, and the reaction in the Russian soldiers was instantaneous. Jaws dropped, and faces looked up, down, right, and left. I expected that they would rush forward to look for us, so I maneuvered Naomi across the side wall to the far corner and then inched toward the back door. My plan was that when the opening was clear enough, I would take us through the back door to the engine.

Thankfully, there were only five soldiers that went to look around the room. They passed us and looked under benches and up into the rafters. I stopped at the back door, which was blocked by two soldiers who were looking around the building for some sign of us.

I was going to wait for them to leave, but the train whistle blew. Could that mean that the train was departing? It couldn't be leaving so fast. It had just arrived. Naomi would know as the daughter of a Way Master. I looked at her, and she seemed alert. I leaned down and whispered in her ear, "Is the train leaving?"

She looked up at me and nodded, her mouth set in a grim line. "Let's go," I whispered. I took her hand in mine, and with a few steps I barreled between the two soldiers. They didn't expect the impact and went flying. I looked to the right, and there was the engine in the distance. Naomi kept pace as I sprinted toward it, still holding her hand.

There were shouts, and I glanced over my shoulder. Thankfully, no one could see us or hear our footsteps in the din of the station. A few soldiers were looking under the train.

We reached the engine, which looked ancient. I was shocked that it was a train that ran on magical power, as it looked like the coal trains that ran in the Old West. The good news was that the engine was large, so Naomi and I weren't noticed as we climbed up.

There was a single engineer who was leaning back and drinking a cup of coffee that was so hot I could see the steam rising from it. Naomi and I moved to the rear of the compartment and into a corner that looked like it hadn't been cleaned or even seen a footstep in years.

We waited.

A few minutes later a soldier climbed up and said some words in Russian. The engineer shook his head and replied, waving his arm around the compartment. The soldier looked around, shook his head, and then departed. The engineer pulled out a pocket watch and checked it. After placing it back in his pocket, he pulled a rope, and a loud, mournful whistle split the air.

I whispered into Naomi's ear, "We don't speak Russian, and I doubt the engineer speaks English. Do you think you could guide this to Paris?"

Naomi shook her head as the Engineer spun around and squinted directly at us. Finally he shook his head, turned some knobs, pulled a lever, and the train surged forward.

As I felt the train move I had an idea. It was risky, foolish even. And it was based on nothing more than a guess on my part. But I felt like it was our only hope.

With the train slowly accelerating to its normal speed, the engineer returned to his coffee. I walked over and slid open the door that led outside. The engineer's eyes went wide, and he stood up.

He took a few hesitant steps forward, looking around and peering at the door which had magically opened. I maneuvered myself behind him, and with two steps of momentum I drove my shoulder into the middle of his back. The engineer stumbled forward. His arms reached for the door frame, but with an additional shove he flew out the door to the Russian countryside.

I hoped he didn't get hurt as he landed, but that was the least of my concerns. I closed the door to find Naomi standing right in front of me. "What the heck was that? You do realize that he's the only one that can drive this thing."

I removed our camouflage and tried to think of a way to explain my plan. I finally gave up and prepared for the abuse.

"I'm the engineer now. I removed the previous one. So I'm going to ask the Marid to guide us to Paris. It's driven these lines for years. It's powering the train. Certainly it could get us there, don't you think?"

Naomi just stared at me and said nothing. It was worse than her screaming.

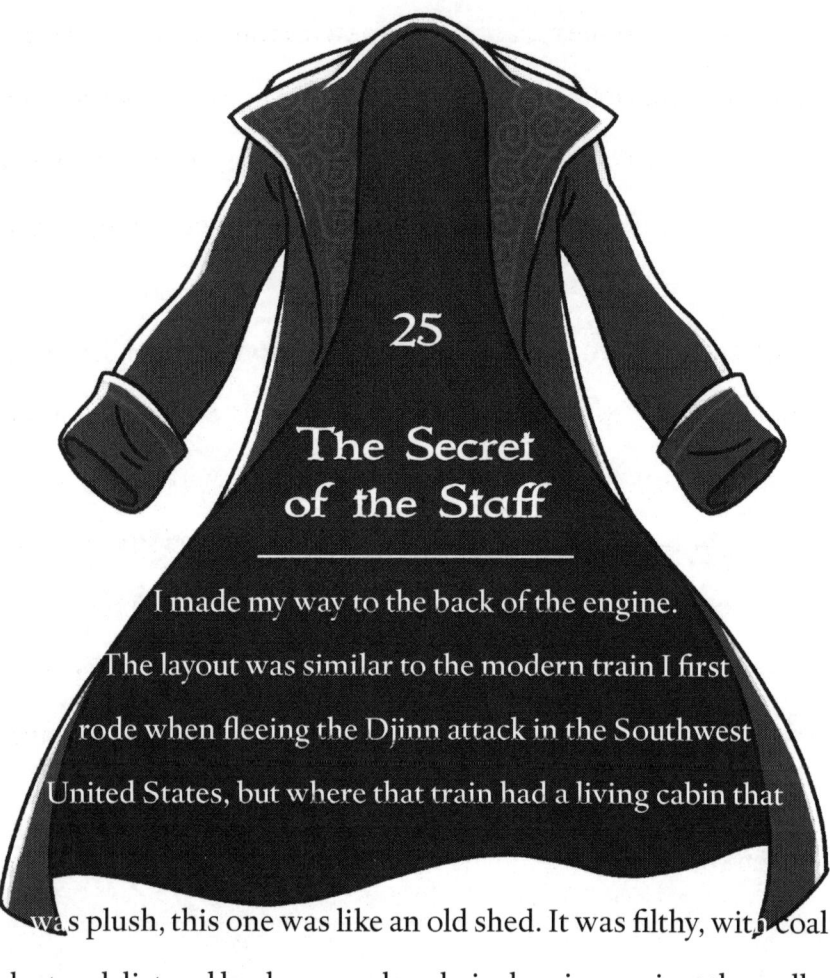

25

The Secret
of the Staff

I made my way to the back of the engine.
The layout was similar to the modern train I first
rode when fleeing the Djinn attack in the Southwest
United States, but where that train had a living cabin that
was plush, this one was like an old shed. It was filthy, with coal
dust and dirt and broken wooden chairs leaning against the walls.

The door to the very back of the engine was iron, and the
handle was so hot I couldn't touch it. I looked around, and on
the floor was a dirty rag. I wrapped it around the handle and
wrenched the door open.

A blast of extreme heat knocked me backward. I looked around for some kind of a protective clothing, but there was nothing. Talking to the Marid would be downright dangerous. The Russians apparently didn't believe in protecting their main engine room from the heat.

I inched forward and peered into the room. It was like those scenes I remembered from the movies, where the heat from the desert would make the image on the screen all wavy. Still, I had been in enough engine rooms to know that all I'd need to do was to take a step or two inside and the Marid would hear me.

I took a deep breath, closed my eyes, held the crook of my elbow over my mouth, and walked in. The air burned my lungs, while the heat scorched my skin. Unfortunately, I had run out of options. I talked fast.

"Mighty Marid. I don't know your name, but I am Tommy Black. I have freed many Marids from slavery because it was the right thing to do, and I will free you shortly. But I want you to hear a request first."

There was no sound but the clanging and grinding of the train's gears moving.

"I am the engineer now, but I don't know how to guide this train. I need to get to Paris. My goal is to free more of your kind, and getting to Paris will help me do that, so I ask you this heartfelt favor—please take me to a station in Paris. That is all."

I was going to take a deep breath, but the hot air was making it hard to breathe. I badly wanted to finish and leave the room, but the burning in my lungs made me cough. My coughing fit over, I hurried and finished. "As the engineer of this train, I am your master, and I free you now. I have no right to be your master. You are free to go. There are no limitations or conditions to my words. You are free."

The train shuddered, and I took a step backward. "You may go, but I ask you again. Please. Take us to Paris."

I rushed out, slamming the iron door door closed behind me. Taking deep breaths of cool air, I walked through the compartments that lead to the front of the engine, marveling over how the magic of the Marid made the train so much different on the inside than regular trains, even as they looked the same on the outside.

Naomi looked at me, and while I saw a glimpse of anger it immediately disappeared. "Oh my God, Tommy, are you okay?" She ran over and grabbed my arms. "You've been burned!"

"I'm okay. Really." I walked over and sat in the engineer's chair.

"Your face is as red as a lobster." She looked around the compartment, but it was as sparse as the countryside. "Is there water?"

I took a deep breath and felt weak from the pain. Sweat was pouring down my face, and as it ran over my cheeks it burned. My hands hurt. I was badly burned, it was clear. "I'll be okay." I said, filling my lungs with fresh air even as each breath caused pain in my chest.

"What happened?" Naomi asked, standing in front of me.

"Well, I am now positive of three things." She tilted her head, telegraphing her curiosity in a way that made me almost laugh it was so cute. "The Marid that runs this train is very old and powerful. He is now free. And he is taking us to Paris."

"Can you be sure?"

"I'm sure. Look outside." Naomi looked through the windows. "This train is traveling way faster than when the engineer was in charge. Plus, the Marid is free right now. He could leave whenever he wants. The conclusion is obvious. He is taking us to Paris, and he wants to get there as fast as possible, so that he can then be truly free."

I kept lightly touching my cheeks, and while they hurt a bit less I wasn't so concerned about the pain. I just hoped that I didn't end up covered in blisters. The last thing I wanted was anyone, especially Naomi, seeing me in such an ugly light. Luckily, it appeared that my burns were not severe. I had a couple blisters on my hands, and a few on the side of my face, but mostly I was unscathed. Each breath was also becoming less painful.

"The engineer's coffee is probably cold by now. Maybe that would help," Naomi said.

I looked at the mug, and the deep brown sludge was not quite what I needed. "No thanks. I think I'd rather go back and talk to the Marid again than drink that stuff."

Naomi leaned over and looked in the mug. "I think that might actually be grease."

We were making small talk while nervously waiting to get to our destination. We both wanted to get settled in Paris and prepare ourselves for seeing Ana. We needed to somehow come up with a plan for retrieving the Coat.

I tapped the cane on the iron flooring, as I thought about exactly how we could do that. Ana could not be hurt. Could she be restrained with ropes or a trap? Or would that be considered being hurt? Magic was too arbitrary for me to know for sure. If we couldn't restrain her or hurt her, how could we possibly get the Coat from her?

Naomi reached over and grabbed my wrist, stopping me from tapping the cane. "Sorry," I replied. "I'm just a bit nervous."

"Speaking of nervous, I wanted to share something with you, but I don't think you're ready for it." I stared at Naomi's face, and the first thought that went though my head was that she was going to tell me that she liked me. I tried to dismiss the thought as being absurd, but part of me wanted to believe it even though I couldn't see us ever being together. Naomi was cute and amazing, but she was also annoying and insulting and all those things that made me want to just toss up my hands and leave any room she was in.

"What's that?" I swallowed hard, which I hoped she blamed on my burnt throat.

"This may take a while, so I'm going to sit down." I got the sense she was buying time. Why was she so nervous? She walked over to the rear of the compartment and slid to the floor, leaning her back against the wall. "So you know what I've been doing for the past two years?"

"Sure. You've been studying magic. I can't believe how hard you must have worked. You're amazing."

Naomi lowered her head, but I caught a smile on her face as she did so. "Yes, but I also studied a lot of history of magic." She wove her hand in the air, and a tiny ball of pure white light appeared in her palm. "The context is important. Merlin's diaries were practically useless, as they were little more than a record of his activities and achievements."

"That must have been disappointing."

"Well, Merlin would discuss other magicians, and if you paid close attention, you could see from his criticisms of their work how he fixed their flawed spells. Do you understand?"

"I think so. You'd find a spell that didn't work from the time of Merlin, and then Merlin's comments on it would give you a hint as to how to fix it."

"Exactly!" Naomi looked up, a huge smile on her face. I got the feeling she had been waiting months to explain to someone her process. I found it interesting and exciting. "So I didn't just study spells, I looked for hints and notes from history, as well."

"That makes sense, but why would I not be ready to know that?"

"Well—" Naomi paused and then continued, "I spent a lot of time studying Jamshid, and—" She paused for a very long time. Finally, she looked up and blurted out, "I know the source of the power of your staff."

"What? Really?" I stood up and walked toward her. "What is it? It's a powerful Marid isn't it? I've been using a slave thinking I was doing something good!"

Naomi's eyes were wide open. "No! I mean, yes, but don't think of it that way." She shook her head. "This is what I was afraid of. You have done amazing things, Tommy. You saved your grandfather. You saved countless enslaved creatures." Her voice dropped to a whisper. "You saved me."

I slid down the wall and sat next to Naomi. She snuffed out her light, pulled her knees up to her chest, and hugged them with her arms. "So what is the history?"

"It's an enslaved creature, Tommy. I didn't want to tell you, because I didn't want to ruin your dream of changing the world and saving magical creatures, and—" Naomi was quiet, so I looked over at her. She was crying.

"What's wrong, Naomi?" I touched her arm, but she pulled it away.

"It was me, Tommy. Me! I love magic so much. I'm not an idiot. I know that I'm probably the only one who can even cast a decent spell that's under the age of forty. It's dying. Magic is dying." She looked up at me, and her cheeks sparkled with her tears, while her eyes shone. "I needed you to save the magical creatures and show the world the power of magic. I don't want it to die, and I'm afraid I can't save it all by myself."

She reached over and took my hand in hers. "I'm sorry, Tommy. I kept this secret from you because I needed you to help me keep magic alive." She squeezed my hand. "Airplanes. Machine guns. Motion pictures. Submarines. I hate technology. It's killing the one thing I love."

I wasn't angry. I was confused. "Naomi, why didn't you trust me? I don't want to see magic die either. I think you're amazing."

She pulled her hand away and cast another ball of light, slightly larger than her previous spell. "I did trust you, Tommy. I trusted you to be a good person. And that's the problem, my problem—you're predictable because you're a good person. I knew what you'd do. You'd look at the staff as something evil. A prison not an artifact. And then you'd want to destroy the prison."

Naomi closed her fist and leaned her head against my shoulder. It was so unexpected that I didn't know what to do. "You are a good person, Tommy. It's one of the things that I love about you. And rather than let you be good, I kept the truth from you."

"I- I don't know what to say," I answered.

"You hate me."

"No! I'm not even sure I'm mad at you. I'm so confused. Yes, I'd want to free the imprisoned magical creature, but maybe I could convince it to help me like the Marid on this train is helping me."

Naomi yanked her head back and looked at me. "I hadn't thought of that." She started casting the light spell again. "I'm an idiot."

"No, you're not. I don't even know if that would be wise. Maybe it would be dangerous."

"Hmm." Naomi stood up and started pacing, casting the small light spell over and over again. "That's a good point. Let me tell you the full story."

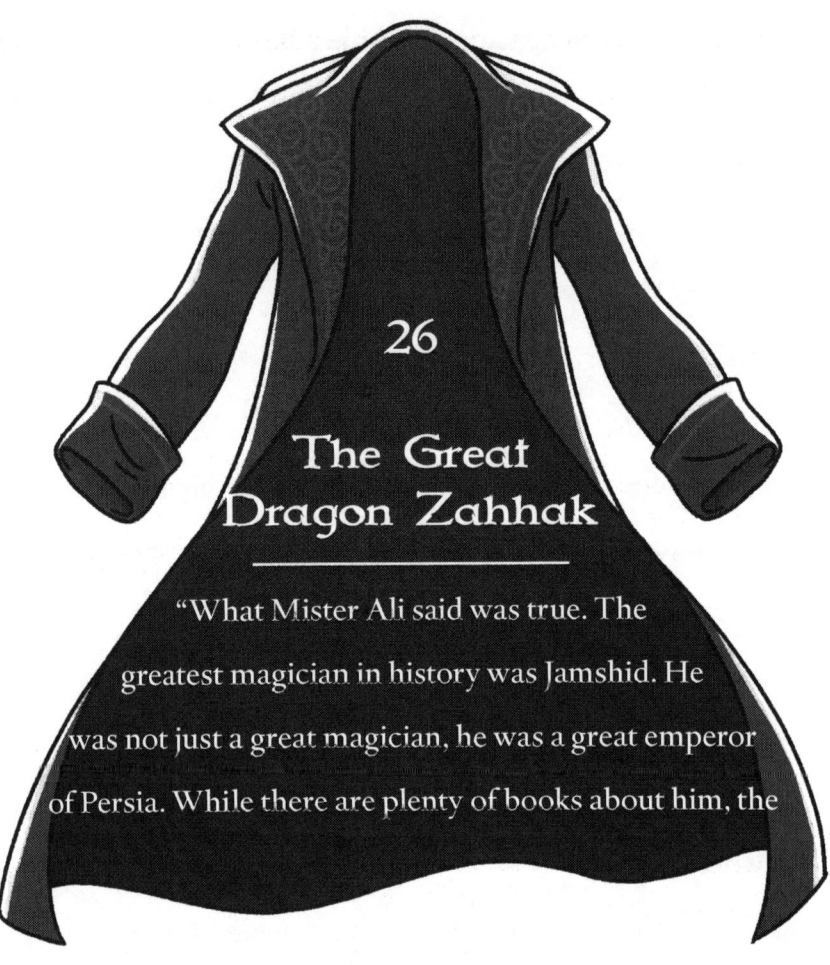

26

The Great
Dragon Zahhak

"What Mister Ali said was true. The greatest magician in history was Jamshid. He was not just a great magician, he was a great emperor of Persia. While there are plenty of books about him, the contemporary magical accounts are rare. So with the exception of very few specific spells, the only things we know are the broadest accounts of his achievements."

"It almost sounds like he didn't want anyone to know his secrets."

Naomi stopped her pacing and looked at me, a big smile on her face. "Yes! He was arrogant and secretive, and while he was the greatest of magicians, he wanted even more power."

"So he bound an ancient Marid into the artifacts?"

"No. He bound the great dragon Zahhak."

I almost dropped the staff. "There is a dragon in here?" I stared at it in my hand.

Naomi nodded. "Not just any dragon. Zahhak, an exceptionally powerful dragon, whose power with magic makes Marids look like schoolchildren."

"He was that powerful?"

"Yes. He terrorized the world with his might. So Jamshid hunted down this majestic dragon and bound him with magic. Even then Zahhak was too powerful, so Jamshid split him into three pieces so that he did not have the power to escape."

"The artifacts!"

"Yes. Each artifact contains part of Zahhak's enslaved essence. Those artifacts were the pieces that made Jamshid's power absolute. No one could defeat him with the combined power of his own magic and the enslaved magic of Zahhak."

I nodded my head. It was all new to me, but it made so much sense. "No wonder Mister Ali said the staff had a mind of its own. It literally has a mind of its own, the mind of Zahhak." Naomi sat down beside me again. "So the Coat and the Cup are the other two artifacts?"

"Yes. Of course they are considered by nearly everyone as nothing more than fanciful tales. Zahhak is a myth. Jamshid is known more as an emperor than a magician, and the artifacts are mere legends."

I could barely control my excitement. I finally knew the source of my family's legacy, even if it was one based on a vile act of enslavement. "Do you know anything about them?"

"Not much more than what Ana said. We know what the Staff and Coat do. The Cup presumably allows the holder to see anything in the universe. You just think of what you want to see, and the Cup shows it to you. There are some who believe it allows the bearer to read minds or even see into the future."

"I'm going to see if I can communicate with Zahhak." I clenched the staff in my hand.

"Will that be dangerous?"

Naomi's comment gave me pause. I hadn't told her that when I was close to the Coat that the staff was exerting a strong influence on my behavior. It was dangerously close to controlling me. Did I want to let Zahhak know that I was aware of his presence in the staff?

"No," I finally replied. I actually didn't know the answer, but I couldn't live not knowing if I could talk to Zahhak and perhaps work with him in new ways to help other enslaved creatures or even free himself.

I closed my eyes and focused on the staff. As always it wasn't really a staff or a cane; it was part of myself. I was Tommy, and the staff was me. Zahhak, I know you are there. I will be the one to free you. I felt the faintest stirring deep within the Staff, but nothing else.

Zahhak, I free you from your slavery. The moment I said the words I knew they were a mistake. I couldn't just free a mighty dragon on a moving train. Plus, I didn't even know if the poor dragon would be grateful. Maybe it would blame us and kill Naomi and me. Luckily, nothing happened.

I opened my eyes. "Nothing," I stated. "But I have a pretty good idea what we need to do." I thought over the flow of energy I felt when close to the Coat. It was obvious what was happening now. As the artifacts were brought together, their power increased but so did the consciousness and will of Zahhak.

"What is that?" Naomi asked.

"I can't free Zahhak until I am wielding all three artifacts. It's like the train. I can't free the Marid unless I'm the engineer."

"So what do we do?" She asked, but I was sure she already knew and was excited about the prospect.

"We get the Coat. And then we travel to Germany and get the Cup."

PART III

PARIS

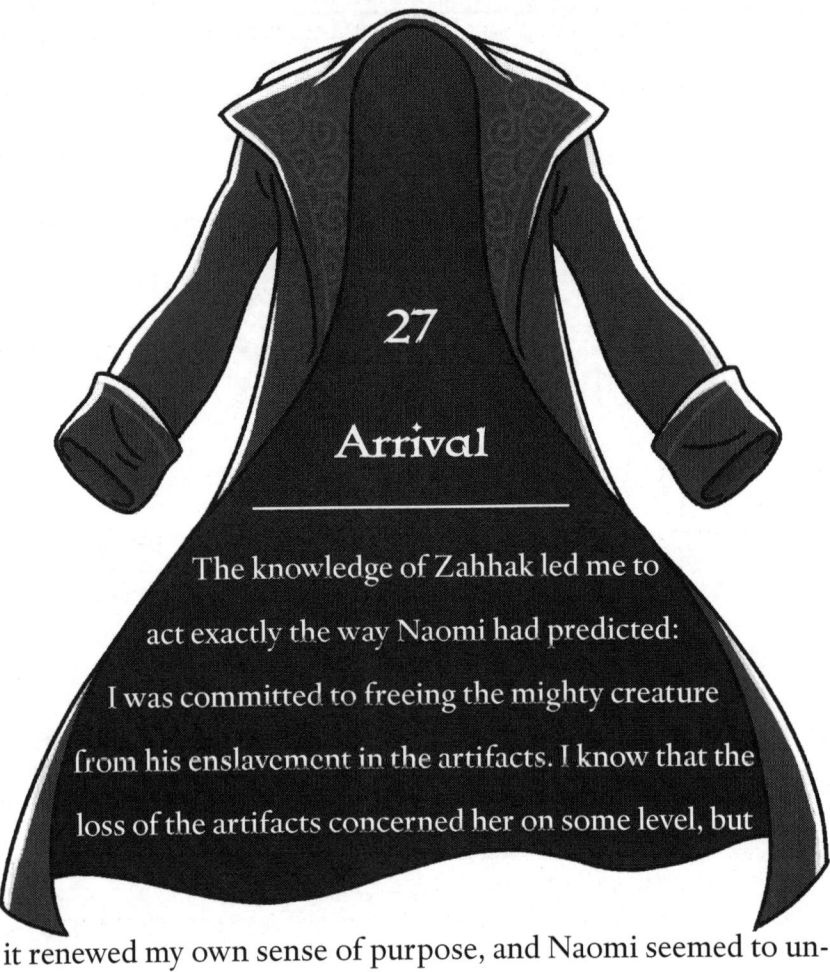

27

Arrival

The knowledge of Zahhak led me to act exactly the way Naomi had predicted: I was committed to freeing the mighty creature from his enslavement in the artifacts. I know that the loss of the artifacts concerned her on some level, but it renewed my own sense of purpose, and Naomi seemed to understand and support that.

She had changed over the past two years. She was more powerful, of course, but she also seemed to have a better understanding of the role magical creatures played in the world. I think she agreed with me that it was wrong that a mighty magician was so thirsty for power that he would enslave an ancient dragon.

The speeding train also made me angry. Even though I knew the Marid was no longer a slave, its route made it clear that all it wanted was to be in Paris as quickly as possible and be free. At times I could see the train hovering over treetops as it sped west. I had no doubt that we'd be in Paris in little more than a few hours.

Knowing what I did of the history of magic and slavery, I found that the only magic I could appreciate any more was that performed by skilled magicians like Naomi and even Cain. It was personal and pure. You could see it in Naomi's eyes as she focused on the light in her hand or cast a spell—it was an art.

It was beautiful in its own way and entirely different from the train. The train's joining of technology and magic wasn't a artistic collaborative thing but rather magic being channeled by a creature forced into service. I couldn't wait for the trip to end in Paris and to watch the Marid explode from the rear of the engine in a violent leap to freedom.

There was a screech and I was nearly thrown to the floor as the train ground to a quick halt. Naomi was thrown forward into the metal controls. As she rubbed her side, she looked outside. "Well, we're somewhere."

"It's Paris." I knew the Marid did as I requested.

"This doesn't look like Paris." I looked outside, and it was a small wooded area with a tiny station. In the distance was a village.

"It's probably just outside Paris."

Before Naomi could say anything, a low growl gained in volume until an ear-piercing scream filled the air. I had heard that sound many times before. "We need to get off this engine now!"

I slid the door open and climbed down the short ladder. As I hit the bottom rung the engine lurched again. I jumped and rolled up to my feet. Naomi was barely clinging to the ladder as the horrific high pitched sound of metal being ripped and torn filled the air. "Naomi, just jump! The Marid is freeing itself. You have to get off the train!"

Naomi leapt and landed awkwardly. I ran over and pulled her out of the way just when a slab of iron landed where she had been lying on the ground. She was limping as we ran along the train tracks, away from the engine. A resounding crash shook the ground.

"It just tossed the engine up in the air like it was a toy!" Naomi said. I didn't look back. I had seen the same thing dozens of times. The magical creatures always completely destroyed the engines that had imprisoned them. The only thing I could do was make sure no one was nearby.

"Keep going, Naomi. It's dangerous!"

Another cry pierced the air. This one was of pure triumph, however. I had also heard this cry many times before. I stopped and looked back. A swirling mass of flame and light coalesced into a creature of pure energy. As the Marid returned to its form, it launched itself into the air, leaving behind molten iron and twisted chunks of metal.

Naomi looked awestruck as she watched the Marid shoot into the sky and then head south. They always headed south, and I had no idea why. "What a magnificent being!"

I nodded. It was. The scene had never failed to move me—a creature that had been enslaved for years was finally free. A large group of people exited the passenger cars and looked at the wreckage, hands covering their mouths. A few of them looked around confused.

"I imagine the Russians are wondering why they aren't in Leningrad!"

I had to smile. While the Marid had taken us to Paris, he had also stranded a large group of Russians far from their home. A few looked in our direction, so I put my arm around Naomi's waist. She squinted at me. "We need to get moving, and your leg is hurt!"

"Actually, it's my ankle." Naomi put her arm on my shoulder and limped along beside me. "And my hip, too. Actually, I'm pretty much bruised all over."

"Well, I'm pretty much burned all over, so I hope we're in France, as we really need to recover before Ana makes it here."

Naomi pointed to a sign. It said Chelle. "That certainly looks like French."

"Well, thank you unnamed Marid. I'm going to assume that this is close enough." I looked up a road but couldn't see many buildings. We appeared to be in some distant suburb of Paris.

"We need to get to Paris, contact the English military, get some new supplies and support, and then set up a base from where we can plan our attack on Ana." Naomi rattled off a plan even as I was considering our options.

"There's only one problem. We don't speak French. We don't have a way to Paris. We don't know where the English military bases are, and we don't even know if the English military will help us."

Naomi smiled. "That's more than one problem."

"Thank you, Miss Optimism." I looked for signs of life on the street but couldn't find any. "So let's tackle the second problem since I doubt either of us will learn French any time soon." We couldn't even hire a taxi, as the remaining money we had was all Russian.

"Any ideas?" Naomi asked, as we rather slowly made our way out to a road that ran alongside the rail line.

"Well, we could walk," I said, not very enthusiastically.

"You mean limp."

"Ugh. I hope we're not too far from Paris."

Naomi laughed, and I turned to look at her. "Well, we're farther than I had hoped." She was pointing to a sign that said "Paris 18 km."

"That doesn't sound good. How far is that in miles?" I was horrible with the metric numbers.

"About eleven miles."

"Why would the Marid leave us so far from Paris?" I asked rhetorically.

We turned down the road with the sign, and we had our answer.

"Is that a British flag?" Naomi asked.

"That is not only a British flag, that is an English army base."

"Well, that's convenient. I'm guessing you told the Marid that we were heading to a military base?" I thought back to what I said to the Marid, and I couldn't think that I gave any guidance other than we needed to go to Paris.

"Maybe." I shrugged.

"Well, let's get some help and then come up with a plan."

I nodded. Could the Marid have helped us this much, taking us to the doorstop of where we needed to be? And how did it know? Did it read my mind? It seemed amazing if it did. That was just one of the many questions swirling in my head. The biggest one was how was I to get the Coat off the back of someone I couldn't harm.

28

A Telegram From Cain

Telegram

From: Black, Thomas, Paris T53X7 base

To: Cain, Fort Belvedere

Followed artifact to Paris STOP Need supplies
and money STOP

Telegram

From: Cain, Fort Belvedere

To: Black, Thomas, Paris T53X7 base

```
I know STOP You were supposed to destroy the
German trains not the trains of our allies
STOP Sending a chaperone STOP He'll have
money and supplies STOP
```

I read the telegram to Naomi for the third time. She clenched her fist and the ever-present ball of light snuffed out. "A chaperone?" She was getting angrier with each time I read it. "I swear I'll learn Ariadne's Net just to tie up the chaperone and then ship him back to Cain." I opened my mouth to say something, but Naomi held up her index finger with a forcefulness that told me just to go with the flow. "He's treating us like children! A chaperone, not an escort. It's insulting! You're the Archmage, and I'm the most powerful magician in the world."

"Yeah," I snuck in before she continued her vent.

"I mean, he may be a better illusionist than me, but he's no match for me overall."

Naomi had never really compared herself to other magicians. Mister Ali had told me that she was a stronger illusionist than Cain, but she appeared too humble to accept that. So hearing her actually say it was kind of shocking. "My great grandfather said that illusionism wasn't real magic."

"He did?" I hadn't seen her smile so widely in a long time. "I always liked him. Is he okay? Still at Balmoral?"

I lowered my head. "He's not doing well. He's retired and, well, just enjoying his garden." I didn't say that there was every chance he was already dead, and that I didn't have a chance to give him a real goodbye or attend his funeral. There was so much that I wanted to say about him.

Naomi must have noticed my change in mood as she walked over and touched my arm. "He is very proud of you. You know that?"

I nodded my head and then cleared my throat. "So what do we do now?" I leaned back on a desk chair. The troops had taken over a local elementary school, and we were in what must have been an office off of the teacher's lounge. I lived with the regular troops, which wasn't so bad, while Naomi was given a cot and a small room in the far corner of the building. We called it "the closet," as that was probably what it was, with no windows, one door, and shelves with stains on them.

She threw herself onto the sofa. "I'm tired of waiting." We had been at the base for two weeks. The Colonel, a man named William Lexington, was nice enough and left us alone. I had originally talked to him about plans to look for Ana, but he dismissed them all. He waved a telegram and said that we were just to await for assistance. I didn't know what he meant then, but he clearly meant Cain's chaperone.

"What we really need are spies who can dig around the Russian community for information about Ana," I noted as I worked on turning Cain's telegram into a paper airplane. "I don't think she's here yet, but that doesn't mean we should just sit on our hands."

"Perhaps we should think about how to get the coat first," Naomi replied.

I threw the paper airplane at her, but it flew nose first to the floor about three feet from my hand. We had discussed plans over and over again, and they all ended with Naomi angry that she couldn't just blow Ana up, and me wondering why the staff, which seemed to increase in power near the Coat, had no effect on Ana, who was actually wearing it. We seemed powerless against her and that just left us both irritable.

Rather than answer Naomi I used the staff to create a light show on the wall next to her. She loved my little shows, and I was getting more and more proficient at them. The key was the manipulation of color. Light contained all colors, and as I worked through what I wanted to see, the staff filled in all of the detail on its own.

Thinking of Zahhak, I created a scene on the wall of a giant dragon swirling around in the air and then landing on rocky ground in front of a robed Persian man. The man held up his hand, and I made the dragon melt into a cup, a staff, and a coat.

"Oh, do that again!" Naomi said standing up and moving closer to the wall.

"What?"

"When you made the cup, the light shimmered and it looked like I could actually touch it." She turned and looked at me. "It had depth."

"Hrm. That was an accident. Let me try to do it on purpose."

I pictured what I wanted to do in my mind, but just like every other time I used the staff, I didn't so much tell it what to do as think of what I wanted. My personal connection to the staff made it happen.

In this case, I thought about making the colorful images extend out like a model train display or a diorama. I didn't even really put much thought into the details. I just knew I wanted to see a light image that looked like you could touch it, even if I didn't know what it was that I actually wanted to see.

"Wow!" Naomi's voice shook me out of a kind of daze. I looked up and the image of Zahhak had changed completely. He was a mighty dragon that was swooping through the air of the room, while the wall had somehow transformed into the mountainside I had pictured for Jamshid. "He looks so real," Naomi said, staring at the dragon.

The only time the dragon looked like he wasn't actually real was when he flew in front of a light source, and I could see through him. In dim light he looked like a real dragon. Tiny, but real.

"This is like an illusion, Tommy," Naomi said. "I mean, it's not like a Cain illusion where you actually can touch and experience it in your mind, but it looks as good as his illusions are."

"Nah. You can see through it in bright light or if there is light behind it." I snuffed out the dragon. "It's neat, though."

Naomi turned toward me looking angry, which was something I was used to by then. "You know, you are maddening."

"I—"

"No! You listen to me." I couldn't help but smile. Like I had a choice. "I love what you did over the past two years, but you've fallen into a very dangerous belief."

"What is that?" I had to admit that I was intrigued by her comment.

"You think that you are powerful because you can do whatever you want when you stop time. That's it. You think all your other powers are useless." The light formed in her hand, and she held it in place. "But even your ability to make light is extraordinary!"

"Kind of as extraordinary as a streetlight."

Naomi looked up with a start. "You know I just say that to tease you. Your light saved us from Shadows. Your absence of light saved the Shadows." She held up two fingers. "Those are two things that no one in the history of the world has been able to do. So don't tell me you're just a streetlight."

I sighed. "I get it. I can do more than stop time, and I shouldn't be disappointed that I can't stop time anymore. But there is nothing I have left that will be able to stop Germans or Ana's allies or—" I waved my arms around. "—Anything!"

Shaking her head, Naomi replied, "You're more powerful than you think. Just remember that what you just did with the dragon is not something to take lightly. That was powerful, and it may save our lives someday."

I tapped the cane on the floor while Naomi went back to casting her tiny balls of light. We each had our own way of calming ourselves. "Didn't you hear? We don't have to worry about saving each others' lives any more. We have a chaperone coming!"

Naomi rolled her eyes. "Yeah. I give him one day before he runs screaming after I'm done with him."

"You won't," I said, feigning shock.

"Oh, I can't wait." She switched her spell and cast one that looked like an ugly green, black, and brown ball. "When do you think he'll get here?"

"I don't know, but you're making me think that whenever he shows up he'll regret it."

Naomi smiled. "That's the idea." She snapped her fingers, and the nasty looking ball disappeared into a noxious smoke that drifted up to the ceiling and faded into nothingness.

29

Iggy

Two weeks later Naomi and I returned from lunch to a young man sitting on the couch in our impromptu home base. He wore an English military uniform with the rank of corporal, yet he looked Indian, with black hair and dark skin. As we walked in he stood up with an exaggerated formality.

I glanced at Naomi, who rolled her eyes. We both had a good idea as to who this was. He was about my height, thin but not frail. He was just what I'd expect from a Cain lackey—Not a soldier, but a desk jockey who was so formal and by-the-book that his very movements seemed robotic.

As I got closer, I got a clear look at his face and was drawn to his eyes, which were so blue that they appeared almost white. The contrast with his dark hair and skin was striking. He was average looking, but his eyes gave him the kind of look that would draw attention from everyone in the room.

"Hello?" I said as we approached. "Can I help you?"

My voice seemed to relax him, as he smiled and replied, "No. Nope. Not at all." He didn't have an Indian accent, so I considered whether his ancestors had immigrated to England generations earlier.

I waited, but he didn't add any more to his answer. Naomi shook her head, marched over, and stood in front of him. Her movements were so aggressive that they intimidated me, and she was my friend. The stranger shrank a little bit as she eyed him up and down. "Who are you?" she asked.

"Ignatius Lazarus," the man replied. "Ig. Iggy. I go by many names. You may pick one that you like the most and use that."

"You're a strange one, Lazarus," Naomi said. I smiled. Of course Naomi used the one name that Iggy hadn't mentioned.

He didn't reply, so I repeated my earlier question. "Can I help you?"

"No. Not at all. You cannot help me."

I closed my eyes and took a breath. As maddening as Naomi could be, this military formality was even worse. "Okay, let me rephrase the question. What are you doing here?"

"I'm here to protect the two of you." Iggy pointed at me and then Naomi. "To keep you from harm. To make sure you don't do anything foolish or risky."

"There's no fun in that," Naomi said. She turned to me. "I think we've met our chaperone."

"I figured as much." I looked at Iggy. He stared at me, which wasn't so much intimidating as it was disconcerting with his pale eyes. I glanced away. "Did Cain send you?"

Iggy looked pained for a moment and then answered, "Cain told me where to find you. He gave me the supplies you need." Iggy turned and pointed to a small duffel bag that was sitting on the couch that I hadn't noticed. "He gave me the direction to come here so I could help."

"Great," Naomi replied before throwing herself on the couch. "Do you know any magic or are you just going to get in the way?"

"Oh, I will most definitely get in the way. Absolutely. No doubt." Iggy smiled, and Naomi and I laughed.

"Well, at least you have the right attitude," I said as I sat on a desk chair. Iggy remained standing. "By the way, stick to that and not the formal language. It's much better."

"I'm afraid I don't understand," Iggy replied.

"You know. Just be honest and don't bother with the niceties. None of this explaining every last detail as if you were organizing some kind of strategic plan stuff." Iggy seemed confused, so I turned to Naomi. "This may be a lost cause."

"Lazarus, what Tommy is saying is that you need to lighten up if you have any hope of remaining with us."

Iggy shrugged. "I cannot get lighter. I'm afraid I'm stuck with this body."

"Aren't we all," I replied, looking at my own skinny arms.

"Ugh. Boys and their insecurities." Naomi looked at Iggy. "Your sense of humor is kind of weird. I like it."

"There you have it, Iggy. Winning over Naomi was the biggest hurdle. You're part of the team." Naomi slapped my arm. "Actually, it was the only hurdle." She hit me again. I turned to Iggy. "So do you know what we're trying to do?"

"Yep. Sure do. Yes."

"Do you always repeat your answers?" Naomi said as she walked over to a chair while casting a spell. Iggy turned and looked at her.

"Not always. But it's good to be understood, so mostly I clarify. So not always but mostly?"

"You're an odd bird, Iggy," I said. "Why don't you sit down?" Iggy bowed his head and sat in a chair that was next to the sofa. "Did Cain have any intelligence on the Angel of St. Petersburg?"

"No," Iggy said. "I'm afraid not." He shrugged. "He was more interested in you two."

"Of course he was," Naomi replied. She turned to Iggy. "I thought you said you knew what we were trying to do. Do you know where Ana is?"

"Yes. She has crossed into France. She is heading to the Russian community in Northern Paris. They are White Russians and consider her their monarch."

"How do you know that?" I replied, shocked at his detailed knowledge. Did Cain have spies looking out to help us?

"Friends. Spies. That kind of thing." He stood up suddenly. "Well, I must be going. I am staying down the hall. Please let me know when you intend on confronting the bearer of the Coat. I am to assist."

I stood up while Naomi focused on some spell. "I'm not sure we'll need your help, but thanks for bringing the supplies. We can take it from here." I reached out to shake his hand.

Iggy stared at me for a moment, and it was the eeriest thing. His eyes held my stare and didn't blink. As I got lost in the pools of icy blue it felt like he was reading my mind, so I turned away and looked at Naomi, who was focused on casting the light spell. There was the stomp of boots hitting the floor, and as I turned back I watched as Iggy left the room.

"That's one strange guy," I said as I turned my attention back to Naomi.

"I think he's probably a student of Cain's," Naomi replied. "He moved like I would expect an illusionist to move. Their more complex spells require very long casting time and movement repetition that lead to moving awkwardly like he did."

"I don't think he blinks his eyes," I noted.

"Well, I'm sure he blinks his eyes, but holding his attention like that would indicate to me that he was perhaps in the midst of casting an illusion." Naomi sat up suddenly. "Do you think he cast an illusion in our room?" She looked around, and I did, too.

"I don't see anything out of place or different," I said.

"Me neither." She stood up. "Maybe he was just practicing."

I shook my head. "Not that I could see even a basic illusion." I wish Mister Ali were here. He'd know." I glanced at Naomi.

Ever since Mister Ali had died saving her life, just mentioning his name created what seemed like a mixture of deep pain and sadness. Instead of clenching her fists, however, this time she just nodded her head and replied, "Yeah. The old knucklehead was useful for that."

I loved that Naomi opened the door to talking about Mister Ali. I had wanted to share my feelings with her for days, but with her hurt and anger and my own confusion the time just never seemed right. "You know, when I think back I wonder why he was so important to me. He gave me bad advice about the staff. He was amazing with his knife but ultimately had to rely on others to save him. He knew just enough magic history to help, but not enough to really provide deeper insight. He was just a nice man that always wanted to help others, even if it hurt himself." I choked up a bit. "Or his relationship with others."

"Maybe that's enough," Naomi said, her voice a whisper.

Naomi broke the awkward silence that followed her comment by slapping her hand on the duffel bag. "Should we just tell Lazarus to leave? I assume we have the stuff we need."

"I don't know. You heard what he said about Ana. He seems to have knowledge that we need."

"I don't trust him," Naomi said. "Even Cain called him our chaperone. Do we really want a Cain spy running around with us?"

"Well, we could probably use an illusionist now that Arkady is gone." Glancing at Naomi, I cursed myself. I just talked about Mister Ali, who had died to save her, and I then mentioned the handsome young man that may have been her boyfriend and had left her for the queen of his motherland, too. I was such an idiot. To move off that topic, I quickly added, "Also, as I said—he had important information for us. We now know Ana is in France and where she is heading. He probably has some inside help from the government, so his intel would be useful."

Naomi opened her palm and started casting spells. "Okay, assuming that he's not lying, and assuming he's an illusionist, I agree. That would be really helpful. Just because we can't harm

Ana doesn't mean that a strong illusion couldn't trick her into doing something rash."

"Okay, good. So let's keep him around until he is more trouble than he's worth."

"So what's next? We still don't have a plan."

"I think our next step is to relocate to Northern Paris and wait. We now have the resources for a hotel room and a base of operations."

Naomi nodded and patted the duffelbag with our new supplies. "It will be nice to sleep in a real bed," she added.

"Well, we should probably enjoy it. I have a feeling things won't be quite so easy once Ana shows up." I clutched the staff, and as I thought about what Iggy had said about her being in France, I realized I had missed a subtle change. My connection to the staff was different—it was getting stronger.

Iggy wasn't lying. The Coat was getting closer.

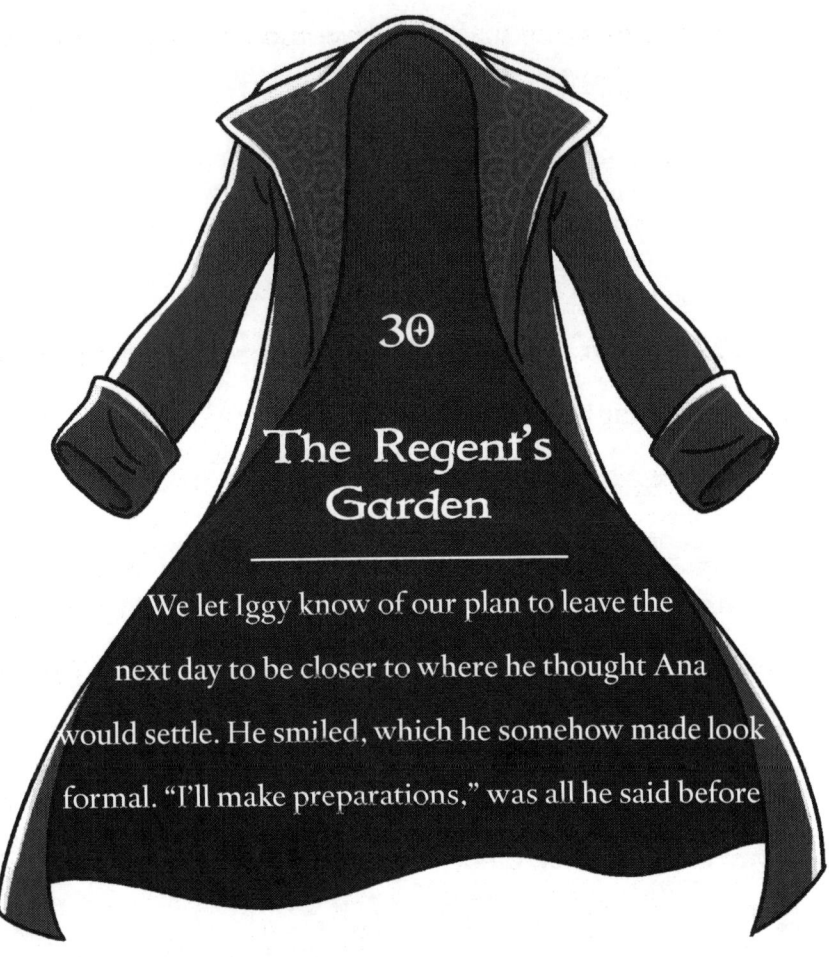

30

The Regent's Garden

We let Iggy know of our plan to leave the next day to be closer to where he thought Ana would settle. He smiled, which he somehow made look formal. "I'll make preparations," was all he said before

walking down the hall without even a goodbye.

The next morning I was immediately thankful for having Iggy on our side. He brought more than just money. He was waiting outside the front entrance of the school with what looked like a new sedan. He was standing at attention in front of the passenger door.

Naomi was carrying the duffel bag, and I had a large carpet-bag with our things, which wasn't a lot. I looked at Naomi and shook my head as we reached Iggy. She noticed and tilted her head. "What's wrong?"

"Well, your face is dirty. Your hair is a mess. You've worn the same shirt and pants for weeks, and your boots were made for small men intending on marching long distances. You don't exactly look like someone setting up residence in a northern Paris hotel."

"You're a real charmer, Streetlight," she replied. Once again, I wanted to kick myself, but I could tell she was suppressing a smile.

I turned to Iggy to hand him the bag and said over my shoulder. "That was more a statement about both of us. I mean, how do I look?"

"You are dirty but would still be described as handsome by most people. Your hair is unfashionably long, and at first glance you look like an older child." I turned my head from Naomi to look at Iggy. He was answering my question. "You have what would be called an air of confidence, but the way you move betrays an uncertain step. But you remain calm in a way that makes others have confidence in you."

"Uh, thanks, Iggy." I looked back at Naomi, who was on the verge of laughter. "What about her?"

"She is as you described." I laughed out loud at that, which elicited a firm punch in the arm from Naomi.

We piled into the car with Naomi and me in the back. "So where are we going?" I asked. I was still a little uncertain of having Iggy suddenly in charge of our plans.

"It is most likely that the bearer of the Cup will settle near Parc Monceau," Iggy replied. "It is not far from the Arc de Triomphe. We will be staying at a new hotel: The Regent's Garden."

"New? Ugh. I hope it's nice, not like those motor hotels that are appearing in America."

"It is a mansion that was gifted from Napolean III to one of his servants."

"Well, I guess that's acceptable," Naomi replied. She smirked when I looked at her.

We arrived at the hotel, and it was a mansion. Just getting from the street to the front door was a long walk across lush grass.

There was a man in a tuxedo who took the keys to Iggy's sedan from him.

Iggy was carrying both our carpet bag and the duffel bag with what looked like the same amount of effort it would take for him to carry a feather. I glanced at the duffel bag, which we had not examined yet. I hoped it was full of money, as the hotel looked extremely expensive. "Can we afford this?" I asked Iggy.

"No," he replied.

I stopped, and both Iggy and Naomi turned. Naomi seemed not to care about what Iggy had just said. I was guessing she just wanted a soft bed and a bath. But Iggy was our chaperone, he should be at least planning ahead.

"Then why are we staying here?" Iggy lowered his head and muttered something. "I didn't hear you. What did you say?"

"We are staying here because this is the most convenient location to attack the Bearer at Parc Monseau and then get out." He looked like he was going to say something else, but Iggy practically shook as he kept his mouth shut.

"Why here and not somewhere that will give us more time to plan or regroup?"

Iggy sighed, and then answered, "This hotel has magical defenses. It is known to me. We don't have to worry about time because when the Bearer arrives we will either succeed or fail. It will not take much time to know, and in either case, coming back here will be unnecessary."

"What do you mean?" I asked.

Naomi put her hands on her hips. "What do you think it means, Streetlight. We'll either get the Coat and flee or we'll die. And if the old hag is going to set up a base of operations then it's better to go after her before she sets up all her defenses." She turned and started walking. "Sheesh." I looked at Iggy, who nodded, turned around, and followed Naomi.

To my shock, Iggy spoke fluent French. He checked us in, turned around, and handed both Naomi and me keys. He had a third key that he slid into his pocket. "Three rooms? Isn't that a bit of a waste? I could share a room with you."

"No. I will have my own room." Iggy picked up the carpet bag and started down the hall. We had three rooms all in a row, and mine was between Iggy's and Naomi's. After Iggy entered his room, Naomi and I looked at each other.

"I don't get that guy at all," I replied.

"He's an illusionist for sure. They're all kind of weird." Naomi replied.

"Yeah, but Arkady was an illusionist—" I said, not in an attempt to get under Naomi's skin but rather to figure out what she meant. I was still convinced Arkady was her boyfriend, or was in the past. Did she like weird boys? Did she think I was weird? And did I like that or not?

"Arkady was weird, too," Naomi replied, a terse tone in her voice. "I'm getting a bath. Let's meet for dinner downstairs later, say six o'clock?"

"Sure, but what about Iggy?"

"He can get his own dinner."

I nodded my head and replied, "Okay," as I opened my door. I had to admit, I was looking forward to a hot bath and a lengthy nap on a soft bed, both things that I hadn't experienced in a long time.

I scrambled down the stairs about fifteen minutes after six. The hotel had a restaurant, and as I ran my hand through my messy hair I looked around for Naomi. I had to do a double take when I saw her. She was in new clothes and had her hair tied back, not in a pony tail but in some kind of fancy braid that fell over her shoulder.

She looked absolutely gorgeous.

What struck me the most was that she was actually in a dress. It was jet black and looked stunning, with long sleeves and a tighter waist that made her look much older. The deep black of the dress also showcased her braided light blonde hair, which rested on her shoulder. I didn't think I had ever seen her in a dress. She looked like a motion picture actress. I walked over and stood next to her chair.

"Uh, hi."

She turned, looked up at me, and then quickly lowered her head. "Hi," she answered, her voice uncharacteristically hesitant. Was she blushing?

"You look amazing," I added.

"Oh, thank you. I just wanted— I wanted to feel human, you know?" She looked back up at me, and I couldn't help but stare. She was at a table next to a window, and the light was shining on her face. I was speechless. She waved a hand toward the outside of the restaurant. "I mean, I've been in a desert with my mom. Then I was in the Scottish highland in a castle surrounded by books and dusty lamps. Now I'm running around hunting a magical artifact while being chased by Nazis and Russians." She turned away. "So I spent some of our money on a dress and time at a salon." I slid into the chair opposite her as she looked up at me. "You don't hate me, do you?"

"Hate you? Why would I hate you?"

"I don't know. Because I took some of our money for something totally unnecessary like this—" She ran the sleeve of her dress between her fingers. "—And this." She flicked her hair with her fingers. "Argh—" Naomi started to stand up. "You're going to just think I'm a girl."

"No! Please. Sit down." She sat down slowly. "Of course I think you're a girl. You're an amazing, talented, powerful girl who drives me crazy with her comments and ability to save the day in the most irresponsible way possible." Naomi smiled. I paused before saying the words, but I thought the time was right. "And you're also beautiful, and you deserve clothing and hair like that."

"You're a real charmer, Streetlight," she said, and this time she couldn't suppress her smile.

Before I could reply, a waiter came over. I couldn't speak French so I just pointed to something on the menu. He nodded and left. The moment seemed to have passed, but I still wanted to talk. Times like this were rare. We never really thought of anything but the present, so we were always alone even when we were together.

"So what's next?" I asked.

"That's a good question. I was thinking we have to restrain Ana without hurting her. Then we can just rip the Coat off her." I paused, and Naomi rushed onward. "I mean, I know it's not a great plan, but I was thinking—"

"Naomi—"

"—That if I were her I would never take the Coat off. So any plan of sneaking in or using an illusion to create a coat rack was just wishful thinking."

"Naomi—"

"I mean, maybe she does take it off for baths. So maybe that's what we do. We use your invisibility power to sneak in and just steal it while she's taking a bath."

"Naomi!"

She looked up at me. "What?"

"I meant what's next later. What's next when I have the artifacts and I free Zahhak. I won't have any powers. I won't even
be a streetlight. And what about you? You're this amazing magician, but even the army doesn't care. It's like you're doomed to
nothing more than a life of study and theory as the world watch-
es magic drift away."

Naomi's brow furrowed. I guess I was too harsh, and I could
tell she was unhappy with my line of questioning, but I thought
it was important to be honest. "First of all, you will always be
the streetlight. It's an honorific at this point." She smiled, and
I knew then she had been pondering the same things. "Beyond
that, I don't know. This is going to sound arrogant, but I have this
sense that I'm going to change the world, that all the work I've
done to preserve magic and re-learn what's been lost has some
kind of higher purpose." She lowered her head and blushed a bit.
"I know it sounds silly, but that's the case." She took a nervous
drink of water and then added, "The truth is, Tommy, that I don't
know what the future will bring, but I know that I'll have a place
in it."

"I wish I had your confidence." I took my own drink of water.
"I look at you, and you're powerful and pretty and seem to know

what you're doing." I motioned my hands along my dirty clothes. "And I'm this boy who is kind of just running from one mess to another." I laughed and looked up. "In fact, I know exactly why you bought the dress, Naomi. I want the same thing, to feel human. To maybe go visit my grandfather and walk to the movies again."

Naomi reached her hand across the table and took mine. "That sounds wonderful, and you will do that again. You should never worry about your future, Tommy. If you want to know what you're future is going to be like, just ask me."

I could barely talk. Naomi was holding my hand, and we were having dinner in a Parisian restaurant. I knew she was just being a good friend, but the emotions that filled me were suddenly about a future where we were holding hands. I swallowed and tried to sound nonchalant as I replied. "So what's my future going to be?"

Pulling her hand away, Naomi laughed in a way that sounded like tinkling bells. "I told you before, Tommy. You're predictable. Your future is you doing good. I don't need to know what it is, I can just be confident that my friend will be a good person doing good things." She leaned forward, and there was this intense look on her face that was impossible to read. "And trust me, Tommy, that's a wonderful future and one that makes me proud to be your friend."

Friend. There was that word again. At least I knew where I stood. I smiled and ran a hand through my hair, doing my best to look somewhat presentable. "That's very nice of you to say. I guess that's a future I can be happy with."

The waiter brought my food, and Naomi and I chatted about magic some more. I couldn't understand any of it, but I loved how animated she was discussing how some magician with a name I couldn't pronounce adapted some fundamental form that I couldn't picture to create an amazing new spell that did something that I couldn't understand.

"Do you want to go for a walk?" Naomi asked, and I immediately pictured us holding hands while walking toward the Seine River.

"Sure!"

Unfortunately, as we were walking through the lobby of the hotel Iggy marched over. "I have been looking for you," he stated in his kind of always formal-yet-excited voice.

"Well, here we are," Naomi replied.

"The bearer arrives in a few days. We need to prepare for the assault."

"Uh, what assault?" I asked. "Naomi and I were thinking that sneaking in and stealing the Coat would be a good option."

"The assault on the Bearer, of course. You cannot sneak in. She has too many guards. She is armed, you understand."

"Tommy will bend light around him so that she can't see him. Or he will do the camouflage thing." Naomi shrugged. "Same difference. He walks in. Puts the Coat on. Walks out."

"I don't understand," Iggy replied.

I looked around. "Look, this is public. Let's talk in my room."

Everyone agreed, and as we headed to the stairs, Naomi pointed to an alcove. "Elevators! They have elevators. I've never been on an elevator."

I looked at her. "You've never been on an elevator?"

"Shut up, Streetlight. They don't have elevators in Way Stations."

I shrugged. "Sure. Let's get on the elevator. It'll be non-stop excitement."

There was a man who looked a bit older than Iggy waiting. The door opened slowly, and as we all piled in, the man looked Naomi up and down. He said something in French, and Iggy snapped an answer, ending with "Anglais."

"Ah, an English girl!" He positioned himself between me and Naomi. "So what is a pretty English girl doing with a dirty boy like this?" He nodded over his shoulder at me. I couldn't see Naomi's face, but I could imagine what it looked like. I smiled wondering what kind of torrent of abuse she was going to unleash on him. But, to my surprise, Iggy reached out and shoved the man back a few feet using only his hand.

"Stop," was all that Iggy said. The elevator finally started to move.

"I can take care of my—" Naomi said, but by then the man had pretty much forgotten about her and turned on Iggy. His face was turning red.

"And what are you going to do about it?" he asked. "I must warn you that I specialize in boxing." The man held up his fists.

"I am going to punch your chest which will break a few of your ribs. I will then grab you by your arms, lift you up, and toss you against the wall. If you struggle after that or speak to the young lady I will break your legs." Iggy's voice retained its formal tone, and he said the words without an ounce of anger. However, in the context of a threat it sounded cold, flat, and thoroughly intimidating. The creaking of the elevator was all that could be heard over the silence. "I have not decided how I will break your legs."

The man stared at Iggy until there was a ding. The elevator door started to open, and the man slowly walked toward them. The doors weren't even fully open as he slipped through.

I looked at Naomi. She was beyond angry. She waited until the doors closed and then launched into Iggy. "What the heck was that all about!?"

"I simply made a comment."

"I don't need you to save me by making threats! I can take care of myself. Trust me, you don't need me on your bad side, Lazarus!"

"I didn't make any threats. He asked me a question, and I answered." Naomi looked confused for a moment, and then smiled.

"You know, Lazarus, you look and talk like this pencil pushing military bureaucrat, but inside you're a joker." Shaking her head, she added. "I can't be mad at you. You're funny in that you're clever."

"I'm not clever at all," was his reply. The elevator dinged, and the door started to open again. Naomi looked at me and shrugged as Iggy shambled through the doors.

"So, Iggy, have you ever broken anyone's legs?" I joked as we walked down the hall.

"Many." The calm formality of his reply was frightening. I looked at Naomi, and she looked equally surprised. We both knew he wasn't kidding.

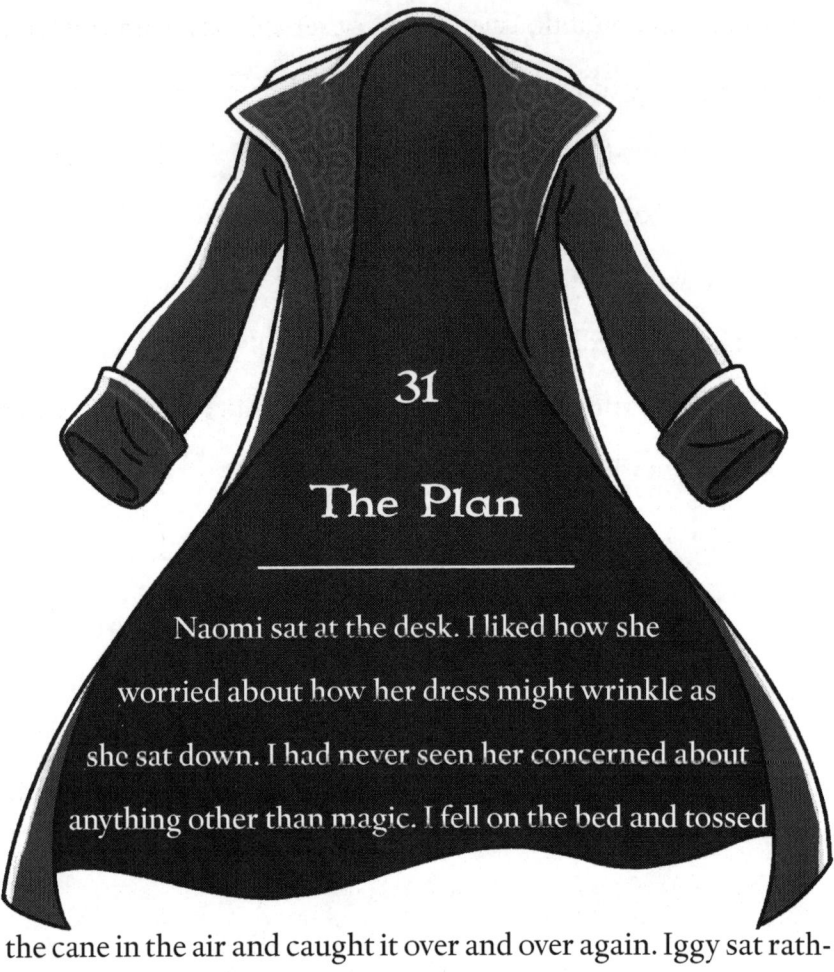

31

The Plan

Naomi sat at the desk. I liked how she worried about how her dress might wrinkle as she sat down. I had never seen her concerned about anything other than magic. I fell on the bed and tossed the cane in the air and caught it over and over again. Iggy sat rather stiffly on the edge of a reading chair.

"The more I think about it, the more I like the plan of a sneak attack," Naomi said. She moved her hands in a way that looked oddly familiar but wasn't any of her normal spells that I'd seen her practice. "We know that she can't be affected when you stop time, but you could do one of two other things: Bend the light around you or camouflage yourself with the color of light."

"Right. Then I'd sneak in when she's bathing and take the Coat."

"Argh." Naomi shook a hand.

"What's wrong?" I sat up.

"Nothing. I'm just working on a new spell." She glanced at Iggy. "What do you think, Lazarus?"

"Your plan won't work."

"Why not?" Naomi asked. She seemed more curious than annoyed that Iggy contradicted her plan.

"Because those that bear the Artifacts can't affect the others that bear the Artifacts." The first thought that went through my mind was wondering how Iggy knew so much about the Staff and Coat. "Your magic won't affect her."

"Well, there goes that plan," I replied.

I was about to ask how he knew this to be true when Iggy added, "And her magic doesn't affect you."

"Wait…" Naomi practically jumped out of the chair. "Are you telling me that Tommy could hurt her?"

"Yes. The Coat of Babr-e Bayan has no power over the Bearer of the Staff of Darius." He paused and then added, "Or the Bearer of the Cup of Jamshid."

Naomi started to pace excitedly. "Oh my gosh, this is great, Tommy. You could just grab a gun, walk up and shoot her. Grab the Coat, and we're good to go! Heck, I'll protect you with the Wall of Babylon and you could just walk in. I mean I've never actually cast that spell before, and I think it takes like twelve hours to prep, but I bet I could do it…" I smiled at Naomi's enthusiasm. By the time she trailed off she was talking more to herself than us.

I tapped the cane against my palm. "That does sound like a reasonable idea, and I'm quite sure you would be able to cast the Wall of Incredibly Amazing Power That Hasn't Been Cast Since Merlin Lived—"

"Babylon."

"Yes, that one. I'm sure you can cast it. But there's one problem: I'm not going to shoot Ana." Even as I said the words I felt strongly tempted to do just that. I'd have the Coat! No one could harm me! And the Staff would somehow be even more powerful with two of the artifacts together. I stood up and started pacing, conflicted over contradictory feelings.

"Well, maybe you just shoot her in the leg or something."

"I'm not going to shoot her! We can do something else that isn't quite so… deadly." I pointed the cane at Iggy, who flinched. "You! How do you know so much about the Staff? Naomi has been researching magic for years, and you seem to know more than she does. Mister Ali was raised in a magical family in Persia, and you know more than he did."

Iggy started wringing his hands. "My ancestors have first hand knowledge of the artifacts." He opened his mouth, but then shut it quickly.

"Is there anything you aren't telling us?"

"More than I could tell in a single night."

"Oooh, this is good." Naomi walked over and stood in front of Iggy. "C'mon, Lazarus. What's the story? What do you know of the artifacts?"

Iggy proceeded to tell us the same history of the artifacts that Naomi had, from Jamshid's battle with the dragon to how it ended. "And then he imprisoned Zahhak in the three artifacts, and when Jamshid died the artifacts were spread across the globe for safety." Iggy held out his hands. "Should I tell you more?"

"No," I replied. "We know the history of the artifacts. I'm more interested in how you know so much of how they work."

Iggy shrugged. "History. Family. Listening."

"You're not going to tell me any more, are you?"

"It depends what you ask," Iggy replied.

"You two are driving me crazy. Let's focus on Princess Hagastasia," Naomi said.

"You really don't like her do you?" I asked, which earned me a glare from Naomi.

"You can hurt her, which means you can restrain her. I still think that our plan should be for you to get to her and just grab the Coat. If she tries to stop you, hit her or something."

"I'm not going to hit a woman!" I exclaimed.

Naomi turned to Iggy. "What do you think she'll do to Tommy if he doesn't give her the staff?"

"She'll kill him."

"Fine," I replied. "I'll forcefully take the Coat from her. But we don't even know where she is."

"She's a day outside of Paris. When she arrives she'll be staying at a residence on Boulevard de Courcelles."

"How do you know this stuff?" I asked, incredulous at how easily Iggy could just rattle off critical information.

"Don't be an idiot, Tommy. Clearly he's some kind of spy. He has informers. Cain's not a fool. He didn't just send us a chaperone. He sent someone who could actually help."

I looked at Iggy. "Is that true? Do you know things from informants?"

He nodded. "There are many that give me information."

"Okay, then the plan is for you to heavily shield me and then I go in and just take the Coat."

"Us. I'll heavily shield us," Naomi replied.

"No. You don't need to go. You can't hurt her, so there's nothing you can do to help."

"Really, Streetlight? Nothing?" Naomi spun around and started walking toward me. "What about all those magicians and guards who will be there protecting her. Do you really think that a single shield would withstand a non-stop onslaught from that?"

"I assumed so. You're casting it, so it has to be really powerful."

"Okay, I can't be angry with you when you are that foolishly complimentary of my skills. Listen, Tommy. I said this before. I love magic. It is my life. But even my most powerful shield cannot withstand a non-stop barrage of spells cast by master level magicians." She paused. "Well, my best shield could probably withstand a barrage for a few minutes, but we would need more than that."

I loved how even when lecturing me she would take a break for a critical self-assessment. That was so Naomi. "Even the Wall of Babylon?"

Naomi sighed. "Yes. Even the Wall of Babylon. Tommy, don't be an idiot. This is not a ten minute operation. You'll need someone to help eliminate those attacking you."

"Correction." We both looked at Iggy, who was holding up a finger. "Anastasia does not use magicians. She is devoted to the machines of war and thinks that magicians are weak."

"I knew there was a reason I hated her," Naomi stated.

"I still can't believe that everyone has abandoned magic," I stated. "The English, The Red Russians. The White Russians. Is there any government that sees value in magicians?"

"The Germans," Iggy stated.

I thought back to our encounter in Leningrad. The Germans used technology, but they also used a group of master magicians. "I could see that." I started tapping the cane on the floor. "Can you imagine their power if they had all three artifacts?"

"No one could withstand them," Iggy replied.

"Well, we can deal with the Nazis later," Naomi said. "First we need to retrieve the Coat."

"I'm just glad the Germans have no idea where we are." I didn't want to admit it, but the might of the Nazis was a little frightening.

"Why would you think they don't know where we are?" Naomi asked.

I smiled. I was hoping she'd ask the question, and I wanted to show off my new understanding of the artifacts. "Well, they have the Cup, which you said allows them see all things. So they're looking for the staff, but since the artifacts cancel each other out, the Cup won't be able to point them to us!" Naomi didn't seem impressed.

"Yeah, because it wasn't horribly obvious that we were near Paris when a Russian train showed up and its Marid was freed."

Naomi shook her head. "You know, that's kind of your calling card."

"Oh," I replied. I hadn't thought of that. "Well, they still don't know where in Paris we are."

"A kid with a cane. Not hard to find, Tommy." Naomi was really starting to annoy me.

"Will you stop it? I get it. We should worry about the Nazis, too. But can we at least focus on Ana first? The odds of the Germans tracking me down this fast are low, and when they do I'll have the Coat."

Naomi stood up. "Well, if we're going to fight Nazis, I need some rest."

"For the last time, we're not going to fight Nazis, at least not yet."

Naomi spun around, her dress swirling around her. "Whatever you say, Streetlight." She walked through the door, leaving me with Iggy.

32

Parc Monceau

I woke the next day, and my hands shook a little as I lifted the Staff. Ana was closing in on Paris. It was obvious to me. I hoped that her getting closer would return my power to stop time, but after several attempts I had to accept that she was still too far away. Either that, or the power of the staff had become completely unpredictable. I tried not to think of that.

The compulsion to leave the hotel and head directly to grab the Coat was strong enough that I had to force myself to relax and be patient. I could practically feel the roiling emotions of Zahhak in the Staff. He had been enslaved for centuries.

At the same time, being cooped up in the hotel was not help-ing. It was nearing lunch time, so I decided to see if Naomi would like to eat and perhaps go for a walk. I knocked on the door to her room, but there was no answer. Assuming she was already in the restaurant, I headed for the stairs.

I scoured the restaurant and lobby of the hotel but couldn't find her anywhere. Knowing that our encounter with Ana was com-ing soon, I changed plans and decided to find out more about how far we were from Parc Monceau, which was where Iggy original-ly said the Russians had settled. After some confused words and waving of hands, the desk clerk called over a woman.

"May I help you?" she asked. Finally, someone who spoke En-glish.

"How far is Parc Monceau?"

"It is a fifteen or twenty minute walk, but don't worry, there are Taxis waiting." She motioned toward my hand. The com-ment confused me until I realized that I was holding the cane.

"Oh, no. That's okay. This isn't a cane. It's a walking stick." I spun the cane in my hand and then dropped the tip to the floor where it let out a loud tap. The other clerk glanced over and his eyes went wide. I ignored him as by then I was used to looks from strangers who didn't know I was the Archmage. "Which direction is the park?"

The woman gave me directions, which were quite easy to follow. I figured I'd walk over, look around, and then come back with some information for Naomi and Iggy. "Thank you!" I said as I spun around and headed out to the street.

The walk was exactly what I needed. I tapped the cane on the pavement, where its the sound reminded me of the days when I would walk with my grandfather and he would do the same thing. I wondered how he was.

He had retired to his apartment in Manhattan, and I had not seen him in months. I had visited him a few times, and each time he happily took me in and listened to my adventures. He was very proud of how I was freeing the Marids. He was a good man who, in his own reckless way, always looked out for those who needed help. Despite his obvious pride in me, I could sense some jealousy—after all, he was a hero during the Great War, and he had clearly loved the role of the mighty warrior. But he never was bitter or angry. More than anything I think he wished he could join me.

I made a left on Boulevard de Courcelles, and it hit me that this was the exact street that Iggy said Ana would be staying on. There were brown stone homes that reminded me of my grandfather's house, and at street level there were shops and cafes. More than anything it felt familiar, as I had been raised in a similar bustling city—New York.

A line of trees started on the right, and behind an iron fence I could see a park. I walked across the street to the entrance, which was a couple blocks further down the street. The sign said Parc Monseau. I assumed the Russians lived in the brown stone houses to my left. Why did they settle here? I thought. Was the park somehow important? Did it remind them of Russia? The sun was bright, and the weather was beautiful, so even if the park was just a distraction I decided to walk through it.

There was a rotunda at the entrance, and ornate iron gates behind it that were wide enough for automobiles to pass through. Despite the war, there were a lot of people walking the well-manicured grounds—couples, families with children, and individuals out for a picnic.

As I moved further along the path around the park I couldn't help but feel it was wrong somehow. There was a wide array of miniature buildings and replicas of things like a Chinese fort and a Roman colonnade. The Roman colonnade was popular, as it sat next to a lake full of ducks. I continued my walk past the lake, and the crowds started to thin the further along I went. The trees became more numerous, and the shade deepened. I eventually came across what looked like a miniature Egyptian pyramid.

I stooped down to get a closer look at its base when something bowled into me and sent me flying through the air. It felt like a giant had just swept me off the path with a flick of his finger. Dazed, I looked up to see Iggy standing next to me. My shoulder was sore and my hip hurt.

"What the heck!" I said as Iggy knelt down.

"They were close to casting at you, Staff Bearer. We must find cover. This was a very foolish place to visit."

"First of all, you know you can call me Tommy. And secondly, what do you mean this is dangerous?"

Iggy looked in all directions, his head darting around. "You were followed by the Germans." I looked around but couldn't see anyone. "This park is full of illusions, and I fear the Germans can use them to harm you." He pointed toward a bush. "We should hide behind that for now." He took my arm and tugged. The force nearly pulled my arm from my socket.

"Ow! Are you trying to kill me?" I stood up, rubbing my shoulder and hip. I followed Iggy toward the bush. "Illusions? What do you mean?"

"You are familiar with follies?" We were in a space behind the bush and near a dense copse of trees. As he spoke about follies, my mind immediately went to Fort Belvedere in London, the citadel that was a folly—a mansion designed to look like a pretend fortress but actually hid a real fortress.

"Wait, do you mean to tell me that all of the fake things in this park are real?" I thought back to the Roman Colonnade, the arch, the fort, and the pyramid standing not ten yards from me.

"Some are real. Some are physical replicas. Some are illusions. The magic in this park is very strong." Iggy must have noticed my confusion, as he added, "Not all illusions are meant to harm or hide. Most of the illusions here are to entertain, but you should never underestimate how a magician could take an existing illusion and twist it to his own uses."

"I didn't even know you could do that," I exclaimed.

"There is a lot you don't know."

"Gee, thanks." I peeked around the bush. "I don't see anyone. Should we try to sneak back to the hotel."

"We should, but be prepared for a battle."

"I don't even know what I can do to fight. I can't stop time, and I don't want to blind everyone. There are children near the lake. I guess I could just create darkness, but without knowing where we are going that will hurt us as much as them." I rubbed my shoulder again. It really hurt. "I wish Naomi were here."

"Yes, she is much more powerful than you are."

"You're not exactly helping," I replied. "So what do we do?"

"The nearest exit is to the east, but we should navigate through the trees and exit through the south. Let us hope that the Germans can't guard all the exits."

It was a well-maintained park, so walking through the trees was not at all that difficult. Iggy would stop every so often, look left and right, and then continue. As we walked I had to give Cain credit—his chaperone was actually helpful.

We exited through some trees and there to our left was a large gate. It was made of wrought iron and, like the gate to the north that I had passed through, was large enough for automobiles.

It was also chained shut.

"That's not good." I said, glancing back into the park. It seemed oddly empty. Where did all the people go? "What do you think?"

"This is a trap."

"Well, for once you're not telling me anything I don't know." I walked toward the gate. "Can we break through?" I was a few steps down the path when there was the sound of scratching and growling. As I turned to see what the sound was Iggy grabbed my arm to pull me back. "Those are Djinn!" I cried out. Four huge Djinn with massive claws and teeth were walking toward us.

"No. They are illusions," Iggy replied.

"Well, I'm not good with illusions, so I'm not sure it matters." I remembered Cain's lesson with the gun. "They'd still kill me."

Iggy nodded. "Wait here." He walked over to the Djinn, who arranged themselves around him. I was sure he was about to get cut to shreds. He crouched down and as they prepared to jump him, he spun around in a whirlwind of amazing speed. His arm reached out and with a pop pop pop, he eviscerated the Djinn, turning them into their elemental essence of air. He was so fast I couldn't even see the knife in his hand or where he pulled it from.

I started toward him. "That was amazing!"

Iggy looked at me and held up his hand. "Stay there, Staff Bearer!" As he spoke an explosion of light hit him in the back and knocked him a few feet in my direction. He lay sprawled on the ground. I ran toward him. It looked like he got hit with a detonation. I hadn't seen a Djinn survive that, let alone a human.

To my shock, he pulled himself up onto his hands and looked at me. It didn't seem like he was in pain. In fact he didn't look hurt at all. "Are you okay?"

"I am injured, but it is not life-threatening." He scrambled to his feet, and stumbled toward the tree line. "We need to escape. There are many magicians. They are coming from the north, but we should expect them to enter from other directions soon."

A loud voice with a German accent yelled out from the distance, "Tommy Black. Where are you, Archmage? I know you are there!" The voice sounded friendly, as if he was calling an old friend. "Come now, Tommy. You know the staff belongs with the other artifacts. Just hand it over to me, and you may leave in peace." I didn't reply, and the voice added, "Or you could join us. You love magic, no? You can help us research and learn. We respect your knowledge. You would like that?"

"I guess the Nazis found us," I said, grimly. "Can we defeat them?"

"I don't know. If you cannot use the Staff, then no. I can only do so much."

I was going to ask Iggy how he could help at all when the German shouted out again. He sounded closer. "Now now, Tommy. Don't be foolish. We know you are protected by an Ifrit, but he will not save you. We have defeated greater creatures with fewer forces."

Ifrit? I looked at Iggy. He was looking out toward where the voice came from. "Are you an Ifrit?"

Iggy turned and looked at me. He attempted a smile, but it retained that comical formality I attributed to him being overly disciplined. I realized the truth—he didn't know how to smile. It was one of many things that I had missed. "I am Ifrit, Enayat."

Enayat. It was the honorific that I hadn't heard used in a long time. The magical creatures gave me the title when I provided a home to the Shadows and started to free the Marids from the trains. It was Persian for "kindness." I had so many questions but no time to ask them. All I knew was that I felt my chances had just increased dramatically. Ifrit were powerful.

"Tommy, I'm afraid my patience is running out." The voice was closer still.

"Can you just transform into fire and destroy them all?"

"Possibly. There are many of them, and their mastery of magic is strong." I was about to tell him to do his best when he added, "But I can only do it if it is required to protect you." "Sheesh, Iggy. I think it's pretty darn required at this point. We're surrounded by Nazi magicians, and the only reason they aren't swarming us now is probably due to them being afraid of you."

"You should use the Staff." I looked at the Staff. He was right. My confidence had been shaken by the loss of my ability to stop time, but I could still make us invisible. Then we could just sneak out.

Just as I was about bend light around us, Iggy leapt in front of me, and a powerful blast knocked him into me and tossed us both back into the plants at the base of the trees. I was a bit dazed but Iggy seemed badly hurt. His body was twisted, although he didn't moan or seem to be in pain.

"Iggy! Are you okay?" I stumbled over and knelt next to him.

"I can heal in my fire form, but—" He paused, and it looked like he was taking a deep breath, although with him being an Ifrit

I wasn't exactly sure what he was doing. "—I am too weak to do that now. I need to rest, Enayat."

"I'll find a way to stop them."

"No. You should escape. They are interested in you, not me."

"They'll kill you!" Iggy didn't say anything. "I'm not leaving you." Before Iggy could object, I added, "I have an idea!" I was going to try something I had never really done before—using two powers of the staff at the same time.

The first thing I did was bend light around us. As I called upon the staff I knew I had done it. In fact, as I became one with the power I was filled with a rush of excitement. I was in my element, using the power of the staff to overcome my enemies!

With both Iggy and me invisible to the German magicians, I shaped the colors of light as I had done in the hotel room with Naomi. I created a massive fiery Ifrit. I had confronted an ancient and powerful Ifrit in Persepolis, and I made this one identical. Burning with fire and impressive in size, my imaginary Ifrit cruised through the air toward the middle of the park.

I left Iggy behind and walked along the tree line, knowing that I couldn't be seen. There were three Nazi magicians straight ahead in a large clearing that marked the intersection of the north-south and east-west paths of the park. One was off to the left, and to the right were two others moving slowly toward me along the tree line.

In total there were six Nazi magicians. A half dozen masters! I had never seen such magical might. I hoped I could scare them away, but seeing them all made me feel foolish. The appearance of an Ifrit may have made them cautious, but it wouldn't make them flee. Still, I had to try. I sent the Ifrit forward, expanding the fire along its arms so that it looked like an awesome elemental being. The three Masters at the path intersection crouched down. I could tell that one was casting a shield, while the other two started hurling spells at my light illusion.

I had the Ifrit dodge the spells, but the Nazi magicians were so fast that a few flew straight through my illusion. If only I could add sound I could perhaps convince them to flee by using the ominous voice that I had experienced in Persepolis. As it was, the Masters were clearly alarmed, but my plan to have them flee wasn't working.

In the distance I heard machine guns and then an explosion. The Germans were bringing reinforcements, and they were troops with machine guns. There was a shout from the left, and

I watched a magician walk toward my Ifrit. I had it expand in size, creating a fire so bright that it would burn their eyes if they looked at it.

The Masters in the middle continued to cast ineffective detonations, while the one to the left shielded his eyes while he continued to walk forward. "Very impressive, Archmage," the magician covering his eyes yelled out. "An illusion of light. You fooled even me." He turned back and shouted something in German. The Masters stopped casting. I worked my way over to the right and the path that led to the pyramid. I was getting dangerously close to the other two magicians.

I had resigned myself to a plan that I had hoped not to need— leaving Iggy behind while I escaped and went to get help from Naomi. My fear was that even Naomi wouldn't be able to handle six Master magicians, even as powerful as she was.

"Where are you, Archmage? We have the park exits blocked. You cannot escape. Are you playing more games with light? That is your talent, is it not?" I had a clear view of the leader. He was in a Nazi uniform and had a lot of medals on his chest. He walked with a bit of an uneven gait. He's a Master illusionist. I shook my head. Why are all the jerks illusionists?

I decided that two could use illusion. I let the Ifrit fade away, and then I created a light illusion of myself running across the path on the opposite side of the intersection from me. Immediately, two Masters cast detonations with deadly accuracy, blowing up the entire area where I would have been. So much for them letting me go without hurting me.

"Come now, Archmage. Don't make this difficult. If you don't run, we won't hurt you." The leader of the magicians glanced around.

I retreated behind the pyramid, but the moment I stepped within a few feet of it, the blocks spread into the form of a mouth and a loud voice said, "Footsteps approach! Footsteps approach!"

I hurried away from the pyramid as all six magicians focused their attention in my direction. At that moment a muffled explosion came from the direction of the main entrance behind the three Masters on the main path. It was so powerful that I felt the force wave push me back. The Masters tumbled forward.

"My, my. That was a very nice shield. I'm impressed." Walking toward us was Naomi. She was in her black dress, and her blond hair stood out against it as a slight wind blew tendrils of her hair around her face. The magicians looked shocked as they got to their feet.

She motioned with her hand and one of the Masters was tossed backward as if he was made of paper caught in a stiff wind. Naomi laughed. "As I said, it was a very nice shield." One of the Masters unleashed a series of detonations, but they thudded against a shield that Naomi had cast.

With another wave of her hand, the second magician went flying, rolling across the lawn. "Naomi! There are two magicians to your left!" I was worried about her being attacked by the magicians she hadn't seen. I didn't even know what kind of magicians they were.

I found out as one of them turned and cast a detonation right at me. He couldn't see me, but he must have aimed where he heard my voice. The detonation missed, but exploded about five feet to my left. I went flying. The only thing that saved me was my instinct in holding onto the cane. I remained invisible.

Clutching the staff in my right hand, I reached down to lift myself with my left when searing pain exploded from my shoulder. It was hanging lower than it should be.

I could barely see through the pain, but what I could see was incredible. Naomi had knocked out four of the Masters, and all four were confined on the ground by some sort of magical restraint. The leader had conjured an illusory wall of fire, which stood between him and Naomi. There was one last master slowly backing up as Naomi advanced on him.

He appeared to be very powerful, as he was maintaining a shield while he cast detonations at Naomi. As Mister Ali had taught me, casting two spells at once was exceptionally difficult. Naomi didn't cast a spell, she just walked forward, her own shield easily absorbing the detonations. She looked completely unconcerned.

The Nazi magician, however, looked terrified. It was extraordinary. Naomi was a vision in black, an angel of deathly beauty as she strode forward. The magician stopped retreating, staring at Naomi. A moment later he conjured a spell I wasn't familiar with. Naomi stopped.

"Okay, so you know at least one good spell. Very nice." Naomi grinned. "But the question for you is whether that spell is stronger than my shield. Here's a hint: It's not."

The magician unleashed his spell, and a green ball of light flew toward Naomi. It stopped a few feet in front of her and then spread around her entire body. The green fire held steady, like a shimmery green cocoon, and then started to squeeze in toward her. As it tightened bit-by-bit Naomi stood still and confident.

I didn't know what the spell did, but I was getting nervous as it didn't stop moving. It was mere inches from Naomi's face when the green fire started to fade. After a few more seconds it died out.

Shaking her head while smiling, Naomi cast the red ball spell, the one that incinerated the target from the inside out. She held her hand toward the magician. "Run," she said. The magician turned and fled into the distance.

"You should join us, Grandmaster!" The voice of the illusionist yelled out. "Such power can only be appreciated by those who share your talent! We would provide you with an honored position. You could help lead us with the heir of Jamshid!"

While the illusionist spoke, his wall of flame had begun to expand to surround Naomi. The flames were hot enough that I could feel their heat from where I sat.

Naomi was moving toward the flames. "Naomi, no! Illusions can still hurt you!" She ignored me and marched forward. She was waving her hands left and right, using a spell to move the flames aside with air, but for every swath of flame that was blown aside, new flames would fill the space.

Changing strategies, Naomi started casting explosive spells through the flames. They exploded in the distance, but I couldn't tell if they were at all close to the Master illusionist and neither could Naomi.

"Naomi! Run! The fire is going to surround you!" The flames roared and spread toward Naomi, only to hold their position as the illusionist spoke. "A pity to destroy such talent. Do not do this! You are not even appreciated by your own allies. Join us, Naomi."

In response Naomi cast a detonation toward the sound of the magician's voice on the other side of the wall of flame. She clearly missed, as the flames marched forward again.

I watched as Naomi fell to a knee. "Naomi, run!" I yelled, but she was casting another spell. At that moment the flames closed connected and completely surrounded her. All that was left was the magician to tighten the fiery noose to incinerate Naomi.

I lifted the staff and willed time to stop. I had witnessed Naomi nearly killed by the flame spell of an Ifrit, and I wouldn't let her get that close to death again. But to my horror time didn't stop. I was powerless. I was once again no more than a streetlight. I pulled myself up with the staff and desperately limped toward her. The flames were burning my face when I noticed movement to my left.

A creature of flame was slowly moving toward the illusionary flames. Iggy! He held out a hand, and a ball of fire shot out, disappearing behind the huge wall of flames that the illusionist had created. There was a cry and then Iggy cast another ball of fire.

At that moment the fiery wall disappeared, replaced by a pillar of fire standing on the lawn in the distance. It burned bright and intense. I limped forward to Naomi, who was on the ground. She looked perfectly fine but was unconscious. I touched her forehead. It wasn't hot at all.

Her chest wasn't moving, so I leaned down and put my lips over her mouth, hoping to fill her lungs with air. The moment my lips touched hers, her eyes shot open and she pushed me hard with her hands. I fell back, jarring my shoulder. I groaned and blinked tears of pain out of my eyes.

"Oh Tommy, you shoulder is dislocated! I'm so sorry!" Naomi looked unsteady, but scrambled over and put her arm around me as she pulled me to a sitting position.

"It's okay. It only hurts like crazy," I replied.

She slapped my good shoulder with her hand. "You idiot. I wouldn't have dislocated your shoulder if you hadn't decided to kiss me while I was burning to death."

I couldn't help but laugh even though I was in searing pain. "You didn't dislocate my shoulder. A detonation from a Master did. And I wasn't trying to kiss you; I was trying to save you."

"We need to get you medical attention." Naomi stood and gently grabbed my good arm, pulling me up.

"I don't know if that's a good idea. We don't know how many Germans are around, and I need to get the Coat."

"I can heal your shoulder." It was Iggy, who had returned to his human form.

"Iggy! You saved us!" I limped over to him. "Are you okay?"

"I am gravely injured, Enayat. My life force is depleted, and by shifting into this form I have used energy I should have used to heal."

"Sheesh, why did you do that?"

"My job is to keep you safe. I can't stay near you for very long in my natural form." Before I could reply, he moved toward me in an odd stutter step, stopping at my side. "Are you ready to be healed?"

"I guess so." I looked at him as he reached toward me. "Will this hurt?"

"Lots," Iggy replied, as his hands and arms grabbed my arm and shoulder. With a yank he pulled my arm into its socket. I am not too proud to admit that I screamed and tears streamed down my face.

Breathing hard, I yelled, "I thought you were going to heal me!"

"You are healed now," Iggy replied.

I moved my arm, and while I clearly wasn't healed, it was at least usable. Naomi rubbed my shoulder, which actually made it hurt more, but I didn't want her to stop so I didn't say anything. "Iggy," Naomi said. "I think our definition of healing is different than yours."

I looked around. There was a small pile of charred ashes in the distance. I didn't need to ask Iggy what it was. There were four magicians secure in some kind of invisible binding spread across the grass. "Where do you think the other magician went?" I asked.

"Back to school, I hope. He knew one good spell, and I had that mastered in my first month of study."

"What do we do with them?" I nodded toward the restrained magicians.

"Leave them for the French," Naomi replied. "We need to get back to the hotel. We're a bit of a mess."

Just to be safe, I made us invisible as we made our way out of the park and along the sidewalk. None of us could see each other, so I held Naomi's hand while Iggy placed his hand on my sore shoulder. We would have looked ridiculous if we weren't invisible.

Shortly after we left the park, Iggy stumbled and I reached for him, but he slipped from my fingers. Beyond the pain of the jolt to my shoulder, I was shocked by the immense weight and bulk of Iggy in his human form. It felt like trying to hold back a tank.

"Iggy, are you okay?"

"I will be fine when we return to the hotel, and I can rest."

"It's not far," I replied, trying to be supportive.

"I will go on my own. I will meet you in my room," he added, his voice coming from further ahead.

I spoke in Naomi's direction. "Are you okay?"

"Just enjoying the Two Invisible Stooges." I was going to object, but she squeezed my hand, and I decided I liked the feeling of holding her hand more than an argument.

Things were quiet as we slowly made our way down the street. I was sore. I was nervous over the possibility of Russians or Germans finding us, and I still didn't know how I would get the Coat. Yet it was a Paris afternoon, and I was walking down the street holding Naomi's hand. I didn't want the afternoon to end.

As we waited at an intersection, I heard Naomi's voice from my right. "What a pair we are. The Mighty magician and the Archmage, beaten by a single illusionist." She sounded utterly defeated. "When are we going to actually win a battle, Tommy? I've studied so hard, and I'm still useless."

"You are not useless!" I exclaimed. "You defeated five Master magicians. Five! No one else in the world could do such a thing. You are amazing."

Naomi was quite for a while, finally replying with deep bitterness in her voice, "But I still failed."

"You could have won, Naomi! You're just too aggressive." I didn't know if Naomi would accept the criticism, but I was worried she'd hurt herself, so I threw caution to the wind. "You need to learn how to retreat and then counter-attack. The illusory fire is a great example. You should have fled and then found a new angle of attack."

"But then he would have killed you, Tommy."

"Maybe that's our problem then," I replied, unable to keep frustration from entering my own voice. "We don't trust each other. I can protect myself with the staff. You can handle yourself with your magic. Maybe we would work better as a team by focusing on our strengths rather than trying to protect or impress each other."

"I never said you had to protect me," Naomi said, irritation in her voice.

"And you don't have to impress me. You're amazing as you are," I replied.

Naomi didn't reply, and we finished our walk back to the hotel in silence.

33

Rest & Healing

When we reached the hotel Naomi
slipped her hand out of mine, and as her
touch faded I became more aware of the pain in
my shoulder and hip. I made us visible, but as I looked

around, Iggy was nowhere to be seen. We were to meet in my
room, so Naomi and I made our way to the elevator, too tired and
sore to take the stairs. We didn't speak as the elevator creakily
took us up to our floor.

Iggy was waiting near the door. He was a mess, and I was sure I
didn't look much better. The only one of us who appeared unhurt

was Naomi. She had quickly recovered from the fire illusion and looked both beautiful and intimidating as she alternately crafted spells and clenched her fists in her black dress.

"Lots to talk about," Iggy said as we approached.

"You think so?" Naomi said, her voice dripping with sarcasm.

"Yes. Absolutely," Iggy replied.

"She's teasing you, Iggy," I said as I pulled the key out of my pocket and unlocked the door.

He didn't reply as we all shuffled into the room. The first thing I did was lay the Staff on the bed and sit next to it, cradling my arm in a way that would support my recently dislocated shoulder. I assumed Naomi would sit on a chair, but she spread out the bottom of her dress and sat on the floor, crossing her legs. She brought up her hands and started casting another spell.

"A very good idea, Naomi," Iggy said as he sat in the desk chair.

"What's that?" I asked.

"She is casting a shield to protect us in case of a surprise attack." I nodded. It sounded like something Naomi would do.

I sighed and adjusted my arm. "So." I looked at Iggy, but he didn't move or say anything. "Why are you helping me? Ifrit aren't exactly known for being friendly to humans."

"You are Enayat, and the artifacts of Jamshid are no longer hidden. You are the one who will do the right thing when they are joined."

I knew exactly what Iggy was saying. No other Archmage would think to free Zahhak. They would all strive to use his combined power. On the other hand that didn't seem at all aligned with what Cain would want. Cain would want me to wield the artifacts for the good of the allies.

"Do you work for Cain?"

"Yes. No." Iggy looked to be in pain. "I report to him, and I am to follow his commands, but I am with you because my brothers and sisters know it is important to assist you."

"I see." I rubbed my shoulder, which was still sore. "Assuming I can get the Coat, who has the Cup?"

"A Nazi illusionist. Goebbels. He is a master of a new magic— voice illusion. He can convince people to do his bidding with his voice."

I nodded. It didn't seem like a particularly powerful magic. "Well, we can worry about him later. First we have to free the Coat from Ana."

Naomi's voice cut into our conversation. "I don't get it." Iggy and I turned toward her as she lifted herself off the floor using only her legs in a single fluid motion, her black dress gathering around her as she stood up. "You speak good English. You are an elemental that can shape shift to human form. Yet there are no historical documents of Ifrit partnering with or even talking casually to humans. Only passages outlining wishes and magic and betrayal."

Iggy stared at Naomi, and that's when I noticed something that I dismissed but had been nagging at me since I met Iggy—he didn't blink. "Djinn, Ifrit, and Marids cannot lie. Humans have taken advantage of that to enslave us for many years. Our only hope was to stop communicating with those who would enslave us."

"You can't tell a lie?" I asked rather incredulously. I tried to think back to all the questions I had asked Iggy. Had he ever lied?

Turning to me, Iggy shook his head. "No."

"Who is the most powerful magician in the world," Naomi said, smirking.

"You are," Iggy replied without any hesitation. Naomi's smirk turned into a big smile.

"I like you, Lazarus," Naomi replied. Iggy smiled, which appeared fake in its formality.

I grabbed the staff. "Iggy should rest. He was badly hurt today." I used the staff to help me stand.

"You were hurt, too!" Naomi walked over and sat next to me, gently touching my shoulder where it was dislocated. "Do you need anything?"

"A sling would probably be good," I replied.

"I will leave you two." Iggy stood up.

"How long will it take you to heal? Should we wait to confront Ana for a few days?" I asked.

"I heal quickly. It is okay. Ana will arrive tomorrow morning. We should plan on retrieving the Coat tomorrow afternoon. A delay would be bad."

Naomi had grabbed a pillow and was removing the case as she replied, "We can't. Tommy's arm will be weak. He needs to be stronger."

"It's okay, Naomi. I can still hold the staff, and that's all that matters." I looked over as Iggy started to leave. "Thank you, Iggy." He didn't reply as he walked through the door.

"Here, try this." Naomi handed me the pillowcase, which she had turned into a sling by tying the corners into a triangle with a tight little knot. I slipped it over my head and slid my arm into it. The length was a little long but close enough that I didn't mention it.

"This is great!" I said to Naomi. She smiled, and I twirled the cane in my right hand. "I'm ready for Ana now."

Naomi's face turned serious. "It will be dangerous, Tommy. You know that."

"Of course. If nothing else, today illustrated that."

Naomi sat down next to me again. "You know that if she resists you'll have to forcefully take the Coat from her. Possibly hurt her."

"I won't have to hurt her. This will be easy, Naomi. Especially with an Ifrit on our side."

"As long as you mean won't and not can't."

"Don't worry!" I exclaimed. "When the time comes I'll do the right thing."

"That's what worries me," Naomi said with a sigh.

34

Artifacts Out of Balance

The next morning I waited in my room for Iggy and Naomi. I had trouble sleeping thanks to my aching shoulder, but the staff filled me with a barely containable energy and excitement. I considered our plan. The good news was that all I had to do was take the Coat from Ana. I had no power over her, but she also had no power over me. The plan was simple: Point a pistol at her and demand the Coat.

But I was worried about her followers. They had guns and perhaps explosives. This would be a fight between magic and technology, and I was afraid that magic wouldn't be enough, even with someone as powerful as Naomi on my side. Her shields could only do so much.

There was a heavy knock on the door. I opened it to Iggy, who looked much better than he had the previous day. He even appeared to be moving in a more casual fashion. "Feeling better?" I asked as Iggy walked in.

"Yes. I am nearly at full strength."

"Do you know if Ana is here?" I had attempted to stop time earlier and failed. That made me think that she was still far away.

"She is here. Yes. She is at the residence on Boulevard de Courcelles."

I didn't say anything as I tried to grasp what was going on. She was close. Close enough that all my powers should work. I tried to bend light around the lamp, making it invisible. I failed.

"Are you okay, Enayat?"

Nothing felt wrong. I knew that I should be able to do everything with the staff. I just knew it. This was different than when I couldn't stop time before. Then I had felt like a part of me was injured. Now everything felt normal. What was going on?

"Tommy?"

"Be quiet, Iggy." I gripped the staff tight and focused on the simplest power, the first I had mastered, the one that made Naomi call me streetlight. I willed the staff to bring forth a beacon of pure white light on its tip.

Nothing happened.

I couldn't breathe. My hands shook hard enough that my shoulder throbbed in rhythmic pain. I tried again. This couldn't possibly be happening. Nothing. I tried again, a smaller light. Nothing. I closed my eyes and focused on the staff, the cane, the artifact in my hand.

Zahhak. I willed him to talk to me. What are you doing? Do not hold back the power of the staff. I need it to free you. Somewhere I heard a knocking. Was it Zahhak? I tried to pass through the bars of his prison, to visit him in the staff. But it was impossible. I knew it. It wasn't a prison like that. It was a prison of existence. Still, I had to know why. Why are you doing this, Zahhak?

There was no answer.

A shock of pain brought me back to reality. I opened my eyes to see Naomi shaking my good shoulder. "Tommy? Are you okay? Tommy?"

"I've lost power over the Staff," I whispered. It took all my strength to hold back tears.

"You can't do anything?" Naomi asked. She was sitting next to me, wearing her black dress. Her face was full of concern. Iggy stood behind her.

"Nothing. I feel a connection to the staff. In fact, it feels stronger now that it ever has. I felt like I was actually close to Zahhak as I tried to see what was happening. It's just that it doesn't do anything."

"Have you tried making light?"

"Of course I have!" I snapped. Naomi leaned back, which made me feel worse. "I'm sorry, Naomi. I'm just upset. I don't know what is going on."

"Zahhak can only serve one master," Iggy said. He stood still as a statue, staring at me with his nearly white, unblinking eyes.

"That can't be true." I tapped the staff on the floor, it's brass tip making the tap tap tap noise that soothed me. "There have been three Archmages for years, and it's pretty clear that all three of us have been able to control the Artifacts."

Naomi spoke as she stood up and started pacing. "But it's become unstable recently. Something has changed." I looked at Iggy, but he didn't add anything to Naomi's comment.

Tap. Tap. Tap. "Something has changed." Tap. "It made sense to me that the Artifacts would start to fail if they were far apart. That would indicate that Zahhak was exerting some power to bring them together. Maybe the Germans have recently unearthed the Cup, and that's what woke Zahhak." I stopped tapping on the floor and clutched the cane in my hand, as if holding it tighter would reveal some undiscovered truth.

"That is accurate, Enayat." Iggy said. "The Germans recently discovered the Cup in a ruin in Egypt."

Naomi stopped pacing and cast the light spell. I wondered if she realized that she was now better at making light than I was. "So that explains the artifacts not working until they were brought closer together, but it doesn't explain why you can't control the Staff now." Naomi turned to Iggy. "Is Ana close?"

"She is walking distance."

"Something has changed," I said. "There was equilibrium. The active Artifacts all worked by themselves. Their powers are different and perhaps even complementary. Even when the Cup was unearthed, the behavior made sense—the closer the Artifacts were together, the more powerful they were."

There was a gasp, and I looked over at Naomi, whose palm was over her mouth. "What if the equilibrium was broken?" Her eyes were wide, and although she didn't look scared, she had the look of someone who had just uncovered a deeply unsettling truth.

"I don't understand."

"Tommy, what if the Germans beat us to Ana, and they have the Coat?" Naomi slumped down into the desk chair.

"Are you saying that the person who has the Cup now also has the Coat?"

"Yes. It's the only thing that makes sense. If someone has both, the equilibrium is broken." Naomi slid her hair behind her ears. She looked like she was preparing for a dangerous but necessary task. "Maybe Zahhak's power is now focused on the Bearer of the Coat and Cup and—" Naomi paused before she said it, "—not you." Naomi lowered her head. "I'm sorry, Tommy."

"But why would this German leader risk coming to Paris during wartime? That sounds foolish," I asked.

"If you were looking for one of the most powerful magical artifacts in the world, one that makes you invincible, would you trust someone else to grab it for you?"

I nodded. It made sense. Zahhak's powers were now focused on the Archmage with two of the three Artifacts. Yet I didn't accept it as indicating failure. I turned to Iggy. "Do you know where the Cup is?"

"No. Its nature makes it difficult for us to find."

"What about the Coat? Is it gone?"

"No. As I said, the Coat is in the residence on Boulevard de Courcelles."

I stood up. "Wait. The Coat is still within striking distance?"

"Yes. Have I been unclear?"

I excitedly rapped the staff on the floor a few times. "It's not too late, and the opportunity is even better! We can attack now and get the Coat and the Cup!"

Naomi looked up at me but didn't move. I couldn't read her face at all. "So you want to take on a building crawling with Nazi magicians, led by an illusionist wielding the Coat of Invincibility and the Cup of Jamshid, and you want to do this with a useless cane, an Ifrit bureaucrat, and me?"

"Exactly."

She sprung out of her chair with a big smile. "I was hoping that's what you were saying."

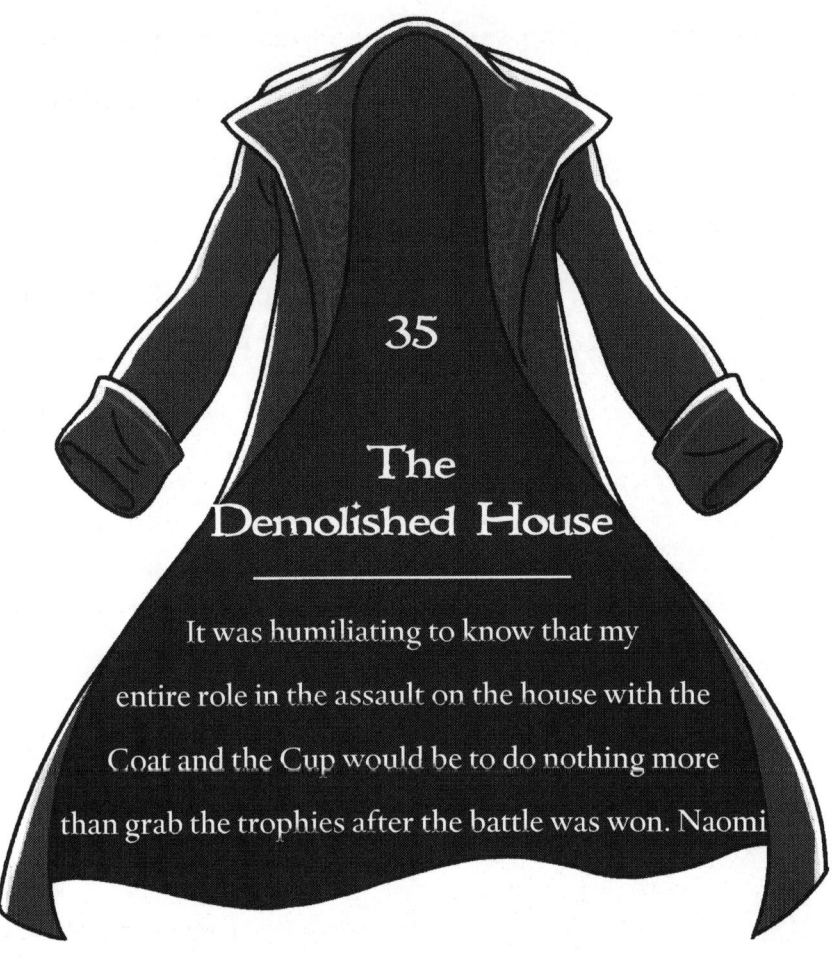

35

The Demolished House

It was humiliating to know that my entire role in the assault on the house with the Coat and the Cup would be to do nothing more than grab the trophies after the battle was won. Naomi and Iggy would be doing all of the fighting. About the only thing I could do was use the sword that was hidden inside my cane, but although that was remarkably sharp I wasn't sure I could actually stab someone. Stopping time and making people invisible were more my style.

We left shortly after noon. Naomi started before the sun came up to cast a shield spell that would surround the three of us. As she stood up after casting the spell she stumbled. "Are you okay?" I asked as I grabbed her arm.

"Fine." She didn't look fine. "It's a… difficult spell." She took a deep breath and steadied herself.

"Is that the Babylon spell?" I looked around. I was used to seeing a slight film or some kind of iridescent glow or muffled sound. I couldn't perceive any of those things.

"No." Naomi slipped her hair behind her ears and tugged the sleeves of her dress up her arms. "It's the Wall of Qin Shi Huang."

"I am unfamiliar with that spell," Iggy said, his voice expressing something close to awe.

"It's from China. It is easy to maintain, but the initial forms are very difficult." I could only imagine. Very difficult for Naomi would be impossible for everyone else.

"Will it stop bullets?"

Naomi nodded. "It's not easy to destroy, but don't expect it to hold up to sustained machine gun fire."

"Then I think we should avoid sustained machine gun fire." I held out my arm toward the door. "We should get going." Iggy took the lead and Naomi followed behind. As I slipped in behind her, I added, "You look fierce in that dress." And she did. It would be easy to get lost in her golden hair and blue eyes contrasting with the deep black, but a closer look revealed her concentration, her sharp features, and the intimidating movement of her hands as she prepared spells. With a background of black, it made her look ominous.

"Why thank you, Streetlight!"

The fact that Naomi called me streetlight when I couldn't even make a flicker with the staff was comforting. She had faith in me and that meant a lot.

"The Germans call you the Black Witch," Iggy added.

"What?" Naomi stopped.

Iggy turned and walked back. "They are aware of you now and call you the Black Witch."

"I love that!" Naomi exclaimed, running a hand over her dress. "I'm going to wear all black from now on."

"Uh, you may have missed the part where Iggy said the Germans are aware of you now," I stated. "That can't be good. No more element of surprise."

"When did I ever worry about the element of surprise?" And with a bounce in her step, Naomi jogged ahead, took Iggy's arm in hers, and tugged him forward to face the German Archmage.

We walked the same street I had followed the day before. I kept glancing about for Germans or Russians. Of course I wasn't expecting anyone to be in a uniform, but I still thought I'd be able to pick out something suspicious. Naomi was doing the same thing.

About twenty yards away from the house that Iggy indicated, he held out his hand and we all stopped. "That is not good."

I stared at the house. It was beautiful. Standing three stories, it had ornate decorative carvings at the top of each level, with a gorgeous deep brown door with inlaid gold. It appeared to be constructed of a light stone or a rough marble cut into blocks. To the left of the door was a short staircase that rose to a lawn with a patio.

"What's not good?" I tried to peer into the windows or find some other evidence of trouble. There was nothing.

"The house is badly damaged. There has been a magical fight here."

"I don't see anything like that," I replied, which elicited a nod from Naomi.

"Oh, I'm sorry, Enayat. It is hidden by an illusion, a very strong one. The house appears normal and well-maintained, but the door is hanging from its hinges, the windows are broken, and there are scorch and bullet marks along many of the walls."

I turned to Naomi. "How good is that shield?"

"Good enough," she replied, marching forward, leaving Iggy and me behind.

We quickly caught up. "Got a plan?" I asked.

"Enter through the front door and blow up anything that moves."

I was going to object, but the truth was that I didn't have any better ideas. "What do you think, Iggy?"

"The weather is warmer than usual. There aren't many people around, and I'm concerned that I won't be able to protect you."

I couldn't help but laugh. "I meant what do you think of Naomi's plan?" I looked around. He was at least right about the people. Perhaps the Germans had created an illusion to drive people away.

"It is simple and direct. She has the power to overwhelm most opposition. However, I fear her shield will be too little to protect us."

"Don't worry about that. Just turn into your fire form or whatever the heck it is you do and make sure to fry as many Nazis as you can."

"I think it would be better if he were to warn us about illusions. We don't have Mister Ali with us."

"Fine. I'll do all the hard work," Naomi replied, starting forward. She sounded more excited than annoyed. Iggy and I once again played catch up.

We reached the door, which appeared closed. Iggy reached out, pushed his hand forward, and the door swung forward easily on its hinges. "They know we are here now," Iggy said, forming a precise frown on his face.

"How so?"

"I knocked the door to the floor. It was hanging by a hinge and fell loudly to the ground when I pushed it."

"I didn't hear anything," I stated.

"Sound is part of the illusion," Iggy replied as we walked across the threshold.

"I guess the illusion ended at the front door," I replied as I looked around the entry way. There wasn't any identifiable furniture, just piles of splinters and broken ceramic and glass. The walls were scorched with marks of fire, and bulletholes were everywhere. There was a relatively clear path to a door on the opposite side of the room, at least.

I took a step only to have Iggy hold his hand out, stopping me. It felt like walking into an iron bar. "This is a trap. There—" Iggy pointed a foot in front of me. "—Is a large hole open to the basement. There are wooden spikes."

"Well, it's crude, but it almost worked," I replied. "Thank you, Iggy." I stepped back. "Why don't you lead?"

"Where is everyone?" Naomi asked, her head darting around as we followed Iggy.

"I'm sure they'll show themselves soon enough."

Iggy paused just inside the next room. A raging fire filled the room from left to right, completely blocking our way. It was clearly an illusion as the top of the flames licked the ceiling but nothing burned.

Turning around, Iggy said, "It is an illusion and cannot hurt me."

"Yeah. About that. It is an illusion, and it can hurt us," I replied.

Iggy nodded. "We will need to go around."

I turned and looked back in the other room. "The wall to the right has to connect with another room. Could we just blow through that?" Naomi stepped past me, looking like I had just given her a present.

Her hands and fingers moving with their typical unworldly speed, a kind of glowing orange smoke appeared in her hand. I guessed it to be some variation of a detonation. Before I could tell her to be careful she hurled the spell at the wall. Rather than explode, this spell hit the wall with great force, as if it was a giant hammer. The wall blew backward into a pile of rubble.

There was a hallway behind it, and before we could consider whether to proceed forward a man in dungarees and a green shirt ran up and immediately cast a spell. It didn't even get halfway to us before it fizzled. The look on his face told the story—his jaw dropped, and you could practically see him trying to figure out what happened.

Naomi stepped forward and thrust her hand out. The magician flew back and slammed into a wall. Naomi dropped her arm, and the man slumped to the floor.

"Was that the Djinn Breath spell?" I asked. Naomi nodded. "I love that spell!"

Iggy didn't wait and stepped through the ragged opening and into the hall, which was now full of the rubble from the missing wall. An explosion flashed in front of my eyes, but I didn't feel anything. Iggy stepped back. He was unhurt. "They have some kind of weapon that hurls large explosive projectiles."

"My shield can't take too many of those. Be more careful, will you?" She muscled her way past Iggy, forming detonations in each hand as she walked through the wall. In the same motion she turned to the right and launched the detonations down the hall. As quickly as she had launched them, she had two more prepared and launched them. She did this two more times.

The effect was immediate. Through the walls to my right I could hear a series of explosions. There was a shout, but then quiet. "Remind me not to get on her bad side, Iggy." He nodded in reply.

Turning our way, Naomi said, "Coast is clear."

The carnage at the end of the hallways was worse than I anticipated. There were two men that I hoped were just unconscious but I feared were dead. They looked like regular men, but I was sure that they were the ones manning the bazooka that lay at their feet. It was little more than twisted metal now.

They had set up an ambush at the an intersection of two halls. The one we were on ended at a "T," and the wall behind the men was partially caved in, with broken plaster and wood showing through scorched wallpaper.

"There are no illusions here," Iggy stated as a fusillade of bullets thudded against Naomi's shield. They came from the hall to the left, where four men were wielding machine guns. It was eerie how the bullets would hit Naomi's shield and then just fall to the floor.

"This is tiresome. Where are the magicians?" Naomi said, as she tossed a detonation toward the men. It hit one of them knocking him backward into two others. As they landed on the floor Naomi marched forward, her black dress flowing behind her as she held out her hands on her left and right. They glowed with an orange light.

One man fled down the hall, while the two that had been knocked down scrambled backward and to their feet, fleeing as fast as they could. It must have been a frightening sight—this woman in black, terrifying spells poised in her hands, her sharp face in a scowl, and her hair and black dress flowing out as if powered by their own magic.

Iggy and I rushed to catch up to Naomi, who seemed dead set on fulfilling her plan of walking through the front door and blowing up anything that moved. I glanced down at the man who had been hit with her detonation. His eyes were closed, and smoke rose from his chest.

Naomi was a few feet in front of us, and there was an explosion of light as she turned a corner. "This is more like it," she muttered as she moved out of view.

Iggy was moving slowly and deliberately, and I tried to push past him. It was like trying to shove a boulder out of the way. I turned the corner to see five magicians in the distance. There was a thick gauzy haze between them and us. One was on his knees, eyes closed, waving his hands casting a spell. The other four were trying to defeat Naomi through pure force. They hurled powerful detonation spells at her over and over.

I expected them to fizzle against her shield, but they landed with something more like a thud, and, as I watched, each one seemed to progress a little further and sound a little louder. Naomi was casting different spells. The first few seemed to be force spells, but they didn't do more than explode against the hazy air.

"Finally, someone who knows how to make a decent shield," Naomi replied as she tried another spell.

"Can you break through that shield?" I asked, rather in awe of the Germans at being able to contain Naomi's power.

"Of course I can break though that shield, but I'd bring the whole house down on our heads if I did it." Naomi stopped casting, ran her fingers through her hair, and then pulled her hair behind her ears. It was awe-inspiring to watch four magicians hurling explosive spells at her non-stop, while she calmly searched her memory for the right spell to use.

I felt a vibration, and that's when I realized that Naomi's shield was weakening. "Uh, Naomi. Maybe Iggy can do something," I replied. I turned to him. "Can you defeat these magicians?"

"Yes, but I'd have to be in my elemental form, and that would set the building on fire."

"I don't need the Ifrit," Naomi said. Her comment caught me off guard. Two years earlier she had been dismissive of magical creatures, but I thought she had changed. Now she was calling someone who had saved us as "the Ifrit."

The time wasn't right to say anything, but it turned out I didn't need to. Naomi stopped what she was doing and turned to Iggy. "I'm sorry. That was rude. Ignatius Lazarus, I do not need your help, but I appreciate the thought."

She said her comment with the utmost calm, even as her shield continued to weaken. "Okay," she muttered to herself. "Something that will blow through a Wall of Gorgan that won't destroy the house."

I tapped my cane on the floor nervously, and that's when an idea popped into my head. "Naomi, will the shield follow me if I move?"

"Yes," she replied, barely acknowledging my question.

"What happens if your shield overlaps theirs?"

"Nothing. Defensive spells don't really affect each other."

"Can I damage our own shield?"

"No. It is attuned to stopping external attacks. Anything you do would simply pass through it. Wait—" Naomi turned and peered at me. "What do you have in mind?"

"I have an idea," I said as I walked forward, tapping my cane on the wood floor, its tap both calming me and filling me with confidence.

"Tommy, no!" she yelled out, right behind me.

It was frightening, walking directly toward Master magicians casting deadly spells at you. The shield in front of me absorbed them, but that was little consolation as their spells got closer to hitting me with each passing second. The interesting thing was the effect it had on the magicians. I could see fear build in their eyes as I slowly walked toward them, step by step, tap by tap.

I reached the gauzy shield and stopped. It was right in front of my face.

"Tommy, I don't think my shield will last much longer," Naomi said.

"How fast can you cast that spell that binds people up in ropes?"

"Ariadne's Net? I just learned it, but it's simple. I can probably cast it in less than a second."

"Get them ready. I don't want to kill anyone if it isn't necessary." To her credit, Naomi didn't argue with me. She crouched and prepped her spells. The Nazi magicians were in a panic, tossing a constant barrage of spells at us.

"Better hurry, Streetlight. We don't have more than a few seconds."

She trusted me.

I pulled my arm out of its sling and held the cane in my hand. With a fluid motion, I slid the blade of the Staff out with my right hand. I paused with the blade poised above my head, and at that moment I knew it would work. The magic of the blade was part of the artifact and could not be turned off. I was one with the Staff, and while it was still full of surprises. I knew this—

I brought the blade down through the air. It reminded me of the moment two years earlier when I was walking with my grandfather through an empty alley, and I used a broomstick to fight imaginary creatures. The feeling of swinging the imaginary blade through the air felt the same as the feeling of swinging this very real blade through the air.

The difference was that it wasn't slicing just through air. It slid through the magical shield with no resistance at all. As the blade reached the floor, the blurry shield fell into smoky tendrils that floated to the left and right. A gash that split the air between us and the Nazi magicians was open and widening.

Naomi wasted no time and cast spells in quick succession. For not being a damage spell, it was wicked looking. Black tendrils of what looked like viscous fluid spread out from her hand with a hiss. The moment they reached a magician the tendrils wrapped around his body, pulling his legs and arms together and tying them tightly.

I had just taken in what was happening to the first magician, when she had three more bound. One of the magicians tried to flee, but her spell caught him before he had taken three steps. He fell forward with a thud.

I sheathed the blade of the Staff, and looked at Naomi. "I couldn't even see your hands move!"

"Child's play," she replied with a smile. She touched my arm. "Great idea with the sword. I'm going to have to come up with some other name than Streetlight."

"How about Deathblade or Slash?" I asked as Iggy walked up.

"I was thinking something more like Butter Knife." I rolled my eyes as Iggy leaned over and looked at one of the magicians. The Magicians' mouths were covered with the black oily bindings that held them.

"These are the Brotherhood of Saturn," Iggy said.

"No way!" Naomi replied. She walked over and looked at two of them. They were struggling to free themselves. "I studied them a bit. I thought they were banished by the Nazis."

"That was just a story to hide the plans the Nazis had for magic," Iggy said. "They are widely considered the most powerful magicians in the world."

I turned to Naomi. "Five of the most powerful magicians in the world, and you beat them!"

"We beat them," she replied. She turned and started down the hall. "Time for us to grab a Coat."

My step was a bit lighter and my shoulder hurt a bit less. Naomi had smiled when she noted that we had beaten the magicians together.

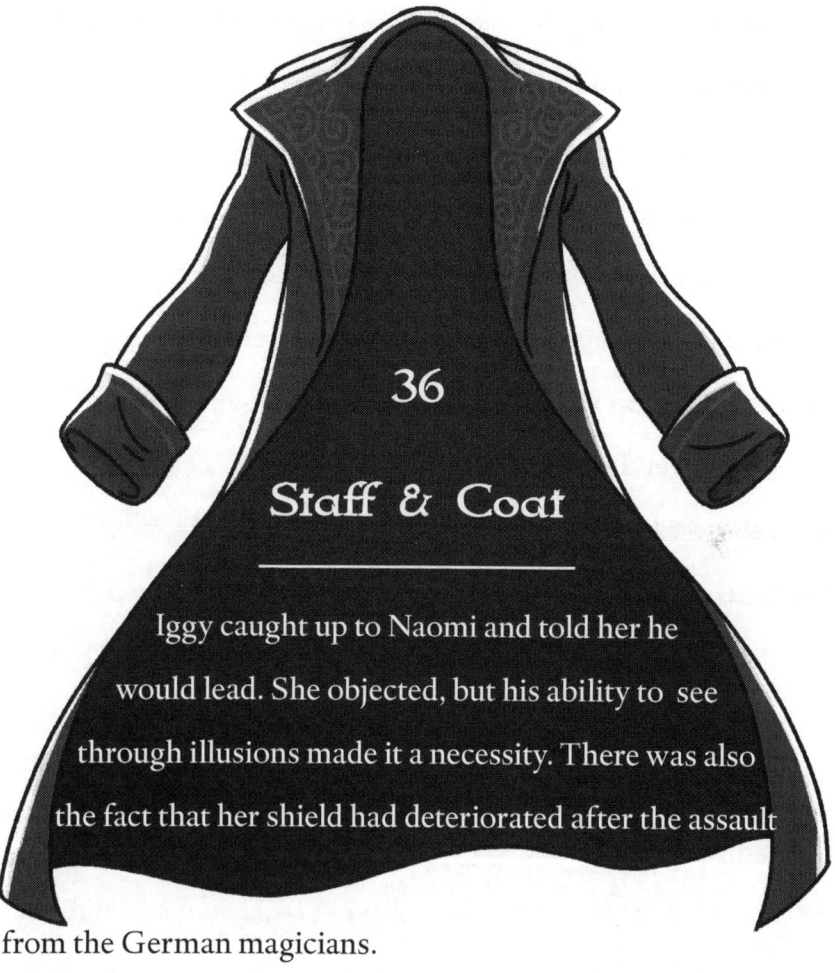

36

Staff & Coat

Iggy caught up to Naomi and told her he would lead. She objected, but his ability to see through illusions made it a necessity. There was also the fact that her shield had deteriorated after the assault from the German magicians.

As Iggy moved to the front, I asked Naomi, "Should we take a break while you re-cast your shield?"

Naomi laughed. "It took me six hours to cast." I didn't reply. I couldn't imagine the physical and mental demands it would take to move precisely and in a certain way while gathering magical energy for six straight hours. It sounded impossible.

At the end of the hallway was a single door. It was a deep brown and polished to a sheen. "What do you think is behind that?" I asked.

"A Cup and a Coat," Naomi replied.

"It will be either the Archmage or more defenses," Iggy added. "We should be prepared for technological weaponry. The Brotherhood of Saturn was most likely his last magical defense."

Iggy shoved the door open, showing no fear of whatever was behind it. The room was dimly lit, but I couldn't see much more than that. Iggy walked in and looked around. "It appears—" His voice was cut off by an explosion, which sent him flying toward us. Even with him taking the brunt of the force, it still knocked me backward.

I ran over to Iggy. His eyes were closed, and flame flickered along his body. "Iggy! Are you okay?" I went to shake him, but yanked my hands back from blistering heat. I looked back just as Naomi finished casting a spell. "Iggy's badly hurt!"

"We're shielded, but don't expect it to handle another one of those." For a moment I was bothered by her lack of concern for Iggy, but the sound of footsteps from the room behind me made it clear that she was being smart. We had to defeat the Germans before we could help him.

I stood up and moved to Naomi's side. "Can you cast the fire spell? Fill the room with flame?"

Nodding, Naomi replied, "That's a good plan. It's a directed spell, but I can lead with it and then just sweep the room once I'm through the door." Not bothering to wait for a response from me, Naomi held up her hand and shot a stream of flame into the room. There was a scream of pain, and Naomi rushed in moving her flame from left to right. I followed.

Two men were running from the room through a door to the right. Their clothes were on fire. It was hard to see details, as the whole room was on fire.

It was a huge library, with bookshelves filled with burning books from floor to ceiling covering every wall. The ceiling was about ten feet high. The entire room was open, with desks, chairs, and floor lamps shoved against the bookcases. Everything was in the early stages of turning into a conflagration.

"Maybe that wasn't the best idea," I said.

"Come in. Come in." The words were spoken with a German accent and came from the far side of the room and the thickest part of the flames. "Oh, pardon me. I'm the only one who can't be harmed in these flames. So I shall come to you."

A man strode through the fire toward us. He was wearing Ana's Coat, and had a cane in one hand, which he slapped against the palm of the other. He looked around. "I should have expected you wouldn't have trouble with my men. A pity you decided to burn down such a valuable library to do so, however."

The flames were growing in intensity, and I grabbed Naomi's arm. "We need to retreat," I whispered. Naomi didn't move. "Remember the park," I said, louder. Nodding, she backed away with me.

"Giving up so soon? Oh, I see, you are worried about being harmed by the flames." He chuckled. "If only you had the Coat."

We rushed out of the room, the heat was intense and getting worse. The German followed us. "My name is Keitel, but you will know me soon as the heir of Jamshid." Naomi whispered in my ear as we made our way back to the front of the house. "Look for a gun. If you find one, pick it up and shoot him."

We weren't very close to the flames, so I stopped. Naomi turned and looked at me. "I have a better idea," I whispered.

Keitel caught up to us but kept his distance. "Don't flee yet. I enjoy the young lady's irrational confidence." He looked at her, a smile on his face as if he didn't have a care in the world. "Feel free to hurl whatever spell you like at me." He touched the edge of the Coat. "You cannot hurt me."

"She is the Black Witch, the greatest magician in history." I laughed. "She is the heir of Jamshid." I knew I was the only one who could hurt him, but I was sure Keitel would know that, too. To catch him off guard, I wanted him to ignore me as a threat by focusing on Naomi.

It didn't work.

"Ah, Tommy Black." He looked at me. "Your confidence is ill-placed. Certainly, you feel it." He said the words as a statement, and as he said them I knew what he meant. The pull of the Artifacts to be brought together was clouding my mind. Part of me wanted to just hand him the Staff.

I gritted my teeth. "You don't have the Cup." It was a guess, but I couldn't see any place he could store it on his person.

"I'm not a fool, young man. I bear the Cup, but it is back in Berlin. I wasn't going to risk it with a trip deep into enemy territory." That explained something to me—he didn't have to have both Artifacts in hand to be the focus of their power. He just had to be the one who was connected to them. Before I could say anything, he spoke up, "Of course with the Coat that is no longer a concern."

"I'd give Tommy the Coat, if I were you," Naomi said. I looked over at her. She seemed nonchalant as she spoke. She was casting the light spell, and it struck me that it was much brighter than those she had previously cast. "He really doesn't like hurting people."

"Black Witch." Keitel practically spat out the words. "This may surprise you, but I assure you that your friend cannot hurt me. You should ask him. He feels it and knows it. I control the power of the Artifacts now." He turned to me. "Go ahead. You are the Archmage of Light are you not? Create a light."

He doesn't know. I couldn't believe my luck. Keitel knew that I had lost the power to control the staff, but as the use of the sword had indicated, I had not lost the power of the staff. He didn't realize I could hurt him. He assumed that because I had no ability to control the power of the Staff it meant the Staff had no power.

I held up a hand in a sign of hopelessness. "It's true, Naomi. I hoped that I could come up with a plan or that you could defeat him, but we can't. Even Iggy can't hurt him." Naomi stared at me. I hoped she would trust me to know what I was doing.

"Iggy?" Keitel asked, but he quickly realized who I was talking about and smiled. "Of course, your Ifrit slave! I must hand it to you, Master Black. I am impressed you were able to enslave an Ifrit." He twirled his cane. "Too bad he is dead."

"What happens if I just give you the Staff?" I asked.

"Tommy, no!" Naomi cried out, and spun her head to look at me, I saw a quick wink behind the mess of hair that had flown over the front of her face. She knows I have a plan. I had to suppress a smile.

"I'm sorry, but it is our only way out. He is too powerful."

The German looked ecstatic. "Of course! You understand! I will do nothing to any of you. I have no need of two teenage children. Be on your way. I don't care." He held up his own cane. "You see, I've been anticipating this day for so long that I had a cane made to match yours." He tossed the cane to the floor beside him. "Hand me the Staff."

I took a step and tapped the cane on the floor. "There is just one problem." I took a few steps closer to Keitel and tapped the floor with each one. He looked nervous as I tapped the cane while approaching him.

"Stop that infernal tapping. Just hand me the staff." After a few more steps, I stopped in front of him, slid my arm out of the sling, grabbed the cane with the hand of my hurt arm, and held the Artifact out. The nervousness on Keitel's face changed to desire, and he reached for the Staff.

I once again held the cane in my hurt hand and withdrew the sword with my right hand. I swung it around and aimed it at his forehead, the blade an inch from his skin. Keitel inched back in surprise, but then smiled. "You cannot hurt me."

I knew that the blade would slice through his skin and bone as easy as it would air, so with great care I pushed my arm forward until the edge of the blade pressed against Keitel's forehead. Despite my care, a small cut opened. "Ow!" Kettle pulled his head back in surprise. Blood beaded on his forehead.

"Move an inch, and I will remove your head," I said as Keitel lifted a leg to step backward. "Don't move at all. If I see anything move I will slice it off." He looked like he was frozen in indecision. I was sure that he couldn't quite believe that I could hurt him, as he was wearing the Coat. His entire plan collapsed due to his arrogance and his faith in something he didn't understand.

I lowered the tip of the sword to the center of Keitel's chest. "You will now remove the Coat and hand it to me."

"Never!" His calm smile was replaced with a mad sneer.

"You have two options, my fellow Archmage. You can hand me the Coat and then return to your Cup, knowing that you will have lived to fight another day. Or you can die, and I'll have to clean your blood off the coat before I put it on." I pressed forward with the sword, which made Keitel step back. "One more step, and you die."

"You will kill me anyway!"

"If that were true you'd be dead already. Now remove the Coat. I really hate doing laundry."

Keitel hemmed and hawed after that but seemed to understand the truth of my words. Still, he replied, "You will hand me over to the French, and they will kill me."

"No. I will let you go."

"I do not believe you."

"Naomi, what do you think I will do?"

She sighed loudly. "You'll let him go, even though that is about the stupidest thing you could do."

"He is not removing the Coat. Should I kill him?"

"You should have killed him already," Naomi replied, sounding impatient.

Keitel stared into my eyes, and I held his gaze. My confidence had grown with each sentence I spoke. Naomi had set me up perfectly, and I was entirely in control. "My patience is at an end. I shall kill you now."

"No! Wait!" Keitel reached up and shrugged his shoulders, sliding one arm and then the other out of the Coat. I gave him more room with the sword, and he reached around and pulled the Coat off. He held it out to me.

I took the Coat of Invincibility and put it on.

Everything went black.

It felt similar to when I stopped time with the Staff, alien and unsettling. Inside, however, I felt enormous power. It was then I realized that I was in the realm of Zahhak's prison. It didn't feel like he had summoned me, more like I had a closer connection to the power of the Artifacts and this was now part of that power—I could get a bit closer to the source of the power, Zahhak himself.

I tried to see if I could talk to Zahhak or see him, but his presence was still beyond me. Some day, I thought, and returned to the real world.

Keitel cowered, loathing in his eyes. I turned my back to him and walked toward Naomi. As I approached her, she smiled widely, her dimples transforming her from the intimidating Black Witch back into my best friend.

"So Streetlight, are you going to really let him go?"

"Yes."

"You are such a softie."

Flames licked along the ceiling, and it suddenly hit me that the room was uncomfortably hot. "We need to leave." Naomi put her arm through mine and pulled me toward the door. I glanced back. Keitel had already disappeared.

We stood across the street watching the French firemen attempt to put out the flames as the house we had just left burned brightly. Naomi hadn't let go of my arm, and we watched the flames in silence. I liked to think we looked like a young French couple.

"So where did Keitel go?" I asked.

A voice behind us answered. "He is on his way to Germany via their network of spies and safe houses."

"Iggy!" we both exclaimed as we turned to see him standing there. Naomi dropped my arm and gave him a big hug. He looked in good shape.

"I thought you were dead," I said.

"Nothing heals an Ifrit faster than a fire." I shook his hand. It was like shaking hands with a marble statue. "It was kind of you to let him go free," Iggy added.

"It was stupid," Naomi replied. "You should have killed him or at least turned him in to the French army."

"Well, I think it's better to know who the Bearer of the Cup is than have that be unknown. Plus, we know the Cup will no longer work."

Naomi stopped and looked up at me. "That's actually quite smart, Streetlight."

I shrugged. "Not that it will make our job much easier. We still have to travel through hundreds of miles of enemy territory to get to Berlin, find Keitel, fight through whatever defenses the Nazis put in place for the Cup, and then retrieve it."

"It's a date!" Naomi exclaimed.

"Wait, did you say a date?" I asked.

Naomi ignored me and turned back to the blaze across the street. She cast a spell, and the pure white light in her palm blazed brighter than it ever had.

THE END

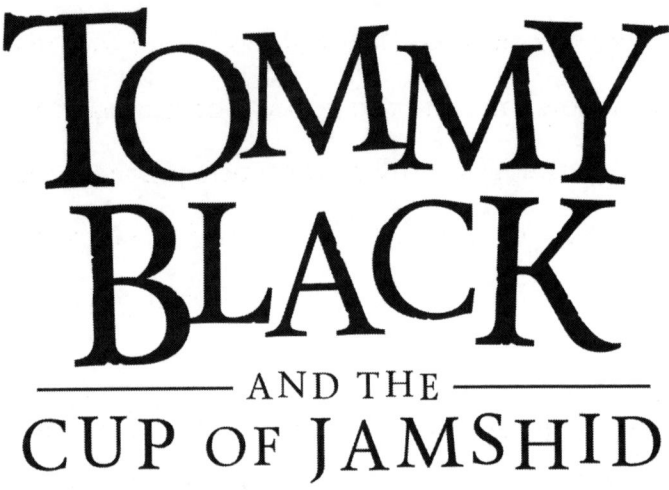

TOMMY BLACK

AND THE

CUP OF JAMSHID

Fall 2016

Acknowledgments

This series started out as a writing exercise at the Writers Garret critique group in Dallas. Many thanks to the Stone Soup crew there, who were instrumental in my development as a writer. The first two chapters of the series were workshopped at the Viable Paradise Workshop. My undying thanks to the instructors and students there who not only made it better, but inspired me to do more.

A number of people helped along the way, including beta readers and editors Sean Patrick Kelly, Aiden Doyle, Eric Jackson, Laurel Amberdine, and Lea Zukas. Ken Liu provided not just moral support, but also the blurb on book one. Rachel Swirsky and Christie Yant sent the right emails at the right time to keep me going. The support of the Codex and Authors Corner writing groups was invaluable. Mike Corley, my fantastic cover artist, continues to help in ways that aren't always seen on the cover.

I will always and forever be grateful to my alma mater, Kenyon College, and the wonderful professors that taught me the love of literature and writing, and my classmates and alumni, who continue to provide friendship and guidance to this day.

Thank you to the people who helped when they didn't need to: John Scalzi, Charlie Jane Anders, John DeNardo, Margaret Brown, Laurisa White Reyes, Matt Mikalatos. Hugh Howey cheered me on and recommended I self-publish. Annie Bellet was a friend and inspiration when I did.

My use of Persian mythology was directly due to the inspiration of Jonathan Stroud and his delightful Bartimaeaus series. The detonation spell is a small nod to him.

Finally, my crazy, wonderful family is the greatest inspiration of all. Thank you, Lea, Zoe, Willow, and Mia.

About the Author

After fifteen years as a music industry journalist Jake Kerr's first published story, "The Old Equations," was nominated for the Nebula Award from the Science Fiction Writers of America and was shortlisted for the Theodore Sturgeon and StorySouth Million Writers awards. His stories have subsequently been published in magazines across the world, broadcast in multiple podcasts, and been published in multiple anthologies and year's best collections. He is also the author of the Guildmaster Thief novella series and the Tommy Black action/adventure series.

A graduate of Kenyon College, Kerr studied fiction under Ursula K. Le Guin and Peruvian playwright Alonso Alegria. He lives in Dallas, Texas, with his wife and three daughters.

www.jakekerr.com

@jakedfw

Made in the USA
San Bernardino, CA
14 December 2016